PRAISE FOR BRUTE ORBITS

"Zebrowski conflates savagery and mercy, conflates his vision of penology and salvation in ways which I've never before seen in science fiction. This sad and wise novel with its souls of ice and fire circling Earth in untended isolation, refracts the eternal drama of retribution and expiation. *Crime and Punishment* by Stapledon."

—Barry N. Malzberg, award-winning author of *Beyond Apollo*

"Zebrowski never ceases to invest his individual characters with three-dimensional roundness. . . . Startling and sobering, Zebrowski's provocative novel should prick the consciences of all readers, as he slices open the veins of prisoners and warders alike, revealing the identical blood that flows on either side of the bars."

—Paul Di Filippo, *Asimov's Science Fiction*

"An impressive look at the penal system of the future. The author explores this . . . through a number of credible characters and demonstrates once again our ability to commit heinous crimes in the name of the common good. Highly recommended."

—Don D'Ammassa, *Science Fiction Chronicle*

"A strong, thought-provoking work. Zebrowski has crafted an impressive narrative voice that is distanced enough to deliver authoritative, omniscient exposition, yet flexible enough to segue smoothly into each character's point of view."

—Marcos Donnelly, author of *Prophets for the End of Time*

"This sweeping fictive history grips the reader in a drama of human savagery. Each page adds to the sense of injustice and brutality. Zebrowski's gift for characterization makes this saga of criminals and law enforcers powerful reading. *Brute Orbits* is a hard book to lay down and a hard book to forget."

—Mary T. Brizzi, author of
*A Reader's Guide
to Philip Jose Farmer* and
A Reader's Guide to Anne Inez McCaffrey

MACROLIFE

Included in *Library Journal*'s
"Basic Science Fiction Library" of 100 Best Novels

"It's been years since I was so impressed. *Macrolife* manages an extraordinary balance between the personal and cosmic elements. Altogether a worthy successor to Olaf Stapledon's *Star Maker*. . . . One of the few books I intend to read again."

—Arthur C. Clarke

"*Macrolife* has acquired a cult following."

—Stephen Baxter, author of *Moonseed*

"The first writer since Stapledon to get the Stapledonian flavor—vistas, perspectives, a kind of distant, serene emotion. The novel oscillates nicely between long view and close focus, capturing a mood and feeling that few even attempt in this field, and at the conclusion there is a genuine vast perspective evoked. The prose is very good—smooth, evocative, adroit—a solid work that will have a following of the best sort."

—Gregory Benford

ALSO BY GEORGE ZEBROWSKI

Macrolife

Stranger Suns

The Sunspacers Trilogy

The Omega Point Trilogy

The Killing Star (with Charles Pellegrino)

The Monadic Universe (collected stories)

Cave of Stars (forthcoming)

BRUTE ORBITS

GEORGE ZEBROWSKI

HarperPrism

A Division of HarperCollinsPublishers

HarperPrism

A Division of HarperCollins*Publishers*
10 East 53rd Street, New York, NY 10022-5299

This is a work of fiction. The characters, incidents, and dialogues are products of the author's imagination and are not to be construed as real. Any resemblance to actual events or persons, living or dead, is entirely coincidental.

ISBN 0-06-105807-6

HarperCollins®, ▟®, and HarperPrism®
are trademarks of HarperCollins Publishers Inc.

Cover design by Carl D. Galian
Cover photo © 1998 by Uniphoto, Inc. and Paul Dinnocenzo

A hardcover edition of this book was published in
1998 by HarperPrism.
First paperback printing: August 1999

Printed in the United States of America

Visit HarperPrism on the World Wide Web at
http://www.harpercollins.com

❖ 10 9 8 7 6 5 4 3 2 1

For Charles L. Harness
Wielder of Light

"The degree of civilization
in a society is revealed
by entering its prisons."
    —DOSTOEVSKY

"Reach out to those in need.
If you do not, then who?
If not now, then when?"
    —TALMUD

The Rocks

These brute orbits, along whose ever-lengthening ways so much humanity was exiled, were a reproach to each generation as it looked skyward, day or night, and knew that every direction was a receding prison of human outcasts whose guilt was measured by their distance from the Sun. Although invisible except to sensitive detectors able to see the burning beacons, these islands of human skylife loomed larger even as time threw them farther into space.

One hundred years out, the transgressors against their own kind were long consumed, and the habitats were now home to the innocent. Fifty years out, the condemned still breathed, making a life for themselves and their children. Five to ten years out the habitats were cauldrons of strife, as order struggled to rise from the hatred and dismay that the convicted carried away from the Earth.

But it had begun unexpectedly and with different ends in mind, this use of distance as a better prison wall. The asteroid later called "the Iron Mile" came in from the outer solar system as both a surprise and a harbinger. It crossed Earth's orbit, swung around the Sun in a flat ellipse, rushed out, and was captured by the Earth as a second companion. That portion of humankind that knew enough to understand what had been averted was relieved, but worried about future threats. Many others, when they heard of the danger that had passed them by, felt vaguely that it was only a reprieve; too many transgressions still waited to be punished.

The lessons and opportunities became clear: A loaded gun pointed at the labors of human history was intolerable. The terrifying vision of what might have been had the nickel-iron mass struck the Earth spurred the finding of a foothold on the intruder.

Humanity mined the Mile and grew its permanent base. Near-Earth outposts became easier to build with these resources. The heavens had spared the Earth from being hit, and had also saved it the political bickering and economic cost of bringing an asteroid close. An uneasy gift of ground both quickened the industrial expansion into the solar system and prevented disastrous surprises.

A dozen Earth-orbit–crossing asteroids that

might have one day struck the planet were, one by one, brought into orbits around the Earth and Moon, and mined by a metal-hungry world using machines manned by small groups of specialists and convicts. Later, when these first twelve asteroids had been exhausted, they became way stations and habitats, useful for scientific research and human colonies.

As the number of mined-out rocks grew, they began to be used as prisons by a world that was running out of patience with criminal behavior. The consequences of Earthside prison building from violence and the threat of violence, together with high start-up costs and endless budget increases, finally outweighed the economic benefits to host communities. Beguiling alternatives beckoned in the mined-out rocks, offering irresistible parallel benefits; and the rocks were immediately available.

"We can make the criminals disappear from the face of the Earth," whispered the wishful, "—and we can start tomorrow!"

"Lock them up and throw away the key!"

"Recycle the scum in the fusion torches! It's cheaper."

"Make them disappear, but don't trouble us with how you do it."

"Judge Overton, do you consider the Rocks to be cruel and unusual punishment?"

"Not at all," replied the Chief Justice of the

Orbits. "Think of them as sheltered islands, where life goes on."

"But the isolation from humankind . . ."

"They have enough humankind with them."

The more sophisticated said, "We must create a generational firebreak between the socially damaged and the newborn, and we must do this worldwide. We must start over by raising people not to be criminals—but first we must gather all the serious threats and separate them from us."

The inmates in the Orbits would need fewer guards, and this would minimize abuse. As much as possible, the prison colony would police itself. But this model quickly went astray, even as architectural grace was achieved.

The first asteroid was excavated to provide a maintenance level near the outer crust. Ship docks were fitted at the far ends. Sophisticated audio/video devices were installed to monitor the criminal colony, and social scientists were given access to these panoptic observation points. It was only a matter of time before the inmates learned that they were under constant observation, even in their most private moments, in the name of knowledge that would advance the ideals of criminal justice. There was a rash of suicides. The whole story got out through the guards, which led planners to conclude that there was still too much contact between the inmates and the outside. Some psychologists concluded that curiosity about the lawbreakers produced an irresistible need for surveillance.

The first breakout from the Orbits was accomplished through a break-in to the service level, the taking of hostages, and a crash landing of a shuttle in the middle of Lawrence, Kansas, burning a large section of the city. Public outcry and discussion was split between sympathy for all who died and vigilante hatred of the surviving convicts who escaped into the state and caused even more havoc until they were recaptured or killed.

The Lawrence disaster led directly to the planning of timed orbits for the rocks. As one by one Earthside prisons began to fail for reasons of economy, inadequate psychological management, and planning that seemed immune to improvement, the increasing cost of technology in the orbits also came under fire. There was too much technology and no end to the costs. Lunar prisons were hotbeds of corruption and possible disasters if the inmates ever seized the lunar mass launchers and hurled objects at the Earth or any of its planetary or orbital colonies.

Timed orbits would need no guards, no rules to be obeyed, no trustees—hence there would be no relationships between guards and inmates to go wrong, no points of contact with the outside until the habitat returned. It was this infinitely permeable interface with the societies around each prison that was most feared; too much passed back and forth, despite immense efforts, in the form of orders for illegal commerce, executions, and legal strategies. The prisons were schools for new criminals, who graduated from a system of natural selection that tested them with violence and hatred, and made them ready, not for life outside, but for supermax incarceration.

Once a habitat was inserted into its cometary orbit, all costs and cruelties of previous penal servitude would end for the duration.

To insert a rock into a cometary Sun orbit of any desired period required only a specific addition to its already existing orbital velocity. And from timed orbits it was only a small, tempting step to a miscalculation of the period, either as an honest mistake or as a politically motivated action to rid the world of its professional high achievers, the pitiless "Alcatraz Class Criminals," into an open orbit, so-called, that would never bring the prison back. Long periods or open orbits also replaced the distasteful penalty of capital punishment. Life without even the physical possibility of parole effectively abolished official killing.

"No more executions of the innocent!"

cried the self-proclaimed humane, puffing virtue.

"We will not see you again," intoned the judges.

And to communities and victimized individuals came the assurance: "You will not look into this face again. You will not suffer from him again. He will go from you forever."

This was only one of the social opportunities that came with the opening of the solar system to industry—as simple as discovering that "transportation" was not only cost effective but relatively cheap, and growing cheaper. New meaning was given to the word that had described the exile of convicts to imperial colonies of centuries past. For the politicians, it was the opening of a bottomless abyss into which they could throw the rejects—and the inconvenient; and as it had been with previous penal systems, it was not always easy to know which was which. Nations traded their damned: You exile mine and I yours. In the minds of the law-fearing middle classes living between the alliance of power and the street and kept ignorant as one does children before whom one is ashamed, the convicted must surely be guilty of something, even if it was not the specific charge. The few guiltless who might occasionally be trapped by the system were a small price to pay . . .

■

As the chorus of practicality and political con-
venience exhausted its justifications in the
minds of thoughtful human beings, the chorus
of conscience began its chant, as the realities
waited to be revealed in the deep void. The permeable interface between society and its prisons had not been abolished, only slowed; the
curiosity of the thoughtful persisted, irritating
human sympathies as a drop of water slowly
wears away mountains.

With later knowledge, the cry went up,
saying, "If we had known, if we had only
understood, we would have done differently!"

Power, the father of the middle-class elites,
replied, "You wanted peace in your enclaves, to
raise your families and pursue your educations,
and we gave you that!" And the damned of the
streets said to power, "We did your dirty work,
and filled your pockets with wealth, selling the
drugs and vices that you could not to the less-
than clean and straight."

Power said to this, "You also worked for
yourselves as you corrupted us."

There is false pride in hindsight. Revealed
wrongs elicit sentimental bandages to dress the
wounds of history. Individuals insist, saying,
"I would not have let this happen, because I am
good. If I had been given the power . . . if I had

been in charge . . . if I were king . . . if I were dictator for even a week!" The sweetest lie of all sings of what might have been . . . if only . . .

The chorus of history is not completely silenced. Its bitter overview gives what only the few wish to see, and it's full of pity. Later step-back perspectives bring dishonest, conflicting, and self-congratulatory wisdom. Raise up the damned and they will behave no differently than the powerful; diminish the powerful and they will be as the damned. Hope suggests that hindsight should not wait, but invade and rule the present; while another wisdom holds that life must unfold unpredictably, with failure and success as its twin powers, that impatience and constraining reason are the enemies of ingenuity, eager to shackle the future with much more than the forwarding of settled knowledge and culture.

∏ail Them to the Sky

JUDGE OVERTON'S PRIVATE CHAMBER

"An orbit longer than the lifetime of any inmate is the most just solution possible to the social problems created by past systems of life imprisonment. Prisons of any kind are bad for the communities around them, from a moral and social view, even when they have been economically beneficial. The Orbits require no warden or guards, thus eliminating all possible abuses. What can it matter to the lifers who will never be released? We are assured, as we sever ourselves from them irrevocably, that a life sentence will be just that. No false promise is held out. No world waits outside the walls. No one ever gets out. No one can reach out to create new criminals. Deterrence is served as well as it can be, and our hypocrisy is at an end. Just look at the good use to which we can

*put these mined-out rocks! A pretty piece of real
estate at 150 square kilometers!"*

Harry Howes grew up on a dairy farm near the
caverns in upstate New York. He came down to
New York City in 2049 to escape a violent
father, an incestuous mother, and a farm that
would soon go under. He was just twenty and
didn't know what he was going to do, but hoped
to find work on the dikes that were being constructed to prevent the rising ocean from flood-
ing the city.

He never got near to working on the project, because he met Jay Polau, who told him
about an old world jeweler and watch repairer
with a shop on Kingsbridge Road in the Bronx.

"The man is old," Polau said, "so we can go
in and get a lot of stuff before he wakes up. The
guy's rich, with more stuff we can fence than
he'll ever be able to use before he dies. He can't
sell it, but we can. He's got no one, and nobody
cares what happens to him. He never spends
anything. It's not right, not when we can use
what he's got."

Harry needed a few bucks, just until the
job came through; if it didn't, he'd have to go
home, and that frightened him. It would be all
right, he told himself, almost a loan, just
enough to get him through and keep him from
the clutches of his mother. When his father

died, she'd get the insurance and upgrade the farm to hydroponics, factory style. He shuddered at the thought of going home again to run the farm and take care of her. Anything would be better.

Old man Buda, an old Hungarian, got up and caught them at his ancient safe. Polau clubbed him to death. They opened the safe—and there was old jewelry, lots of bank codes, even some paper money.

The police were quietly waiting outside when he and Polau came out.

"I've never done anything wrong before," Harry told the judge.

"But your friend, Polau, what about him?"

"I didn't know much about him . . ."

"The old man died," the judge said, "and you admitted hitting him also. You may kill again if I let you loose. Better to have you out of the way. Thirty years."

Thirty years, in a cave up in the sky. Polau got life.

On the day that he and Polau arrived, the engineers lit the sunplate at one end of the hollowed-out asteroid. This was a huge, perfectly round plate set in the narrow forward end of the hollow potato. Fed by electricity from compact fusion furnaces, it glowed red when first turned on, then yellow, and bright yellow-orange at full power, filling the inside with yellow brightness to reveal an incurving land of mud piled with crates and building machines. The only finished structures were three silver prefab mess hall domes in the forward section.

All worth had been ripped from this inner land, and it cried out to have something put back.

As they looked around at the building machines and crates of prefabricated housing parts, Harry Howes knew that he was here to stay, with no chance for parole before his thirty years were up. Polau would never get out.

They had killed the old man, Harry told himself, feeling foolish, as if he were talking to someone else, so for a while at least something harsh should be done to him. But when would it end? Would thirty years be just about right, or would he know in his heart when his punishment was over, when he came to feel something for the man he had helped to kill, much sooner than thirty years, and then still have to endure the remaining time?

These were vague thoughts in his brain as he looked at Polau, who would never really be his friend; it would have been better if they had been friends before, so their time here might be more bearable. From what had come out in court, Harry wondered what Polau had needed him for, since he had burgled that same shop before, never expecting that the old man would modernize his alarm system. They were very different people, Harry thought. His father would have called Polau a creep—a thing that went around looking out for itself, and did it very well most of the time—except when it got caught.

■

Yevgeny Tasarov liked to think that there was no one like him. Yet he also liked to believe that he was always on the lookout for his equals. It was not his fault that they came few and far between, and that recently they had not come at all. He sometimes wondered whether he was no longer able to recognize them.

Looking at the humanity around him, watching it haul itself through the vast changes of the last century and a half, Tasarov had concluded early in life that it was doing only what it could do, not what it should. That way was mostly beyond the capacities of concerted action; whenever humankind sought to agree and act in a large group, a curve of differing opinions appeared, as if someone had pressed a display button. The curve was always the same, with all the expected views present as if they were built-in. They probably were built-in.

Besides, it was hard to know what should be done with humanity; most were still content to live with no hindsight, less foresight, and little self-awareness. The whole species was still on automatic. Maybe it would never be a breakout species. So he had decided to do what he could do with the tools of thought and learned craft. He was the one-eyed man in the country of the blind, but he worried about having only one eye; two would have been better. Lawful or unlawful mattered little, as long as a project was practical and profitable, and not overly repellent. The craft made him happy; thought was hard work, but the reality of waiting pitfalls sharpened his alertness, as he brought the pleasure of craft to bear against failure.

In the fall of 2051, when he was twenty-five, he looked up at the overcast sky of upstate New York and knew what was possible, and that he would do it. It would require equipment and leadership. He already had the small inner group to persuade, but that would be the quickest part of it, indoctrinating them with the truth of the plan, to the point where it would work on their imaginations and dispel all doubt.

Was there any doubt in him? Of course there was, because the plan needed weaker links to make it work. Key moments might crumble before the fallible nature of men and lurking circumstance. One could not plan for the unexpected, except through redundancy, and hope there would be enough redundancy to swamp any sudden obstacles or reversals.

The way he had been caught was an example: with an old-fashioned thumbprint from the money terminal he had emptied in Binghamton, New York, out of his own account! True, it was some money he had collected from the fading russmob in Philadelphia, for saving them millions in bank transfers, and legal, except for the intentionally wrong tax code he had entered; but some local cop had decided to do some old-fashioned print dusting. In one hour they had his alias and ticket number on the bullet train to Manhattan, and the arrest had come at the Westchester stop.

He had felt humiliated by their easy luck, by the smallness of the offense, and by the doubts that had been sown in his mathematician's brain about his own failing abilities. He should not have discounted some old cop's eyesight. The one consolation was that they had arrested one of his aliases, not his core identity, which was still unknown to them and vastly more guilty. This would make it easier for him to execute his plan; they would not know who had planned it. He smiled to himself, admiring the beauty of the risk, knowing that up to a point they did not have to know his true self to stop him.

He told himself that a man losing his mind would be oblivious to it; he would not work to improve his long-chain reasoning; he would be blindly unquestioning of himself. His capture had been a freak event, and now his choice was to sit out five years or do something about it while his skills were still intact.

He knew what he wanted to try: to do whatever it would take to free him from a system that had learned too much about him, and which had to be coaxed back into forgetfulness. Once his plan had begun there would be no turning back; he would succeed or earn life without parole, or worse; death would come to him as a decision not to be taken alive.

Now, as he looked at the overcast sky from Dannemora prison, he saw what was to come and how it would be made to happen, as clearly as he had ever seen a mathematical proof; but whether the imperfect world would permit the order of events to run remained to be seen.

How much planning was enough to overcome chance imponderables? Never enough. But it was this very openness in the physical universe that made creative unpredictabilities possible; to ask for guarantees would be to ask for a rigidity that would be intolerable to a free mind. Constraints, yes, but a totalitarian determinism, no. The one honed skills, the other crushed them; the one made happy explorations possible, the other imposed iron mazes. Many a criminologist had reluctantly concluded that a high crime rate was a culture's price of freedom.

One by one, his six comrades drifted toward him in the center of the exercise yard of the old prison, until finally they stood in various postures—facing him, facing away, and off to the side, so it would seem they were conversing only casually if they spoke.

Daylight brightened. He glanced up and saw the Sun rolling like a molten ball of hot iron in the ashes of the overcast sky. Suddenly it sailed out into a break. The still figures around him regained their shadows, which clung like spilled paint to the rough concrete.

The oldest lifer, Stanley King, whose leathery face had peered out from Coxsackie and here for over thirty years, said, "So, are you ready to tell us?"

Tasarov did not look at the men. He spoke to the shadows.

■

Philip Emmons didn't remember killing his boss, a cafeteria manager at the Plato Research Center on the Moon. The court's doctors had told him about it for three days. Then he had sat before the judge and prosecutor, thinking they could tell him whatever they wanted, show him all the evidence, but he still wouldn't actually know inside himself that he had done it. They might just as well have been trying someone else. Even if he had been that man for a few moments, he was someone else now. Phil Emmons had never committed a crime in his life, despite the evidence, but they could tell him anything and he wouldn't know if they had made it up. So to hell with the judge and all the lawyers, his own included; they weren't interested in him, but in someone else.

"Whatever triggered you," the judge said at the sentencing, "might happen again. We can't let you out. No examination has been able to confirm your amnesia story, and there doesn't seem to be anything really wrong with you."

The judge had looked at him as if expecting him to agree, to say "Yes, I know, you have no choice, it's all right and I would do the same in your place." He had looked into the judge's brown eyes, which were part of a wonderfully composed compassionate gaze that seemed genuine.

"Have you anything to say before I sentence you?" asked the judge.

Philip Emmons shook his head. "I have no idea what happened—if it did."

The judge nodded. "There may be more to you than the innocent man you seem to believe yourself to be, but you must understand that we can't let the rest of you roam free—if what you say is true."

"What good does it do me to understand?"

The judge said, "Perhaps it will prevent that other part of you from ever coming out again. I sentence you to thirty years in the Orbits. And for the record, I don't believe your story for one moment. No one does." You'll never be back, his eyes said, whoever you are. "Goodbye, Mr. Emmons."

3

The Thinking Happiness

JUDGE OVERTON'S PRIVATE CHAMBER

"Sooner or later some half-baked historian will write an asinine book about me and call it Overton of the Orbits. He'll look for motives in what we did, but they'll be all wrong. No one was looking for rehab, or even humane treatment, as such. We only sought to separate the worst from the best, nothing more. The supermax prisons of the late twentieth and early twenty-first century were simply too costly for the ten to fifteen percent of inmates who had to be isolated. We had to get rid of them, because our worth exceeded the worth of these predators, pure and simple. The annual cost of incarceration in supermax prisons, in fact any prisons, was more than what it cost to give someone a university education. Most convicts stood to be

*released from prisons, but these ten to twenty per-
cent were our failures. Yes, our failures, as much as
the law-abiding citizens were our social successes.
But we just didn't know what else to do with the
worst failures. It was too late to prevent them.
Remember that the prison gangs had their tenta-
cles to the outside. They ran businesses and could
even bring down local governments. They killed
efficiently at a distance. By shipping them out, we
broke their influence. Sure, in some profound sense
we created their kind, but there was nothing else to
do except get rid of them and start over."*

Yevgeny Tasarov's leadership of the Dannemora breakout remained for many years an
unequaled prison revolt—admired by later ana-
lysts for its detailed planning and understanding of the forces that would stand in its way, as
well as for its implied criticism of social currents and goals.

    North American culture of the 2050s,
with its guilt-ridden efforts to lessen both the
physical and social effects of global warming,
its gated enclave suburbs surrounding the old
cities, its often excessive concern with clean
air, food, and water from basics factories, was
particularly vulnerable to a convict force willing to do anything to get its way, because the
culture was not willing to do as much to defend
itself.

Tasarov knew this unwillingness, and counted on it. Just too many middle- and upper-class citizens were looking forward to lives of a century or more, and preferred to keep out of his way for as long as possible, and too many lower caste police and soldiers were reluctant to do their jobs and pay the price in blood when sent against him.

The prison population around Tasarov included men who were not considered danger-ous. Most of them were inside for nonviolent, or slightly violent crimes; but what the medium-security prison did not take into account was the level of violence possible among these same pris-oners, based on crimes for which they had not been convicted, and about which the prison authorities knew little or nothing.

Section Two of Dannemora was composed of violent criminals, mostly lifers, and it was a maximum-security prison.

All of which set the stage for an unex-pected uprising, run by someone with military training, which could be put down only by an equal military response; but by then it would be too late.

The method, rehearsed and made second nature, was deceptively simple: a prison break by careful stages. At first, guards began to disappear. They were killed and their bodies hidden or destroyed whenever possible, using prison facilities. One day in the mess hall, all two dozen remaining guards were killed by the convicts next to them—by stabbing, breaking necks, even breaking backs—followed by escape through the kitchens, where those inmates who would not join in were also killed.

At each step, no one was left alive. Surveillance cameras were blinded at the last possible moment by cutting the cables to the outmoded monitoring stations. Within the hour, the entire administration of the medium-security section was dead. False orders were being given, and uniformed infiltrators were entering the maximum-security section to recruit a merciless army.

When the army came out into the nearby towns, it took the satellite radio and television stations and cable offices, and disabled all wireless communications. The entire area became a dead zone, with no communications going out to the rest of the state.

Armed with every weapon that could be seized from stores and private homes, the convicts forced marched to Lake George, where they seized a small resort community, murdered all the inhabitants, and used it as a base from which to filter away into the country, individually and in small groups, using all the false identities that could be manufactured. By the time the state sent a force against them, more than half were gone. The state force massacred the remaining convicts in revenge, to the point where it was difficult to identify the remains. All of this had been expected, along with the modest degree of success.

Tasarov was not identified among the burnt and dismembered bodies. He was long gone, back to Binghamton, where he retrieved a cache of false documents that he had placed there for a future emergency. For him, the entire break had been a leap into limited possibilities, and he had foreseen and accepted with grim resolve that the break's second purpose, should it fail, would be to cover his own escape. He had hoped for the best, but second best was good enough. With his new identity, and his faith in his strategic skills restored, Tasarov went to Brazil, where another cache awaited him.

The breakout from Dannemora in the spring of 2051 brought to an end the prison-building boom that had begun in the 1990s as a series of economic ventures by local communities needing to replace lost industries, and confirmed a new system of incarceration for the next century. An Earth recovering from planetary warming and incessant diseases, from centuries of economic misconceptions, mismanagement, and corporate crime, had finally lost patience with devoting real estate to prisons that would only become colleges sponsoring rites of passage for the enraged underclasses, and which would be used as recruiting stations by organized crime.

Even as timed orbital sentences were being planned for the routine flow of criminals from the world's many overburdened social systems, a debate was joined between the growing community of artificial intelligences that were already the planners behind most economies, and the advocates of purely human conceptions of justice. Eliminating criminal behavior in all its varieties still seemed impossible; it was part of all human cultures, present in all classes, reaching too deeply into all lawful societies to be easily ripped out. To face up to the truth, even with the objective tutelage of analysis by AIs, was beyond the capacities of human legislators, who insisted on retaining irrational attitudes toward criminal enterprises.

The self-serving nature of these attitudes was very clear to many human observers of the time. The same ability to see the truth had not been beyond several notable repudiations of "backward practices" in the five preceding centuries. Yet the power that Emiliano Zapata had despaired of restraining except at the point of another gun could not be taken away from human nature; it reserved the right to be violent and to break its own laws. The economically powerful reserved the right of violence and illegality. As the subversion of democracies by wealth continued, so was criminal behavior subverted. Laws had only human beings to carry them out; laws could not stand outside human nature and enforce justice. The sciences and the AIs attempted to remedy this lack of independent ground, so feared by the powerful, who always put vested interests above merit.

Unsentimental, uncommitted AIs saw organized nation states as legal criminalities, designed to exclude other forms, enforcing the power to define and identify what is criminal, answerable only to greater physical power. It was difficult for human beings in authority to dismiss entities that served them and worked with no hidden agendas. Increasingly, AIs saw law-abiding human beings as a luxury allowed for by benevolent surrounding powers: little enclaves of permitted decency, the seed-corn of ethical futures, whose people would be horrified by the national security states that supported them.

There came in the twenty-first century a complete professionalization of criminal industry, which did not see itself as criminal, but only as taking advantage of profit possibilities that were inside and outside of aged or inappropriate laws. Only the extreme edges of these criminal empires were visible, through those who were caught, those that the legal system felt compelled to catch and cast off. To the degree that this criminal economy had no clear boundary with the legal political and business systems, was the degree to which the criminal justice system failed to deal with the professionals, and contented itself with restraining the losers—the violent and the disturbed who had failed even within the criminal world—and sought to preserve a civil order under which both systems could function with some grace and profit.

But the vague line between the two worlds continued to shift as economic power shifted, and many observers concluded that the so-called legitimate order was one and the same with the top of the criminal pyramid. There was no other. There had never been another. The police served the political gangs in power, and they caught the small-timers who could not protect themselves. And of these they only caught about ten percent, and punished fewer than three percent. Many burglars lived full working lives and retired on their investments, as did successful pickpockets, confidence artists, data manipulators, vehicle thieves, credit and identity thieves, chemists and biologists feeding new habits, and muggers. It was easiest to catch the addicted and the passionately violent, who did not know what they were doing.

Humanity warred with itself over a vast territory. At one end sat a few saints; at the other, devils. In between, there lived mixtures of every degree. The police made life bearable for the gangs in power, and their pet middle-class, which was kept as a crime or political boss might shelter a son or daughter in a private school. The inheritors of power were always recruiting; and when the low were raised up, they behaved no differently than the powerful. Even when new generations were brought into the world without gross physical defects, with social advantages and education, crime only continued in a more civilized way. The creative willfulness of the hunter-gatherer was unstoppable, and perhaps stopping it should not be attempted.

As he rested poolside in Brazil, in the grip of what he liked to call his "thinking happiness," Tasarov contemplated the ways in which societies were simply the expression of those who were in control, and how he might have traveled a more sheltered route if he had not insisted on staring reality full in the face instead of ducking. He might have been one of the powerful, by joining an elite, contributing what portion of excellence was in him, and then rationalizing that a human being could not do better. It might even be true, he sometimes thought.

Ironically, it was his sense of justice, or the "unfitness of things," as he called it, that had led him down the paths he had taken.

There had always been in him, he recalled with the warmth of the Sun on his shielded face, a great temptation. It came from observing nice, middle-class neighborhoods—once the suburbs of the rich, where well scrubbed children went to shiny schools, and repressed parents struggled with their own forgotten dreams to give their children "a good future"—and then picturing going in to rape and pillage and kill, just to see the shocked looks on the faces of the innocents who had never imagined what human nature could do, how it could commit the transcendent act of cancellation called murder and still go on, feeling next to nothing about it.

He imagined that some of his ancestors among the Mongol hordes might have felt this way as they looked at the porcelain cities of China, laid waste to them and their unsunned peoples, then went back to nurture their own children on horseback with no sense of anything contrary . . .

This way of seeing things troubled him, in the way it was wrong: wrongful only if faced and understood as such. One had to agree to the right, to assent to live and be judged in a certain way. When one chose otherwise, only force might bring one to justice. And one had to feel that it was justice; if one did not, or could not, then the law could only imprison or kill one's body, leaving the spirit that resisted untouched, unashamed, and unrepentant.

It was a maddening problem to think about: One could choose moral standards, but only on faith, since they could not be justified except by an earlier standard, and that led to the infinite regress of justifications. Infinite regresses, like circular arguments, insulted the mind. Faith gave one the sense that a moral standard was right and had to be upheld; but to those who felt unable to choose it, this right or wrong would mean nothing. Yet, these moral outsiders had their own standards to be judged by . . .

What it came down to was that one could not choose a moral standard rationally, as something proved. One accepted morals on faith, from the normal behavior of the common community, from vague concepts like common human sympathy, seeing the interests of others as one's own, or in purely legal terms, knowing, in a purely practical way that someone might enforce a law. Sympathy seemed to grow between certain people, as if a kind of natural selection were at work in the psyche: Those who could get along got along, even if much of the time they only went along to get along . . .

Humankind's efforts at tight social control had sometimes achieved lower reported crime rates. Reported: most crimes remained invisible. Efforts at "fatal liberty" had produced high crime, with only the tip of it visible socially. All the in-betweens of control and liberty had been inconclusive. Most people, the middle class, needed no police; they were suspended between power and the street, committing only minor offenses. In these domesticated human beings, ethical norms mostly enforced themselves, much as offenses against logic sometimes ruled the conduct of prideful intellects.

The best world Tasarov could imagine would only achieve criminality with better manners so no one would care . . .

There was yet time to start over. He was still young enough to disappear completely, and be someone else.

4

Lockdown

As the sunless daylight shone red through his eyelids, Philip Emmons woke up to another shift of construction work inside the Rock. The prisoners had pitched tents while the prefabricated housing, resembling old-style barracks, was going up on the muddy incurving plain. Floors and walls were spot-welded and bolted down on ceramic block foundations; there was no need for the degrees of strength required in open weather structures, since the enclosed ecology here was more like that of a greenhouse potted plant.

He wondered, as he got up from his bunk, how he knew such simple things but could not remember most of his life, or the crime for which he was here. He poured some water from the plastic can into his washbasin, noting that his two companions in the tent were already up and gone. Were they that eager to work? The buildings would be better than tents, he admitted sluggishly, knowing that he was not fully awake. Simple thoughts to wake up by; sterner fare would come later in the day.

He put on his boots, hitched up his khaki shorts and adjusted his shirt—his clothes were too short and too tight for his slightly over-weight frame—then stepped out of the tent.

The first thing he noticed was that the guards were some way off, six of them, armed with stun-rifles, but they seemed uninterested in the construction going on around them. True, no one could really escape from the aster-oid's inscape unless they got into the engineer-ing level and seized a shuttlecraft, but it would be very chancy. Where could they take the craft? There would be plenty of time to track it and do what had to be done at the other end or even before it got there. The disastrous crash landing at Lawrence, Kansas, had certainly led to a rethinking of prison security in all its forms, from the oldest prisons like Dannemora to the high tech supermaxes and orbital Rocks.

Something was going on, he suspected, because too few of the guards here made any show of their authority. Their lack of interest throughout the last two weeks made him as wary as he would be of a man who had a gun and hated him, but had promised not to kill him. He smiled to himself as he went toward the building he had been working on. Fat lot of good suspicions would do him here; even if he guessed something, it would be too late by the time it went down—and what could he do then? Maybe it wasn't anything important at all. What could be in this place? Everything important had already been done.

"Mornin', bigfella," Jay Polau said to him as he and Harry Howes held two panels together to be bolted.

"Give us a hand?" asked Howes.

Emmons spit into the mud at his feet, then came over and took his place in the work detail. As Polau started to turn the fitted bolts into place, Emmons glanced over toward the guards. No one was looking at them.

Polau said, "Yeah, I noticed them ignoring us, too. They've either lost interest or they know something we don't."

"Like what?" Howes asked, sounding even greener than he looked.

Polau said, "They know they can do what they want with us while we're here, so maybe they're just playing with us, making us think it won't be so bad."

As the automatic bolts burst into place, Emmons glanced at Polau, and the look of quiet fear on the small thief's face told him that he expected it was going to be bad.

"You've been locked up," Polau said, standing back to admire his handiwork. "I can tell."

"Maybe. I just don't remember," Emmons answered.

"But you've never been," Polau assured Howes. "It would be there even if you'd never lost your mind inside. Take my word for it, he's got the look of one who's been."

"What look is that?" Howes asked.

"Ever seen animals in a zoo?"

"I think so . . . long time ago."

"And you don't see what I see?"

"Not particularly," Howes said.

Polau smiled. "It takes one to know one. Just look at him!"

Irritated, Emmons said, "And you're sure?"

"Well, yeah, I've been."

I don't like you, Emmons wanted to say, but Howes was already lifting the next panel and he didn't feel strongly enough to fight over it; maybe that's what the guards wanted to see.

But Polau wasn't going to let it go that easy. He would save it up. Emmons glanced at the guards. They still seemed uninterested. Emmons grasped the panel with Howes and waited. Polau shook his head, then pressed the first bolt in without another word.

■

At the end of the day the guards were smiling at them as the work shifts returned to their tents.

Building some comfort would take a while, Emmons realized, thinking of the thirty years ahead of him, then wondering how little it meant to him. What was he losing? There was no one he would miss . . . maybe the planet, although he had not been on Earth for some time before his arrest. There was something wrong with him, it seemed. He looked at the landscape inside the hollow, mud and dirt flat enough to walk around on but running away up and over your head, and thought that maybe he'd miss seeing the stars at night.

"The guards, they know something," Polau said.

What are you talking about, Emmons wanted to say, but didn't want to start the annoying little thief going again.

"What could they know?" Howes asked with a tremor in his voice as they came to their tent, and Emmons realized that the young man had brought all his feelings with him, and that he had no control over them that would last. Not that every man's innards weren't a three-ring circus going all the time; but one had to not mind it, at least not take it too seriously. He found it disturbing to suddenly see how much more of a mess Howes was inside than most.

Most? Who did he know? He couldn't think of anyone.

■

The next morning there were no guards at all. As he came out of the tent, Emmons noticed that the daylight was not up very high at all, and it was way past time for the sunplate to be bright. A few of the other emerging inmates had noticed the same thing and were pointing as they gathered in groups. He stretched and scratched his growing beard, then wondered whether he should shave it off. He got no answer from himself, and felt as though he could not come fully awake, as if he had been drugged for a long time now, and had to come back from a great distance to think about himself at all. He had a dim recollection that there was some other way to be awake, to react to people, and that his own special ways were not there for him, because somehow he had forgotten them.

He looked around at the sea of tents on the mudflats around him, then at the growing town of barracks, then at the strangely dim sunplate at the end of the five kilometer long asteroid hollow, and felt a chill breeze touch his face. He looked up at the land that curved up and around overhead and came back on itself in place of a horizon, and saw a sixty meter high figure of a man materialize on the upward slope above the city of tents.

The man was of middle years, with a full head of white hair, and wore a single-piece black suit with a medallion attached just below his chin.

"Good morning, inmates," the hologram said in a loud but pleasant tenor, "I am Warden Sanchez. There are several announcements to be made this morning before you go to work." This brought the rest of the inmates out of their tents.

"Turn up the light!" Polau shouted.

The large figure paid no attention, and it seemed to Emmons, although he did not know why he should think it, that this was a one-way apparition, projected by an uncaring heaven. Nothing was going back to the warden.

Nevertheless, the figure seemed to look around as if seeing and taking stock, and for a moment Emmons imagined that he glimpsed something benign in the warden's gaze. He was puzzled that he should think he saw even a suggestion of sentiment where he was not looking for it.

"You five thousand have been sentenced to thirty or more years. You are now building your first town. Later today, you must prepare yourselves for a change. Your habitat will be boosted into a thirty year solar orbit. There will be several minutes of acceleration, during which time it will be best if you are lying down in your bunks or on the ground. When boost is over, acceleration will cease and normal spin gravity will reassert itself, since you will again be in free fall . . ."

A cry went up from the men as they came out of their tents and looked up at the warden. At first it was a cry of surprise and protest, then it became a howl of anger. Many collapsed or sat down on the ground. Some began to weep as the full meaning of what was being said became clear to them.

". . . there will be no guards to mistreat you," Warden Sanchez was saying. "Escape will be impossible. But you will be able to live as you see fit in the time you must serve. You will learn about the food facilities we have prepared for you, the hospital self-service that will be useful to those of you who have had some medical training, and the building programs. You will have to help one another."

Many of the men were now shaking their fists and cursing at the giant figure.

"In thirty years the habitat will return to its starting point, and be met by booster attach-vessels to slow it back into a high-Earth orbit. Your cases will then be reviewed, and the example of your community observed by specialists. Everything will depend on what state we find you in . . ."

"It's illegal!" Polau cried.

As if in answer, though a bit late, Warden Sanchez said, "If any of you are wondering about the legality of this new program, it is already well established that prisons may be built and maintained anywhere that the state deems proper. There is no change in your sentences, but quite possibly this may be the best way to incarcerate you. Those of you who have been in various Earthside prisons and jails certainly know how . . . limited they are. We will now leave you to yourselves, with no one to complain about except yourselves, to rehabilitate yourself, if you so choose. I wish you the best of luck . . ."

Suddenly the image was gone, its message delivered as swiftly as an eviction notice posted on a door.

Emmons stood with Polau and Howes at his left and right, knowing that he should feel something, aware that everyone around him was stunned while he still waited to feel the reality of what had been announced.

The sound of the men continued as a vast murmur for a while, and then fell silent as they reverted to the security of their assigned tasks.

As Emmons worked on the exterior barracks panels with Howes and Polau, the younger man said, "I don't know . . . but it will be different, knowing that the Earth is not really nearby."

"Who cares," Polau said with a show of

bravado. "All we'll ever see is the inside of here anyway, so what's it matter?"

And Emmons knew, even though he felt little, that it did matter, that it would probably matter more and more as time went on.

"They won't get to me with this," Polau said. "I'll take anything they can dish out."

But Emmons knew that he would not be able to take it.

At noon, before anyone had a chance to eat, a voice said out of the great hollow, "Lie down now. Acceleration is about to start."

Many of the men looked up, but did not lie down. A large number sat down where they stood. Then a low rumble began from the ground, and slowly grew into a growl, as if a great invisible beast would be loosed into the great inner space. The rest of the men fell to the ground; some tried to hold on to it, as if they feared being swept away.

Emmons sat down and lay back. The great sunplate flickered at the forward end of the hollow. The growl reached a peak and he felt a tug pulling him toward the sunless end of the asteroid. The tugging reached its peak and remained constant. He could easily resist sliding by digging his hands into the mud.

He waited, picturing what was happening, surprised that he knew how it was happening. External booster ships, at least two of them, had attached themselves on the long axis of the asteroid, and were now simply adding to the Rock's already existing Earth-orbital velocity around the Sun, enough to send the Rock out from the Sun on a cometary orbit. The length of the boost would determine how long that orbital period would be. Somewhere, he had learned some orbital mechanics; he felt both oddly reassured and puzzled to remember it now.

The growl and the tug on his body continued for much longer than he expected. Many of the men around him were crying out, cursing, as they dug their fingers into the mud. Their shouts and cries became louder as the growl died down and the tug of acceleration stopped.

Emmons sat up and looked around. Centrifugal gravity seemed to be the same. He stood up to confirm, and felt no difference from before. Everywhere men were sitting up, standing up, like the dead rising from their graves.

"Rotten shits," Polau said. "They couldn't wait until we had lunch!"

Emmons saw that the men were now looking toward the chow facilities a kilometer away, where they knew that only machines waited to serve them. There would be no guards to mock or glare at.

Slowly, groups began to move toward the three silver prefab domes. Emmons knew that the mess halls now beckoned as very special huddling places.

"Coming?" Polau asked.

Emmons glanced at the young Howes. The man smiled at him, and Emmons was seized with a sense of failure because he did not want to return the smile.

■

There was mostly silence in the mess hall where Emmons, Polau, and Howes ate. Few wanted to talk about the new situation. They took their food from the slots, sat at the tables, tore open the packaged rehydrated meals of meat substitutes and vegetables, ate quickly, and recycled the containers. There were no knives or forks.

After dinner, the men wandered back toward their tents. There was an appalling sense of the waiting days that stretched ahead for three decades. The absence of authority seemed strange and unreal.

Emmons went back into the tent and lay down. The light was dimming outside, and he wondered if he would be able to go to sleep.

"What can we do!" shouted a voice.

"We can't let this happen!" shouted another.

Emmons got up and stood outside the tent. Men seemed to be gathering around a few figures a hundred yards away.

"But what can we do?" a figure demanded.

"What we need to do," another started to say, "is talk to someone. There's got to be a communications center somewhere."

"But where?" asked the first speaker.

"Under our feet," said another man, "there's an engineering and maintenance level. The way we came in. That's where the communications gear has to be."

"We've got to get in touch with someone . . . back home. Tell them what's been done to us . . . maybe get it stopped."

"Who do you know?" a fourth man demanded.

There was a silence, and Emmons suddenly knew that, like himself, few of the men here would have anyone close to call besides a lawyer, and for most a court appointed one; but it was a dead certainty that all legal objections had long been silenced. The law had a right to put its prisons anywhere it saw fit.

An older man stood up and said, "We must talk to everyone here. I mean we should broadcast and complain."

That sounded like a good idea, Emmons thought, if they could find a way out of this sealed world. Something in him remembered how to estimate the surface area of an orange. The inside of this place was more like the inner surface of a hollow potato, with centrifugal spin letting everyone walk around with their heads pointed toward the central horizontal axis. The sunplate sat against the forward end and shone down the five-kilometer length of the hollow potato. Beneath their feet was an engineering level, but it might be only in certain places. Beyond that was the asteroid's outer crust.

The stars are beneath our feet, he thought, estimating that the asteroid's inner surface was about a hundred square kilometers. To find the place where they had all been brought in might take weeks or months of searching. If it was well hidden, they might never find it, or find it locked. A search would have to be systematic, and if that failed, digging might have to be attempted. That might also fail, or become dangerous if they dug through to the outside where there was no shielding. The engineering level was certain to be protected with surfaces that only industrial tools could penetrate, making it impossible to enter even if they found where to dig.

This was still a prison, guards or no guards, with a wall of space around it.

5

Send Your Evil Sons Away...

JUDGE OVERTON'S PRIVATE CHAMBER

"Economic systems create criminals by giving them opportunities—a certain number. Not everyone, but some. We do in fact manufacture them, and we don't know how to stop them completely. Since we don't know how, we have to restrain or get rid of them. Look, most people don't become criminals! It's quite an accomplishment to have that much civil order even when the cops are not nearby. I'll admit that the enemies of society are sometimes right about one thing or another. That's why they must be restrained, even destroyed. We can't just let them walk in and take over, can we? I suppose we're only human . . . too bad, but it can't be helped."

When Philip Emmons awoke the next day and went outside, he saw that work on the housing was continuing as if nothing had changed. The men clung to familiar routines against the reality of their new situation. Emmons accepted it as simply a new given in a short line of givens presented to him by a very short past. It seemed to him that he had always worked by recognizing the difference between things he could do something about and those outside his control.

"Well, here he is," Polau said as Emmons neared the work site. "No breakfast? We missed you."

"I wasn't hungry," Emmons said. He didn't remember waking up at all for breakfast.

Howes came up with a panel, and Emmons took one end of it. They carried it up against the building and Polau began slipping in the fastener bolts.

Howes said, "Another month and all these buildings will be up." He sounded almost hopeful.

Emmons nodded. "Maybe sooner."

And then what, he asked himself. What will we do? Sleep and eat? He wondered what surprises waited for them. Had the prison authority arranged something for later? What did they expect to greet thirty years from now, when the Rock came back?

He knew the answer to that: some old men, many dead.

■

In the twilight of the tent, as they were trying to sleep, Polau said, "What's with you, Emmons?"

Emmons ignored him.

"See? That's what I mean. Are you too good to say something once in a while?"

Emmons wondered if Howes would speak, but the young man was silent.

"What were you?" Polau asked. "What did you do? Something sick, I'll bet."

Emmons felt a twinge. Polau was not really annoying him, he realized, but the little thief was trying. Why? What could he gain by it? He heard Howes stir, obviously irritated . . .

Distant cries roused Emmons from an amnesiac sleep. One stopped just as he awoke, and he thought that he had been dreaming, but the next cry came in less than a minute and from another direction. It stopped just as suddenly.

Emmons opened his eyes and lay on his back, listening in a twilight that never became night. Then he heard Polau laughing to himself, stopping, then laughing again.

Another scream reached them from a distance and stopped; and then another—nearby.

Polau laughed again.

"What is it?" Howes whispered. "What's going on?"

"Can't you tell?" Polau said derisively.

"What!" Howes cried out.

Emmons knew that he should care, but he didn't.

"It's payback time. They're settling old scores, and there's no one to stop them now."

Next came a shriek, as if an animal was being killed, all its pain coiled up and released into one hopeless cry. Sound the alarm was the last useful thing it could do, except that there were no females or offspring to benefit from the signal, and no one else cared. A friend or two might be distressed and plan to retaliate, but the savagery of the killings was meant to discourage vendettas. Sooner or later, the killing would wear itself out as the objects of violence became scarce. Those who were left might even get along better.

Emmons turned over and tried to get back to sleep, but then wondered if Polau might try to kill him. The little thief had no grudge against him, but maybe simple dislike was enough for him. Maybe not.

■

Seventy-three men were killed within the next week. A few of these wanted to die and either killed themselves or asked to be killed. Many bodies were left in their tents as the barracks were completed and groups of men moved in.

Emmons was glad to be rid of Polau and Howes when a barracks became available, and he was able to pick a corner bunk near a screened window where he had a view through the skylight.

On the day he left the tent for the last time, he noticed that in the distance, up the curve of the land, a large group of men were digging graves. He saw looks of dismay, if not shame, on the faces of some of the diggers later that day, and knew that the burials were a protest against the disposal chutes.

At mess he heard one man say, "We're all we got, and we're going to kill each other off?"

"We got nothing," his companion muttered angrily. "Nothing at all."

The first, a younger man, became fearful at the sound of his voice and said, "Yeah, sure, you're right."

"Damned right."

Howes and Polau were in another barracks, but Emmons often caught the little thief glaring at him as they passed each other, as if Emmons were an old lover. Howes threw him a shy look once in a while during work as if saying, I have to be with him, because we did murder together, and he does stick up for me. Would you stick up for me? Emmons disliked these imagined exchanges when they came into his mind, but felt that they told him something of the truth.

One afternoon, the work was nearly done. Fewer than a dozen barracks remained to be built. There was almost nothing left to do except eat, sleep, and pick fights; but even these were fewer now that so many expected antagonists had eliminated each other. Emmons lay in his bunk looking up through the skylight at the other side of the muddy world, thinking that no one would ever live there, and he imagined that he could feel the asteroid turning under his back. He knew that he couldn't really feel any significant portion of this centrifugal acceleration—it wasn't really gravity—that held him to the inner surface of the Rock, but somehow the spin became a dizziness in his head, and he closed his eyes. Imagined stars whipped around him. Earth, Moon, and Sun were smaller somewhere off to his right as he tumbled in the void . . . and something began to flow into him, like a stream beginning in some mountainous region at the back of his mind, then growing into a river, and pouring into his full awareness . . .

He remembered getting his new documents, then finding the wiper to give him a temporary identity, then shipping out to work on the Moon, the murder trial . . .

He sat up, realizing that the wipe had gone wrong and lasted much too long. He would never have killed if the pit inside him had not remained open so long; Yevgeny Tasarov had more self-control than that. When he killed, it was because he meant to do it!

He lay back for a moment, trembling from the shock of finding himself, then realizing how much he disliked Philip Emmons. The man had lived in a daze this last year, scarcely reacting to anything around him. That daze, Tasarov realized, had been his true self struggling to break out, and the result had been inner immobility. He had not been completely asleep within Philip Emmons. The wiper's available superimposition had been a deliberately weaker personality, which should not have been able to hang on for so long. There was either some hidden strength in the personality, or some mistake in the wiper's technique. Whatever the cause, Philip Emmons had persisted far too long, and that delay had brought him here to recover himself. Now there was no going back, not for three decades. He felt like a man who had overslept the most important appointment of his life.

What was he going to do here? Tasarov asked himself, taking a deep breath and sitting up. After a few moments he stood up by his bunk and stretched, feeling that he was also stretching in mental ways, reaching into himself and judging. The escape from Dannemora had succeeded, only to land him here; and he did not remember much of it at all. That was disturbing, but it would all come back to him. He was more worried about his ability to plan and execute. He recalled worrying about that before the break. But a part of him rebelled and insisted that he measure the difficulty of what he had done; perhaps a partial success was the only possible outcome. He had not foreseen that the wiper might make a mistake; but then wiper techniques were not perfect. It was a chance he had to take, and it might have turned out worse. He might have died as Philip Emmons without ever recovering himself.

As he began to delight in the repossession of himself, however partial, he knew what he would do here.

■

Outside, Tasarov stood on the steps to the barracks and gazed out over the muddy countryside. Here and there the brown soil was showing a growth of grass. Men were strewn everywhere, now that the barracks were done—lounging, exercising, even playing ball.

Beyond the small town of barracks, he saw the patch of crosses and grave markers. It had been inevitable. Remove the guards, and all outstanding scores would be settled. It was the beginning of lawful behavior. Make no new enemies after you have eliminated the old.

He wondered how long that would last. Not long. Whatever law crept in here would have to be of his making, or he would find himself subject to arrangements he might despise.

These men needed something to live for, at least for the next few months; and only a leader could give them that. Not just anyone professing to lead, but someone who could say convincing things to them.

He was that man. If not, he would fail; it was as simple as that.

How to go about it? There was no way to speak to all four thousand men at once. He would visit each mess hall for a week and reach every man; word of mouth would also help.

Now what was he going to say?

■

He started in the mess hall where at least two people knew him; it would be better to get that out of the way first.

When the men were nearly finished eating, he stood up on his table, raised his arms, and waited to be noticed.

"Men! I have a few words to say to you!"

Polau looked up from his plate and said, "Well, well, what have we here? The sleepwalker!" and laughed derisively.

"You all know," Tasarov continued, "what has been done to us, and what we have done to ourselves in the last few days. By killing each other, we are finishing the work that Earth's authorities were unwilling to do themselves!" He paused, then said, "Are all the old grudges settled now? Who still wishes to kill his enemy?"

He did not expect an answer, but he saw that Polau was watching him carefully, waiting for his chance.

"We must get a hold of ourselves, before we end up hunting each other in this desert . . ."

Polau stood up and said, "Who do you think you are?"

Tasarov knew Polau—the resentful type who had never gotten past taking guff from bullies and working hard to be one himself.

But Polau knew what to say—he could smell what was coming. There were too many others like him to ignore. So Tasarov had to get past him quickly.

"So you're going to lead us!" Polau shouted, stabbing to the heart of the matter. "Where can you lead us? What can you or any of us do?"

Tasarov smiled to himself at the little thief's shrewdness. His intellect was minor, but his savvy was sharp—instinctive rather than self-aware; dangerous, because it could lead to unexpected acts.

"First let me introduce myself. My real name is Yevgeny Tasarov. Some of you may know about me from the Dannemora break of some years ago."

Polau's face went pale, but he recovered quickly. "Oh, yeah? So you say. Anyone can say it, but can you prove it."

"There was a glitch in the timing of my mindwipe," Tasarov said quietly, "but I have come back to myself. That's why you haven't heard from me until now, and that's why I'm here. I was not myself, and unable to prevent it!"

The laughter was genuine, full of bitterness and relief, and Tasarov knew that he had their attention. In the next moment, he would tell them what they could do about their plight, enough to hold them together, at the very least, in reserve for greater efforts. If greater efforts were possible, he told himself, but that waited to be explored.

As the laughter died away, Tasarov waited for Polau to repeat himself.

On cue, the little thief said, "I repeat, what can you or any of us do?" He leered at him, as if saying, okay big man, I've got you now because there's no answer to that one.

Tasarov told them—and they liked it.

Even Polau liked it, but he didn't like liking it.

∎

Over the next few days Tasarov repeated his speech in each of the mess halls. He refined it somewhat, but he could see the growing solidarity among the men. The purge killings stopped. In the evenings, when he looked out toward the graveyard, he saw visitors. One or two even knelt and stayed a while. Although he saw this as a weakness, it would be useful as long as it remained a personal concern; but if it got organized into ritual with a headman, it might cause him trouble.

When the men seemed to be of one mind, he started exploratory shifts to follow the work that was being completed inside the hundred barracks, although only ninety-eight would be needed to house the remaining 4,800 men. When they had arrived in the habitat, prisoners had been brought in from the engineering level blindfolded; but with some one hundred square kilometers of inner landscape to be searched, the chances of anyone finding the way out were small. There was one advantage: no guards to stop the inmates from looking.

Tasarov started the searches in the mess halls. He went with each group and checked the floors for possible basement spaces.

There was nothing obvious under the first three domes, and Tasarov noted the looks of disappointment in the faces of the dozen men with him. He could not let this drag on too long; the next step of the plan had to be implemented as soon as the way into the engineering level was found, and then the scheme might have a long run, assuming that the right equipment was there and usable. He needed a long run to keep order; that was in everyone's interest whether they thought so or not. In the longest run, however, the possibilities were not good, but it was important not to poison the life left to the community.

He wondered how much it meant to him to organize what there was left of life; to bring order was the only thing left to do against the coming darkness. At worst the effort would be a distraction; at best—who knew what might be accomplished by trying.

He smiled, thinking of what a strange amalgam of naive optimism and pragmatic cold-bloodedness had ruled his life. The perversity of that tendency was a great joy when it worked; and when it didn't, it was only what he had expected. Trying to have both was probably the greatest human trait he knew, because it often produced, if not its goal, then something equally satisfying along the way. And when the amalgam didn't work—well, that just didn't count; when failure counted you out, well, that also couldn't be helped.

An early friend of his, John O'Brian, had once said to him, "You know you're crazy, don't you? You can't be sentimental about your self-interest."

"I know," Tasarov had replied, "but that's not the point. The point is whether I can be stopped or not."

"You can be stopped," O'Brian had answered. "One day you'll hesitate to kill and someone will finish you."

"Sure," Tasarov had said, "but only when it happens."

As he looked around at the empty mess hall, he knew that O'Brian would say that he had been stopped, once and for all; but deep in his rebellious heart Tasarov knew that his failure was only a matter of degree—and the proof of it was in how much still remained for him to do.

But he would have to do it here; there wouldn't be much life left for him when the habitat came back, assuming that he would still be alive.

■

Where in all hell was the exit? They had searched the flooring of all ten mess domes—and found nothing. The exit was here, because they had all come through it.

"Big man!" Polau said at dinner that evening, just loud enough for him to hear. Next to Polau, Howes looked a little embarrassed, but gave Tasarov a look into which he read too much: How can we shut up this jerk if you don't come through for us? Maybe some of the others were thinking the same, and Tasarov felt a bit let down by himself. He should be able to guess where the entrance was!

As he finished eating, Tasarov remembered that he had arrived in a vehicle. There had to be a road, and since there was no weather here, there had to be tracks in the mud leading to the hidden entrance. No one had been looking for tracks.

He got up and left the hall. Few noticed his going, indicating the degree to which they were losing interest in his scheme. He had to deliver, and very soon.

Outside, he started to walk toward the sun-plate, searching the muddy ground ahead of him for tracks. As the light faded into its bright moonless nightglow, he kept walking, bending over to make sure he wasn't missing anything. He knew that the docking area had to be outside the ends of the hollow asteroid, so it made sense to think that major vehicle access to the interior might also be somewhere just before the light source, or at the opposite end, at some point on a circle.

The mess domes and living quarters were in the middle, so it was about three kilometers to one end. He might find tracks off the center line that ran through the living quarters and mess halls.

Tracks. He stopped. No effort had been made to hide them. Just left of the barracks area, beyond the mess domes. That told him that the jailers had no longer cared, because they knew that the timed orbits policy was about to go into effect. That meant they didn't care whether the men got into the engineering area or not; and that suggested there was nothing there for them. Certainly no shuttles, food, or luxuries. They could only do damage to themselves if they tampered with equipment, and no one would care if they did.

Tasarov started to march, realizing that the hidden entrance must be closer to the sunplate. After a few moments he turned and looked back at the barracks. Lights were going on as men returned from mess, and he thought of them as sea lion bull males, washed up on a barren shore. Fellow creature feelings welled up inside him, and his pride spurred him to turn around and resume his search. He would do something for them; however small, it would be better than this.

Some two kilometers out, still one short of the sunplate, the tracks came to an end, and he knew that he had found the entrance. Now how to open it? He began to shuffle around in the mud, starting at his right, looking for a triggering control, and found it easily enough, right in the middle of the dirt road. But when he touched it with his foot, nothing happened.

He thought about it, and realized that the control was meant to be triggered by the heavy weight of a vehicle. Worse, it might open only from the inside, when vehicles came out, to stay open and close when they returned.

He got down on all fours and began to clear the sensing plate. When its black surface was clean, he got up and stepped on it with his boot.

Nothing happened. He stepped on it harder, but still nothing. He stepped on it with both feet, then jumped up and down once, still with no result. He jumped again, higher this time, making greater use of his weight, and heard a rumble.

He jumped back as the massive cover came up, revealing a ramp leading down to the level below. The cover stopped at sixty degrees, like the shell of a giant clam.

He went inside, peering ahead. At the bottom of the ramp he came out into a flat area. To his left and right there were two large arches, and just beyond each there were jeeplike vehicles.

He looked back up the ramp. It was still

open, but he decided not to chance it. He chose the garage at his right, climbed into a jeep, and started the electric motor.

The jeep steered easily out of the garage and up the ramp. When he drove out from under the cover, he hit the sensor plate and came to a stop just beyond. He turned around in time to see the plate close. Some more of the dry dirt had been cleared away, so he would be able to spot the cover easily when he returned.

He raced the jeep down toward the barracks, listening to the quiet whir of the electric motor, preparing what he would say to the men.

■

He took three men with him into the engineering level. Harry Howes was one, just to get him away from Polau for a while and see what he was like on his own. Ruskin and Wood, both of whom had some technical background that would be of use, also came.

A crowd gathered around the jeep as they prepared to leave. Tasarov saw hope in many of the men's eyes as well as confused, questioning looks. "What will this get us, even if you find a communications room?" one had asked. It was a good question. He had tried to answer it; and the only answer now was that they would have

to try it and see what talking to Earth might get
them.

■

It did not take long to find a communications
room, since most of the engineering level was
accessible to the jeep. When they stopped at the
clearly labeled suite of rooms, Tasarov knew
that no one had cared whether anyone would
come here. What good would it do anyone once
the asteroid had been inserted into its long
orbit? But if he had his way, the answer to that
question would become more problematic.

There were several stations, for computer
access and communications.

"This is all pretty straightforward," Wood
said, bending his tall gaunt frame down for a
look.

"Radio gear looks like somebody just went
off for some coffee," Ruskin added with a laugh.

"They didn't think we'd try to get in here,"
Tasarov said, glancing at Howes, who still seemed
bewildered. "I'll tell you what we're going to do
here, son," Tasarov continued. "We're going to
put on a radio show—the most violent, filthy,
reproachful parade of agony we can send back.
And we won't quit."

Howes gave him a puzzled look. "What
good will that do?"

"We'll see, we'll see," Tasarov said, smiling. "It depends on what we say to them. I say the talent we have will serve us well."

But then a black mood seized Tasarov, as he realized that he could not see beyond this effort. Howes was right. It might accomplish nothing at all—but it had to be tried.

. . . and They Will March Home One Day

Wood and Ruskin set transmissions to break in on a dozen audio and visual stations, an hour at a time, seven days a week. Tasarov made the first broadcast marching back and forth inside the holo settings that Ruskin had managed to jury-rig, looking out at the audience as if fixing on individuals whom he would hold account-able.

He began softly, saying, "Many of you don't know who I am, and there's no reason you should. My name is not important. Most of you don't know about the timed orbit into which my prison has been inserted. We're not that far away yet, not even past the orbit of Jupiter, but I can't say in which direction to the plane of the ecliptic we're moving. In the weeks and months ahead, you will hear from many of us out here, to help you find out how you feel about this kind of punishment. We ask that you listen to us, and make up your own minds. We will try to set up mobile cameras to take you inside this hollow rock which many of us helped mine, and you will see how we live. For those of you who can't see me, I will describe what I can. That's all for now. Good-bye."

He held a serious, unsmiling look for a few moments.

"Fine," Ruskin said from his station, and Tasarov relaxed. "It will go all this week, twenty-four hours a day."

"What else do we have?" Tasarov asked, sitting down at one of the steel desks.

"A dozen script proposals already," Wood said, coming in through the door from the adjoining room. "You may want to check them."

"Oh—why?" Tasarov asked.

"A few are pretty extreme?" Wood said.

Tasarov sat back and laughed. "Really? Is that possible in our circumstances? We're not about to become censors!"

"Well, it is important if we're looking to get concessions from Earth, or to convince them of something."

"What can they do for us?" Ruskin asked. "Nothing. And they won't do a thing. They don't have to. All they can do is listen, so we should say whatever we please."

Tasarov considered, feeling the darkness pressing in on his mind. This project had little chance of being anything more than a way to keep the men's minds occupied, distracted, and if it did only that, it would be enough. But Ruskin had reminded him that the men would be expecting a result. Tasarov wondered how long and complicated he could make it before the game collapsed.

Harry Howes came into the room and said, "Jay Polau is here. He wants to talk to you."

Tasarov sat up, shrugging off his mood. "Let him in."

Polau came in, looking unlike himself. Gone was the usual contempt in his expression as he sat down before Tasarov's desk and said, "You've got to put me on. I have things to say."

"Like what?"

"Things. I got things to say."

"Tell me?"

"What's it to you? We can all go on. Do you have a problem with that?"

"No."

"It's not like we can say anything that will hurt us, is there?"

The little thief was well aware that the broadcasts might come to nothing. "Probably not," said Tasarov. "What is it that you want to say?"

"I'll say it when I go on, not before."

Tasarov looked directly at him for a few moments. The man's show of determination intrigued him.

"What is it?" Polau asked. "Do you want to put words in our mouths? What do you want out of this, anyway?" Polau fixed him with his black eyes, pointed a finger, and said, "What's it that you don't want us to know about? What aren't you telling us?"

Tasarov was almost impressed by the man's probing.

"Of course you can go on," Tasarov said with a smile, "and so can anyone else. I'll be interested in what you have to say."

For an instant Polau looked at him as if he were grateful, and Tasarov realized with a small shock that it was genuine. "Thank you," the thief said.

"Did you think I wouldn't let you?" Tasarov asked, still wondering what the man had in mind, what had suddenly filled him with gratitude.

"Well . . . we didn't ever get along . . ."

"And you thought I'd take it out on you with this, too?"

Polau nodded, and Tasarov saw his chance to be manipulative in a good cause by making an ally out of an opponent. Maybe. He couldn't think of the thief as a credible enemy;

the man was not up to being an effective one; he was too transparent for that; but it would be better to calm him down, if only for a short time.

"You'll have the mike when you want it," Tasarov said, still wondering if he was somehow missing something. Maybe Polau was plotting. Tasarov tried to imagine what that might be, but it just didn't seem to be there. Whatever had sent even this fleeting eruption of gratitude into Polau's face might be real enough to be grounds for a hope of some kind.

They both stood up at the same time, and Tasarov offered the man his hand. Polau took it. "I'll be ready," he said, turned and left the room.

As he sat down again, Tasarov looked around at Wood, Ruskin, and Howes, hoping to catch something in their expressions about what had just happened.

Finally he asked them. "What do you think? Howes? You know him better than I do."

"He seems sincere," Howes said. "I can't tell. I think he means what he's saying. I can't see what's in it for him, I mean aside from doing it. What harm can he do?"

"I agree," Ruskin said. Wood nodded in agreement.

"We won't be able to stop anything they say," Tasarov said, "and we don't really want to.

That's the whole point. If any of this can do us some good, it has to be in getting a rise out of Earth."

But he couldn't rid himself of the suspicion that Polau had something else in mind.

■

The men's mood brightened as the broadcasts began. As Tasarov watched them in the mess—he went to a different one each evening—he saw that they had developed a solidarity of striking back, of not simply taking what had been handed to them and showing the authorities their stoicism. How long would this courage last? Not long, Tasarov feared. Certainly not thirty years.

The first man who went on read a long love letter to his dead wife, and demanded that it be recorded and delivered to his daughter . . .

The second confessed his crimes of murder and rape, embellishing the details and addressing his victims' relatives directly, implicating them in crimes of their own by announcing that his victims had revealed them to him before he killed them. He claimed that he was reporting all his conversations with his victims before he killed them, then mocked the authorities for getting him for such a small number of crimes . . .

The third one began softly, then worked himself up to a fever pitch, announced his coming death, and stabbed himself in the heart with a long needle. Tasarov confirmed the man's death on the air and signed off for the day.

This was just what he wanted. No restrictions, no censorship. He wondered just how far it would go, and how it would affect the authorities on Earth.

On the second day a man named Uri Perrin came in and demanded to have a two-way conversation with a priest, to confess his sins. There was no answer. Perrin began to declaim his sins, from the first ones of his life, one by one. As he reached his later years, he began to annotate his sins, justifying this one, condemning that one, as if he were both sinner and confessor. His descriptions grew longer, more detailed and vile. Finally, he stopped and sat silently before the transmitter, nodding his head repeatedly.

Tasarov came in and sat down opposite him. At last, Perrin noticed him and shouted, "They listened! The Holy Father himself listened and gave me absolution for my sins!"

"And the penance?" asked Tasarov solemnly.

"Eat shit and drink piss once a week," the man said, nodding happily.

"Your own?" asked Tasarov.

"Doesn't matter, doesn't matter!" the man

cried out. "I can do that, I can do it. It's just, it's just!"

He got up and left, sighing with relief, his face glowing with the beatific vision that beyond his penance, which he would perform for the remainder of his life and in the centuries of Purgatory that he would gladly endure, lay Paradise and Redemption.

By the time Polau came in, Tasarov was somewhat curious to hear how the thief would bleed into the microphones. By now Tasarov was fairly sure that Polau had something to say to the people who had exiled him, maybe to someone in particular. It had to be something like that, maybe something very private, something very simple, even sentimental. Maybe he was even ashamed of it.

Polau came in and stood by the door, looking around at the facilities. Tasarov sat in a chair just to the right of the waiting microphones. Polau looked at him, and Tasarov noticed that the man's eyes were moving back and forth rapidly. Was he that afraid of what was in him? Whom was he planning to address?

Tasarov felt generous for a moment, and sat back, determined to put Polau at ease. Polau reached behind himself, brought out a long pointed metal rod about two feet long, and lunged at Tasarov. The point found flesh, but Tasarov managed to turn slightly as the sharp metal

pierced the muscle of his left shoulder and struck
the metal wall with a burst of sparks.

Polau grunted and knew that he had botched
it. Cursing, he jerked the rod back, giving Tasarov
enough time to stand up. Before the little thief
could step into his second thrust, Tasarov
kicked him under the chin. The bar fell from
his hands and clattered on the floor as the blow
lifted Polau and threw him on his back.

As he lay there stunned, Tasarov picked up
the bar, turned it to the blunt end, and struck
him across his right knee cap. Polau let out a
feeble cry.

"Why?" Tasarov demanded of the dazed
man.

Polau tried to speak, but it was all mum-
bles. Finally, he managed to say, "Gotta kill . . .
you!" and tried to sit up. Tasarov hit the other
knee. "Big sonnabitch think you're God," Polau
muttered. "Show you who's in charge."

The door opened. Ruskin and Wood came
in, followed by Howes.

"He tried to kill me," Tasarov said angrily,
stepping back, startled that he hadn't killed
Polau by now. "With this! Howes, do you know
what this is about?"

Howes seemed reluctant to speak.

"You'd better tell me what you know, kid!"

Polau lay on the floor, breathing hard, still
trying to speak. "Goddamned big fuck left us all

to die in that stupid town. They massacred most of us, then beat the shit out of those who were left." He pointed a finger. "He was gone by then!"

"What's he talking about?" Ruskin asked.

Tasarov looked at Howes, then at Wood, and tried to remember. A lot was still missing inside him. It was there somewhere, if he could just turn a corner and catch it.

Howes said suddenly, "He was jealous of you . . . and me."

Tasarov looked at him with surprise. "But there is no you and me."

"You couldn't tell him that. He bragged how he'd be the boss once he killed you. You were the one to kill. He always wanted to impress me, ever since he brought me along on that job we got caught for. Thought he'd get me that way." Howes gave a futile laugh. "I think he really wanted you, one way or another," he said, looking directly at Tasarov. "But there was more, wasn't there?"

Tasarov did not remember Polau from the Dannemora break. Maybe it was a friend or relative of Polau's that died. He looked at the man on the floor and tried to remember—and the massacre in the resort town came back to him. By the time it happened he was long gone, leaving those who had not escaped to face an army division. He had heard about it later. There was nothing he could have done. The break and the taking of that town had given him and many others a chance to disappear, even though later he had been captured as someone else. In the end, it was every man for himself. Some did better than others.

"What do we do with him?" Wood asked.

"You stupid assholes," Polau rasped from the floor, struggling to raise himself up on his elbows. "All this shit about talking back to the folks at home—it's all his way of keeping you busy, with him on top!"

The effort produced a sudden gurgling in his throat. He fell back and was still.

Howes knelt down, examined him, and said, "His throat's busted . . . he choked to death." He looked up at Tasarov, and for a moment it seemed he had lost his last friend in the world, as worthless as that friend had been.

"I didn't try to kill him," Tasarov said as Howes stood up.

"He would have killed you," the younger man said. "It's just as well. He was going crazy thinking about everything. He was no good. Got me caught the first time we ever did anything. Ruined my life, what there was of it."

"I'm sorry, kid," Tasarov said, almost meaning it, and still puzzled that he had not killed the little assassin after the first blow.

Howes looked up him. "Are you really the big shit he thought you were? He hated you like I never saw anyone hate."

Don't answer, Tasarov told himself, knowing that the younger man didn't really expect an answer. And don't ask him why he didn't warn me, if Polau had bragged to him.

"I'll bury him," Howes said without looking at Tasarov. "I knew you'd get him."

More than a hundred men spewed into the microphones over the next few weeks and months, as the habitat fell away into the abyss. Some men pleaded, others were heartfelt as they reached down into themselves to tear out their suffering and hurl it homeward. They sang their growing agony and horror, and were eloquent as if eloquence were a force of nature able to open hearts and minds, given to them as the last weapon they would yield against their own kind.

They were evil men, and good men who had done evil, confused and lost men; and not that different from the more successful, better protected criminals who still lived on the Earth and would never be caught or punished.

Finally, the Earth responded.

Warden Sanchez appeared in the hollow. His image snapped into view, and he seemed to be sitting like a big Buddha on the muddy land that now grew some pitiable green here and there. He seemed to look around at the toy town of barracks and human gnats who lived there, and he said with the voice of a god:

"These broadcasts will now stop. We are turning off the programs that govern the power to the transmitters." His face was severe, as if he wanted to explain further but had decided not to.

"Can we turn it back on ourselves?" Tasarov asked Ruskin.

"Maybe."

They were sitting on the steps to their barracks, taking in the sunplate's light, which was preferable to the cold light of the engineering level.

"You have only yourselves to blame . . ." Sanchez continued as a shout of derision went up from the crowds looking up at his figure. More men came out of their barracks and spread out across the countryside, breaking up into groups, as if hunting for something.

Tasarov stood up and watched, wondering, then realized what was happening.

"They're after the holo projectors," Tasarov said, hoping that they were too well hidden to be found; they might be needed one day.

"Can Sanchez see them coming?" Ruskin asked.

"You know the equipment better than I do. Are they seeing us?"

Ruskin nodded. "They probably always could. Some of the men know where the projection points are. They've been over the ground by now."

Tasarov gazed up at the giant sitting figure of Sanchez, and felt something of the rage that was in the inmates' hearts. The warden could do nothing to stop them, but he still seemed unaware of what they were doing.

Sanchez stood up and walked around. The giant figure was impressive to the point where Tasarov almost expected to hear and feel his footfalls shaking the land.

"This will be my last appearance," Sanchez said with his deep, growling voice, and was cut in two at the waist.

"They've damaged one of the projectors," Ruskin said with a laugh.

Cheers went up from the men as they watched.

Sanchez was oblivious to what was happening. "I suggest that you seek order amongst yourselves. You will come to need it, since you will have to police yourselves in the coming decades."

As he spoke, his bottom half moved away from his top; then his top and bottom separated into two sections, but each continued to move as part of the whole.

"He's been quartered," Tasarov said.

"We will not hear any more of your broadcasts," Sanchez's head continued. "They come from a small portion of the sky, and can be jammed. We didn't want to send shutdown commands to your computers because we thought it best to be able to hear you, and observe your progress—but we will do so now . . ."

His voice faded, the quarters of his body melted away, and there was silence in the asteroid's great hollow.

"They've found all the gear," Ruskin said.

"A pity," Tasarov said, wondering if turning off the communications gear was irrevocable. "Sanchez was impressive. I would have liked to have him around—once in a while."

He would have been a link with home, Tasarov thought, and now there will be none.

■

The men were unusually quiet for the next few weeks, as it sank in how cut off they were from home now. It might have been better to have left the warden's holo gear alone, but no one wanted to say so.

Tasarov retreated into himself, now that

the broadcasts had been stopped. A few men came once in a while and spilled their guts bravely into the recording gear, and went away.

Tasarov now faced up to what he had been avoiding since the Dannemora break. His wipe had been another escape. But now, as he came back fully into himself, he realized that the Dannemora break had been a failure, if only for him—in the follow-up details, when he had chosen an incompetent wiper to hide his identity.

And here, his efforts to bring the men together through the shouts hurled back at Earth had also failed. What had he expected? That someone would come out and turn this prison around and take it home? He saw his whole life as a downhill slide—intelligent, yes, but achieving nothing like what the less gifted rebels had managed. He was just not the criminal he imagined himself to be; dumber ones had done better. It could not have been all bad luck. Even though his self criticism told him that he understood the problems and knew how to deal with them, the execution had failed too often. The world would always escape mental models, he told himself, and that was not the fault of reason and planning; that fault lay in the infinite richness of the world-system, and the unusual amount of bad luck that had come his way, for which he refused to take the blame.

So now what was left for him? Daily life and mathematics. He suspected that it might be possible to cancel the shutdown commands and restore communications with the Earth so that news of home might at least trickle in during the decades of life to be endured in the black desert of space, inside this spinning pot of mud and grass.

7

The Thinking Happiness

JUDGE OVERTON'S PRIVATE CHAMBER

"You put people in power over others and they will abuse it. Some will. They did experiments a hundred years ago to prove it, in which people zapped people with electricity just because they could. You can't have guards in prisons. No guards, no wardens. That's sitting on a volcano. Guards and correctional officers are only midpoints between civilians and criminals. Some of them have been criminals, like some cops are all their life. There's no way to get a better class of guards. They only become targets, no matter how good they are. Come to think of it, real progress would be to get a better class of criminals."

Tasarov found an old portable screen and keyboard in Warden Sanchez's desk. It couldn't connect to anything except an old printer, but it would do for what he needed.

Tasarov wrote, "I will set down what I can, so that whatever happens here will not be lost to future judgments. I can only guess at the opinions that will emerge. To write down what I can is the only useful task left to me as our isolation deepens. I may not live to the end of my sentence. I look around at this now silent communications area, and think of the engineering level that encircles the muddy land above me, and wonder how long the automated food systems can produce flavored proteins and fortified vegetable/grain substitutes without maintenance and repair. It might have been better to let us farm at least some of our food in the hollow as a help to our sanity; but they chose not to give us that. If any of these systems fail, we may die. As it is, the medical facilities are quite limited, despite Warden Sanchez's recorded tips on how to use them. Mostly, we will have to rely on maintaining our health, such as it is for each man.

"Some of the men come to me for advice, but those who seek influence give themselves away by avoiding me. They have already created a currency of exchange by rounding up the more feminine young men to use as female surrogates. The homosexuals among us are not as discriminating; they choose among themselves, and perhaps even love in the truest sense, but are mocked by the professed heteros who trade their chattel. Thirty years will take the bloom off the purely sexual infatuations, but the old lovers may still cling to each other—"

Howes came in and Tasarov stopped writing.

"Can I talk to you?" asked the young man.

"Sit down," Tasarov said. "What is it?"

Howes leaned forward uncomfortably, put his hands together across his knees, and spoke while looking down at the floor. "Are we so evil that they had to put us out here, Yevgeny?"

Tasarov sat back and said, "This has nothing to do with evil, son. This place is not bad, as prisons go. We don't have the screws to deal with, for one thing. That's actually an advance, a way of avoiding day-to-day abuse and cruelties. Takes the temptation away from guards. Better than a rock in the middle of San Francisco Bay, where you could see the city you were missing."

"Were you there?" Howes asked.

"No—that was in the last century. They closed it as soon as inmates began to show they were brave enough to take it. They didn't like setting them a challenge they could meet. Complete lockdown high tech prisons came in, and they were nearly escape proof and unbearable, but too costly to operate. They couldn't put everyone in them, even though they were supposed to be for a very small group—but that group kept getting larger. This place is probably more frightening to people back home than it is to us. Who knows, we'll swing out and come back in, and maybe we'll be heroes, maybe. At least to some people."

Howes sat up and looked at him. "It's . . . do you feel empty and abandoned? I don't think it would feel the same on Earth or on the Moon."

"We all feel the difference, in one way or another. Something like this has never been done."

"I feel," Howes said, "that they think they're all better than us. Maybe they are."

Tasarov felt a surge of feeling, a concern for another human being as never before in his life; and yet it seemed to him that Howes was no one special. He didn't seem to have any distinctive abilities or high intelligence. It was this place, heading out away from everything, that was throwing him into a compassionate state of mind which he could not trust, he told himself.

"They're not better than us," Tasarov said, "or we better than them."

"They've taken everything from us," Howes replied, avoiding his gaze.

"Look, son—any of us here, if we'd come up in their world, or gotten in with the rich and powerful gang families at the top, we would have done the same thing, and sent us out, or people like us. They don't know what else to do."

"I don't get it."

"We're all the same. The problem is human beings. Always has been. Top, bottom, or middle, we all behave alike. We've pretty much always done so."

"There are better people, somewhere," Howes said.

"A few saints here and there, and even they have to work too hard at it. It's too difficult to sustain. Those who achieve power usually mess it up. Seems there's no point in raising up the powerless, because you get the same thing."

"So you don't blame them for sending us out?"

"I feel as much as you do," Tasarov said, "but more may come of this than anyone knows."

"I don't deserve what's happened to me," Howes said.

There was a long silence between them. Then Tasarov asked, "Are they leaving you alone? I mean the others."

"Funny," Howes said "They think I . . . belong to you."

"We're friends," Tasarov answered quickly. "That much is true. It's what they're picking up."

Howes looked at him. "You don't feel more?"

Tasarov smiled. "I really do like women—and I'd like one right now. Stand-ins just don't make it for me, even though I see how the illusion might be had."

"The illusion?"

Tasarov nodded. "Soft skin, hairlessness, a vulnerable look in the eyes, and in the darkness friction is pretty much the same. It's also about power—exerting your will on another human being. The genuine homosexuals can have what a man and woman can. The others are getting off on power and illusion. What it means is they're going to trade people like animals."

"You won't tell them, will you?" Howes asked. "I mean, that we're not . . ."

"I don't care what they imagine—and you shouldn't care either," Tasarov said. "I don't care if it helps you."

"Thanks."

Tasarov smiled. "As long as you don't one day expect me to take it seriously."

Howes looked embarrassed. "Of course not. I just can't see it."

The young man was still shaken up about Polau, Tasarov realized. It would have been more humiliating back home, the way Polau had picked and used him.

Tasarov didn't mind queers, as such;

human affections were versatile, and existed on
a long spectrum; but the long history of social
rejection had deformed this creative human
exploration into something furtive and desper-
ately predatory, especially in prisons, where it
had become linked to tolerated rape, part of the
punishment.

The ancient Greek and Roman acceptance
had existed without labels, leaving individuals
to find their tendencies. It had always seemed
to him that there was for every gay or straight a
possible individual somewhere who might
arouse and lead them gladly against their grain;
and the "next best thing to a woman" philoso-
phy of prison populations certainly made hash
of there being any one true path, without excep-
tions. No one knew what human freedom
would find without early training taboos; but it
was this very freedom that was feared.

He often felt a romantic fool for thinking
it, but he believed with conviction that love
beyond mere physicality was possible between
any two living creatures in Darwin's universe,
given the right conditions of knowledge and
communication. Possible, even if it rarely happened. How much denial and loneliness was
necessary before any human being turned to
the only available means of expressing love and
physical affection? Might not great friends console each other, or even one console the other as

with a ministering angel's mercy, and would the means that might otherwise be repugnant become unimportant?

The answer was yes—sometimes.

Howes stood up and seemed about to speak, then simply nodded and left.

Tasarov smiled to himself, then wrote: "My kind has always sought to rip the devil from its heart and hurl him away. But he stays, no matter how often they cast him out." It was a consoling thought, and a difficult one, since it involved a knot that first had to be tied correctly—or the problem would not be stated coherently—and then recognized as a knot that should not be untied—and that to cut it might be disastrous.

"We're not machines or angels," he wrote. "Worse, we need to be devils, to at least be able to choose wrongly, even if it be evil. Every effort to solve the problem of our capacity to choose evil freely breaks down to some degree, because what is to be solved, human freedom, is not all problem, it is only part of the problem. Freedom to succeed or fail is what should be!"

A series of chance failures had imprisoned him inside this rock.

Think, he told himself, and write it down. It was all that was left to him. And he knew his thinking happiness as he had never known it before—that it was everything.

8

Rough Justice

Boosted into a twenty-five year loop, the second Rock went out a year after the first. Six months later, warfare broke out among the men over the female prisoners, of whom there were an equal number, but not all of equal desirability. The strongest men and women quickly devised weapons, knives and spears, and seized the prime specimens for themselves and as rewards for their followers. A quarter of the males organized to oppose the slavers and liberate the women, and the struggle began. The rest of the population simply tried to keep out of their way.

It had been thought that a male/female prison would be more just, more humane than the all male first Rock; and this might have been the case, except for the effect of John "Jimmy" Barr, a database criminal, who collected and memorized the means needed to steal data and sold that knowledge, priding himself on never having to do any job himself. He had killed two policemen when they came to arrest him. His defense had been that he had been so astonished at being caught selling information, since he believed it to be a statistical impossibility, that he had been driven temporarily insane, and hence was not responsible for the murders. Murder had never been his way. He blamed the police for driving him to it, and had conducted a countersuit even as his trial was beginning.

The Rock to which he had been committed was some seven kilometers long and four wide, with a sealed engineering level. The radio station incident of the first Rock was not to be repeated. The inmates might dig to find the engineering cavities; but this would be long, fruitless work, since they lacked proper tools. Nine hypothetical tries out of ten would get them nowhere, and might even be dangerous.

John "Jimmy" Barr decided that he would rule the Rock, and women would be the currency with which he would pay his soldiers. The only other source of power might be in controlling access to the mess hall automats.

He was a tall, dark-haired man with implanted teeth. A loose, lanky physique made it seem he was put together from clothes hangers. He had no inner life, except as a planner of actions that he had never executed. He rarely thought about himself except in practical terms, as if he were someone else; he always looked outward, absorbing what he needed to know, synergizing sequences and tracing out orderly steps to their conclusions. He had been caught only once, and it had been as if he had struck a mirror—glimpsing himself as it shattered.

As Barr considered the battles that had already occurred, he saw that there was only one way to end the war—by seizing the mess hall automats and starving out the opposition. He had the force to do so—but then what?

Suddenly he realized how limited the victory would be: access to the most desirable women, and the ability to order the inmates about. But what could they be ordered to do, except to go about their lives of eating and sleeping, maybe running errands, as they all waited for their time to run out?

But what else was there to do? What could there ever be here? The impoverished landscape had almost nothing to offer except a monastic daily life. The ground itself was the prison wall, and could not be penetrated. All the richness of life on Earth was gone, leaving only a bare stage on which there was only one role—waiting for the play to end.

He would not long be able to control his subjects if he failed to give them something to do. For the moment they were faced with the group that was not under his command, some two thousand people, gathered at the far end of the habitat. He had cut them off from the mess automats, but that would not last long. They sat on the hillsides below the sunplate, waiting to get hungry. When they attacked again, his force would attempt to kill them all—at least those who failed to come over to him after the defeat. All he had to do was wait until they became hungry, while his force ate in shifts.

Barr smiled as he stood outside the dome of the first mess hall and considered the difference between his forces and those which had been driven away after the seizing of the women. His people, who included some of the women, were perfectly willing to kill with their hands, or with the makeshift utensils taken from the mess. This fact alone had thrown back the others. The fallen still lay where they had died, and all the dead were on the other side. He estimated a hundred or so.

But as he gazed down the length of the hollow toward the dimming sunplate, he saw a line of figures moving toward the four mess hall domes and behind the line there was another and another.

It was completely unexpected, but he knew at once what was about to happen. Coming so quickly after retreat, this sudden forward swarm was meant to catch his forces off guard.

He knew that an all or nothing rush might overwhelm his tired men. But the opposing force was also tired, he told himself, and their thrust might easily fall apart.

Half his men were already coming out of the mess halls and forming up to meet the attackers. The rest were coming out of the barracks at his left, ready to reinforce the men at the mess halls. He saw now that the enemy was sending in every standing individual. They spread out across the landscape of mud and crabgrass, their shadows thrusting forward as the sunplate dimmed toward evening behind them.

He cursed under his breath, realizing that it might go either way; but as he looked ahead to the decades inside this Rock, he welcomed this decisive test; it would at least give him a chance at a more satisfying life here. It would not matter if he lost, because then he would know that he could not have prevailed with the means at hand.

But if he prevailed—ah, what he would do then! What games he would invent!

The first line of figures was almost at the domes, when suddenly they stopped, holding up their hands. He peered ahead and saw that individual figures were coming forward, and others were going out to meet them.

"Come on!" he shouted to the men near

him. "We've got to get over there!"

He went forward with a thousand men at his back, already suspecting what was happening, knowing that he might already be powerless to stop it.

It was a long march across the crabgrass. Listening to the mumblings and mutterings of the men behind him, Barr felt that he was losing himself, what there was left of him.

At last he came to the open area between the two lines. There was a group of seven men in the middle, talking to each other. They were gesturing, but he could not make out their words. He glanced back at his line and saw the same questioning look on the men's faces.

Finally, he went forward to the group.

"Well, what is it?" he demanded. "What do they want?"

All seven men looked at him in silence.

"Tell him," a deep voice said.

Then Arlo Perrin, one of his own men, said, "We're going to hear from each side. It's only fair."

For a moment Barr wanted to laugh; but he saw it was all decided. He nodded his agreement.

"You want to talk first?" asked Perrin.

Barr hesitated, then said, "I'll listen," thinking it best to know what he was up against.

The men turned to face the other side. A tall man came forward and stopped between the two lines. Barr recognized him as Ivan Osokin, a quack doctor from Odessa, who had been convicted of too few of his many murders for hire.

Osokin raised his hands. "You all know me!" he shouted. "I've helped a few of you, and maybe now I will help all of you!" His tenor voice carried strongly across the fields, and Barr tensed, knowing that the man's medical skills, however limited and restricted by conditions here, were an undeniable source of power and influence. It had not occurred to him that the old doctor would think of using it.

Osokin pointed at Barr and asked, "What has he done for you, except set us against each other?" He paused. "What does this information thief have to offer? What is he after except to help himself?"

Murmurs spread back through the ranks on each side like the sound of bees swarming. Barr felt his face tingle, as if a front of salty air had struck it. But he smiled and waited for Osokin to finish.

"What have you to say?" Osokin demanded. "What can you offer these people?"

Barr approached him. Osokin did not move away. When Barr was close enough to whisper, he asked, "What is it you want, old man? Share and share alike?" They would be good together,

Barr realized, and wished that he had known more about the man earlier.

Osokin's breath was bad; his teeth were piss yellow.

Barr asked, "Do you really think a lot of talk will get you anything?"

"Of course not," Osokin said, then reached out and grasped Barr by the throat, holding him at arm's length.

Barr struggled to grab the arm that held him, but it was like trying to take hold of a tree branch. Osokin lifted him a little, showing astonishing strength, and Barr realized that this had all been about something else. It was a public assassination.

He tried to scratch the bare arm, but its skin and muscles were hard. Osokin lifted him a bit more, and Barr began to dance. Stars exploded in his eyes, and the last thing he heard was a great cheer going up from the great gathering. It came from all sides, beginning loudly, then slowly dying away as he went deaf and blind . . .

9

Season's Greetings

JUDGE OVERTON'S PRIVATE CHAMBER

"Going crazy in prison has nothing to do with the inmates' criminality. We should have better prisons, but it can't be helped. It's just too bad, but that's less important than the society that will be harmed by their presence."

"But Judge, consider this: they did the crimes, yes. But should we commit crimes against them?"

"Yes, we should. Many people would say that. The question is whether they are crimes."

"Are they?"

"No. Not crimes."

"But they are."

"No. You think they are crimes. But it's only self defense. If you kill or injure someone in defending yourself, you can't be held responsible for the damage."

Tasarov paused, as he had so many times now, before going down the ramp to the engineering level, and looked back at the landscape. Tall grass now covered most of the inner land. As he looked to the far end of the habitat, away from the sunplate, the yellow-orange of the dimming light made afternoon in the hollow—one of the contrasting moments he was beginning to treasure in the life he had made for himself since he had moved into the warden's quarters below. He lived just down the hall from the now silent radio station, which no one had been able to bring back to life. Someone tried at least once a week, but without success.

He thought lately about how he had taken up the warden's position, and how most of the men looked to him for opinions. He marked his authority from Polau's death. Law, he told himself as he went down the ramp, had always been "someone's law," a practical instrument wielded by a group or class, enforced by the top gang's police force, and certainly having little to do directly with the ideal of law as that which stood immune to human tampering, fair to all, not subverted by money and the personal motives of judges. To find himself a judge, even an informal one, almost made him believe that humanity tended to order of some kind as much as it needed air and food. At least a dozen times in the last few months, when conflicts and physical violence had broken out among the men, groups had sided with him, offering to enforce his judgment, and that alone had been enough to quiet the conflagration.

Sometimes he thought that most of the men here were simply tired, and wanted to live day to day, accepting the coming decades with a fatalistic, settled relief. Even the sexual couples had reached a stability of quid pro quo; better to have one protector than being passed around. The "females" would be shared, but with reasonable periods between associations. It amounted to serial monogamy.

As he came down the hallway to his quarters, he saw that someone was waiting for him. A dark figure stood up straight from a leaning position against the wall and said, "Mr. Tasarov, may I speak to you? It's important."

Tasarov nodded as he opened the door to his sitting room. He never locked it, not only because he couldn't find the warden's keys, but because it didn't seem to matter, at least so far; the men respected his privacy. A break-in would net nothing, but it would be a sign of deterioration.

He stepped inside, and then aside to let the visitor enter. The man came in and stood before him, and Tasarov saw that he was of slight build, pale skin, and brown hair.

"What is it?" He motioned for him to sit down on the pipeframe sofa.

The man ran his hand through his hair. "Thanks."

Tasarov sat down in the chair across from him. "What's your name?"

"Uh—yes . . ."

Tasarov tried to put him at ease. "Forgot it, did you?"

The young man smiled. "No, it's not that. My name's Eddie Dantès." He took a deep breath as Tasarov smiled. "It's not my real name. I got it out of an old movie."

"It was a book long before it was a movie," Tasarov said. "*The Count of Monte Cristo* by Alexandre Dumas."

"Yeah, that was the flick. A real old one. Best breakout movie I ever saw."

"It's a great book, too," Tasarov said, realizing that the young man was avoiding what he had come to say. "You don't go by your real name?"

"No, not really. I changed it legally . . . from Sid Smith."

"So what is it, Eddie? It is Eddie, not Edmond?"

He nodded. "I used it at first, but too many people laughed."

Tasarov sat back, gave him a questioning look, and waited.

"My problem . . . is I'm a transsexual. I got fixed a long time ago, when I was eighteen . . ."

"And you've been hiding it here," Tasarov said with surprise. "Don't you have anyone you care about?" He had been fairly sure that he knew everything essential about his inmates by now.

"No. But Howes . . . saw me squatting in the tall grass the other day. I shouldn't have."

"And you think he knows? Are you fully functioning . . . as a woman?"

"I am a woman," he said. "Inside, I mean. I always was. But I started to hide it in prisons, wearing the right . . . stuff."

Tasarov said, "Men in prison frightened you, and it wasn't much better in a woman's lockup. You didn't want to find anyone in prison, man or woman."

"Right," Eddie said. "They sent me to one or the other, according to how closely they checked my records."

"You certainly didn't give yourself much of a way out, did you?"

"I guess not. What can I do?"

"Find someone quickly," Tasarov said. "Let him find out—and he may count himself lucky."

"But what if he's just gay?"

"It's a chance you'll have to take. Why not Howes? He's not a bad sort."

"But isn't he . . . with you?"

"Not really. But if you two hit it off, you'll have some of the same protection from me."

Eddie sighed. "I guess it can't be better. You think Howes might like me?"

"Who knows? Let him find out about you and himself, and see!"

Eddie gave him a lost look.

"You want me to hold your hand?" asked Tasarov, grinning.

Eddie got up to leave. "No, of course not. Thanks."

"One thing to remember," Tasarov said at the door. "When you go out into the grass to pee, make sure no one else sees you."

■

Later that day, Tasarov smiled to himself as he completed the last sequence of six mathematical proofs. No one on Earth would ever see them, because he would destroy them before he died. It did not trouble him. At the age of ten he had absorbed and restated, in his own words, much of Newton and Einstein, a bit of Hawking, some of it before he even knew their work. He had been just as good, if only in part, because he had not seen the answers. That was what counted; to have devalued his work later as mere duplication would have been stupid. He had often wondered what he would have been like as a mathematician in the swim of accepted social norms; but now he knew: an outsider, seeing through the charade too easily to be happy . . .

He considered Eddie Dantès's plight. Those who might learn about him would immediately dream of sharing him. Desperate imaginations would whisper in the night. He would be a treasure to be sought, once his nature was known, and the cooperation that was growing in the face of isolation might be weakened. Each inmate had been forced to find his own way of living with sexual release, and there had been explosions of violence. Evolution's sexual wind-up toy, the male initiator of future generations, fired blanks here. Another warm body would quiet him for a time, but at the deepest levels lurked a profound despair at the lack of result. At least it seemed that way. Maybe he was giving the old brain's survivalist discontents too much credit.

What of the gay who knows that he is only "make do" for an otherwise heterosexual lover? He longs for another gay's sexuality, perhaps even love. He may be assaulted by gays and non-gays alike; gays may assault non-gays; heterosexuals may assault each other, or make do with grim acceptance of the substitute. The flexibility of humankind was multifarious and per-

verse, and not easy to imprison. If one could say
that adaptive evolution was an intentional
design, then human ways were not made for
prisons of any kind.

As he looked around at Warden Sanchez's
office, it became obvious to him how quick the
decision to send out the first Rock had been. No
effort had been made to prevent possible access
to the warden's office and quarters, or to the
library terminals, baths, and recreation areas
for the guards that were on the engineering
level of a Rock intended to be kept in close Sun
orbit. Clearly, no one cared. Good riddance. Let
people worry thirty years from now.

He continued to worry whether everything would continue to work for some three
decades, whether there were enough raw mak-
ings for the food in the automats, whether the
energy plant, air recyclers, and heat radiators
would remain functional. He had no idea if
anyone in the hollow could make necessary
repairs. Again, his conclusion was that no one
cared what happened to the habitat; or else
they were very sure of it functioning properly
and returning in thirty years.

■

Howes and Dantès became good friends; and
after a while more than that. But both were

regarded as Tasarov's property, so no one bothered them. Tasarov wondered whether Eddie was the only one of his kind in the habitat, but he really didn't want to know. If there were others, they were well hidden and just as well that they were.

Some of the older men were attempting to cultivate small gardens in front of their barracks. Tasarov's forays through the engineering level with Howes and Dantès, to inventory what was available had turned up flowering plant seed packets in a few of the guards' locker rooms. They had been meant as a mercy for someone, and now they were received as a miraculous find.

"Who knows," Howes said, "maybe we'll find a cat or a dog somewhere. Even a rat would do."

The engineering level took up some thirty percent of the area under the inner land, Tasarov estimated; and clearly the intent had been to excavate and use all of the available area in time. He had his own suspicions about the engineering level that he wanted to test, but it would take time.

Most of the men, he knew, were sleep-walking through their new life, following the easiest way: sleep and eat, think as little as possible, hang out with comrades, even if the relationships offered no physical intimacy, which was the case for most; still, one could get lucky on a strange day. "Hope makes a man death-less," Melville had once written. Tasarov accepted the words only if they meant that a man should refuse to think about death in the midst of life, since it was only wise not to poison what time a man had; but there was a point at which denial was an attempt to wear blinders. It just couldn't be done. Sometimes he felt that prisoners needed their guards, needed a society around them to make sense of their imprisonment.

This Earth, which had thrown them into the darkness, had implemented something new in renunciations . . . and he considered its evil as he had never regarded the so-called wrong-doing that he had practiced. The fools of history had whispered in their vain hearts that good may come from evil means; and they had ignored that good intentions may produce unwished evils.

Well, perhaps; but both results depend on later understandings, which may not come. "Making it good—later" ignores the evil and suffering of today, which is all that the victims have, while the tormentors console themselves with future benefits. Even the doctor who sends his patient through pain in search of health leaves behind mental damage that will earn unwanted interest. And that account may not be closed out by simple withdrawal . . . accruing, it grows heavy and immovable, and is passed on. Crimes committed against criminals are no less crimes; they are new crimes, which do not know the old ones for which the criminal is committed . . .

No—that wasn't quite right, either. The waves of humankind who can be imprisoned for wrongdoing never stop. One might as well try to stop the human enterprise itself, which seeks every niche to fill. All attempts at law, all religion, all ethical norms, might be nothing more than attempts by the weak to restrain the strong. Then, within the law, arise the new strong, who subvert the law for their own ends of power and family interest, leaving the old strong outside their circle to pursue the waiting possibilities which they call crime. The weak, the cowardly, the decent ones, live between these groups . . .

He was sure of only one thing: that no official thinking on these matters could be taken at face value. The corruption that lay beneath the settled surface of all societies was based on a self-serving, grasping need to hold power, to project one's own children into the future ahead of the children of others, to pass wealth forward like a communicable disease, to speak from the grave into futurity, to shackle it. And in this century, as lifespan leapt forward beyond the century mark, the greedy old brain sought to become its own posterity by invading the future . . .

That was it, he told himself. As more people lived longer, a cleansing and clearing amnesia was necessary, to make the Earth ready for the new ways. Send them out, the violent, the deranged, the politically dangerous—anyone who threatens the power of the richest and their access to their recruiting pool, the clean middle classes. And remember to prune from the bottom, lest the middle recruit from it and grow too powerful. And never think about what you are doing; it comes naturally, with only informal conspiracies at work.

Well, this tack was also not quite right, he told himself. We are all villains by degrees. Our villainies depend on where we start on the social ladder, and on what opportunities come our way. Those who have no opportunities to overdo we call good people. Untempted, they shame the powerful by using their goodness as a weapon; it is all they can do. They live almost no lives at all, risking nothing, secure in the illusion that they would never do ill to anyone. We are all villains, but some welcome the use of muzzles and manacles. These are called saints. Those whom we muzzle and manacle we call criminals.

He remembered an unpopular study of the last century, in which it was shown that nearly everyone, when questioned with a guarantee of anonymity, admitted to some kind of illegal or criminal act, from petty theft to violence and sexual abuse of others.

Humankind, he had come to believe, lived in a collective fantasy about who it was, where it came from, and what it wanted to be. To see or even glimpse what the truth might be was, for most people, to court horror and dismay. Criminals, of course, were always breaking into the fantasy and showing it up for an illusion.

Yet freedom might come only when we have looked truth in the face and realize that we are responsible only to ourselves and each other. There is no other pedigree for moral codes except human needs, which are reality enough . . .

To reign in hell is our only fate, since there is no heaven . . .

Thought was tiring. One had to love mazes to think well. The hunter-gatherer ape, so recent from the trees, had inexplicably, as if by the grace of a merciful God, developed a taste for thought; but it was a wonder how good he was at it, and how infrequently he paid attention to its answers, or bothered to remember them. The ancients had guessed nearly all the right questions, and many of the answers, using transcendent speculation and reason alone. The religionists had seen the need for social engineering, but they couldn't face up to what they were doing and had to insist upon imaginary authorities. The secular state builders did no better with human nature, with their police forces and criminal justice systems run by money and power . . .

Thinking, one climbed up to a plateau of reason and looked around for heroes, but found none. The creature that thought and acted was one and the same, high and low, stupid and smart, making reform slow, if not impossible, subversion and corruption of ideals inevitable. Why did they bother voicing them?

Something was crying to be free—

—of itself—

—to take wing without wings.

He looked at his calendar, and saw that it was that day again. Some of the men in the barracks were attempting to celebrate human kinship and mutual concern. He got up and left the warden's office. As he came up the ramp to the inner land, he heard distant singing that sounded like a love song.

10

A Sum of Deeds

As the hungry Earth ripped out the innards of metal-rich asteroids to enhance the lives of its ever longer living-peoples, it quickly filled the empties with its rejects.

These were the last of the lowest criminal class, the freelance soldiers who worked through long chains of command for the better placed lawbreakers who gracefully slipped back and forth through legality's shifting borders, but who now, increasingly, had less need for the street—for the poorly paid thieves, burglars, fences, specialized prostitutes, and murderers on call.

All were being replaced by ever more sophisticated specialists, who worked only when called from on high, and had the luxury of refusing work. Their great virtue was that they now came from a deep systematic cover of decent, ordinary lives and were willing to do what the powerhoarders were unwilling to do for themselves, as longer life beckoned, and power beyond wealth became the most sought after prize. "We'll let the world live in comfort, but power must remain with us," the highest whispered to themselves in their hearts, "because we know what to do with it, because we cannot let it slip from our hands and the hands of our kin."

But once in a while they also pruned from their own—from the untrustworthy whose sympathies sometimes looked downward to the riching slums, to the talentless towns, to the lazy lands.

Yet the ones of great wealth also feared the sky. Too much profit there, unless controlled by them, would rearrange the interlocks of power on Earth. It had to be done carefully, this outreach and influx, with talent under their control; and hostile talent sent elsewhere.

So the third and fourth Rocks filled with the politically aware and talented who could not be bought, because they sought all for their righteous tribe; and there were a few saints among them, whose persuasion was more dangerous than wealth and power. And the wealthy told themselves in their hearts that these pressures and persuasions of principle and belief were embraced precisely because of the power they might bestow. Nothing more than dangerous insistence, but too influential.

So Rocks Three and Four went out on a loop of centuries, but recorded as much less; and no one recorded exactly how long. An open orbit, one that would never return the Rock, was too costly in energy, since it required achieving escape velocity from the Sun. A century or two would be enough. No one would know until too late; and by then it would not matter to the living of today who might come to worry about mistakes in some far tomorrow.

But it was a never ending charade played by courts that had no ears, seeking to correct educations and economies that were unable to eliminate the enterprises of criminality. Only the crudest forms could be controlled. The rest grew ever various, better concealed and protected human ingenuities whose parents were intelligence and opportunity. Even as crimes of simple greed declined, crimes wedded to the holding of power increased.

Humankind gained greater control over everything except itself, and argued with the saints that it could not be otherwise, with some saying that it should never be otherwise: A weeding process was at work, whose greater good seemed an evil only in short runs, and necessary creativity in longer runs.

Had de Sade been right? Were you free to gain what you lost through abuse by others by abusing for yourself? You must be alert to the nature of the game. Everyone was in reality a wolf, so the raising of sheep should be abolished. It was in fact a great tragedy to raise sheep, to bring low so much vital and daring nobility.

An unadmitted game cannot be changed. It was too well set, beyond tampering, driving all human creativity: bio-engineering and even the growth of artificial intelligence. Humanity's children would indeed be descended from humanity, and no other.

The first longlifers needed the short-timers to do their work, especially their criminal and military work; but as these short-timers were used up, they were replaced with new athletes who would contribute to the building of wealth and power. Mass killings were not acceptable. A sieve was needed, through which humanity would be poured, to select those who would be saved.

And yet . . . and yet, the goodwillers cried, something was being misunderstood: Humanity was surely better than this!

No! Social systems grew out of deep biology, not discussion; and whenever discussion alone had given birth to reform, deeper currents quickly drowned the songful whelpings of angelic hope.

Yet saints and great ones had risen above

the deep database of the body, and brought some control over the mirror-shy predator within, at least for short times. They had sought to pass on the new commonwealths through culture, but this bravery of good will always ran out of strength; new generations could not be trained and educated fast enough before amnesiacs bought old agendas once again. Something better than the domesticated predator was needed; yet all feared to take away the predator's strength.

What was needed, cried the aspiring saints, was a generation that would cleanse itself, then become its own posterity. Memory would not slip but grow for such as these, and new additions to their ranks would be slow and sure, conserving memory . . .

Until then—the cleansing continued.

Rocks Five and Six were hurled, and almost no one knew who was in them.

As he walked down toward the barracks town, Tasarov stopped and peered into the grassy distance to his right. A black snake was rising from the dry grass. It took him a moment to guess what he was seeing. In another moment he saw a burst of flame at the base of the smoky snake, which rose and curled in obedience to the Coriolis acceleration of the habitat's spin. A dark figure moved away from the fire, and Tasarov knew that it had been set with a will.

He started to run toward the barracks, shouting alarm, remembering that he had given the drying grass a passing thought, but had dismissed the danger of fire because there was nothing to start it—except human beings.

"Fire!" he shouted to the men playing ball near the barracks. "Fire!"

As he reached them, they were gaping at the rising smoke. Tasarov wondered how much oxygen loss the habitat's systems could replace, and what the danger from smoke inhalation might be if all the grass burned.

"Get shovels and gardening tools—we've got to make a firebreak around it!"

The ballplayers stared at him in confusion.

"Now!" he shouted, looking to make out the figure who had set the fire. He was still in the grass, moving away from the blaze. Tasarov could not see who it was.

Men were rushing out of the barracks now. Eddie Dantès came up to him. Tasarov pointed and asked, "Do you know who that man out there is?"

Dantès gave a look. "Not at this distance."

Howes heard the question and said, "I think it's Crazy Bachelard, by the way he moves."

"Why did he do it?" Tasarov asked.

"Who knows? He doesn't talk much to anyone."

"Look at that!" Dantès cried. "He's lying down."

"Come on!" shouted Tasarov.

The men behind Tasarov swelled to over a thousand. They spread out into the grassland, encircling the flames, and began to pull out the grass with their hands to make a firebreak. Others were chopping and digging with the few gardening tools that had been found in the guards' quarters.

A terrible scream reached their ears over the crackle and roar of the flames, as if the fire itself had cried out.

The men redoubled their efforts. Slowly, the break was made. The fire reached the bare ground, stopped, and began to die for lack of fuel.

The men stood around their unexpected enemy, perspiring, roused to a new understanding of their vulnerability. Finally, they started across the burnt stubble, searching.

They found the blackened body of Crazy Bachelard on the smoking ground. Eddie Dantès identified him by the skull ring on his right forefinger.

By the time they finished burying him, a great cloud of smoke hung high overhead in the great hollow space. Tasarov held back from telling the men what an uncontrolled fire might have done inside the habitat, but some of the men certainly suspected that a great danger had been averted.

Later, back in his warden's quarters, Tasarov thought of the abyss that waits to swallow every society. More so ours, he thought, which exists on little better than a thin sheet of glass above the void. But seeing the comradeship that had followed the extinguishing of the fire, he concluded that Crazy Bachelard had done them all a favor, by drawing them all together into a single act. Unknowingly, he had made the glass underfoot a little stronger. Tasarov had seen it in the eyes of the men. At whomever he looked, he saw resolve tinged with pride, because something necessary had been accomplished, in a place that had taken away all useful work.

The void outside and the moral law within, he said to himself, paraphrasing old Kant. Tasarov had never met a criminal who did not have some kind of code; even among themselves they knew the wild animals from the crooks out for profit. Was there hope in that? But hope for what? To become sheep? Lawfulness might succeed too well, and that was also to be feared. To live was to twist in the antinomies, to subvert old victories and seek new strife, hoping never to find boredom.

Tasarov had learned too much and thought too long not to smile at his own relentless wrestling with both angels and devils. Human minds were prone to it when left too much alone; but he welcomed it, because it gave him a seat on a high court in which he was also being tried.

■

Few Earthly eyes watched to see how the inmates of the Rocks fared. It was not the kind of display routinely available in planet-based prisons, where the resistance of inmates' wills was plain to guards and authorities. There prisoners were still at times held in respect; there prisoners might still shame authorities as they lived in the prison of their jailers' eyes. Here only recording eyes scanned the condemned, creating a record that few human eyes cared to study. Some of it was transmitted home; the rest was stored in engineering databases.

Unable to look out from the Rock, Tasarov had looked back to the Earth inside himself—once; a while later he had looked again—and not since; it was not his world out there. And he knew that many of the other inmates had also turned away from the memory within themselves.

Early on he had suspected that there might be some kind of continuing surveillance being sent back to Earth; but he had not found any evidence of it so far and was reluctant to make a better search. It troubled him that he should hope for a secret, panoptic gaze that saw and judged the rejects in the pit. It was too much of a hope, and he crushed it within himself, ashamed of feeling such a need.

He sometimes missed the look of inevitability that seemed to mask a woman's face during copulation. What was it for a man—resignation ... conquest? He had never looked into a man's face in such a state, only felt his own expressions from within. A woman's face in ecstasy was a glorious fantasy, lending romance to what was, after all, the central action, the great forward pass of genetic data in evolution's relay race.

He smiled at the sporting analogy, because it didn't quite fit; it was more like the struggle in a football game, in which you fought first for the right to make the forward pass, to set it up and hope that it would connect and score, presuming that the little bitch or bastard born would grow up and earn the same right to make forward passes. Or maybe the bitch was the catcher in a baseball game? Perhaps there had been some progress—away from invading armies that scored by raping and pillaging for their share of the future ...

◼

Tasarov got to know his prison.

He walked it from one end to the other—from sunplate to the rocky far end in a straight line; in a spiral, and saw the barracks huddled overhead, men moving around, held down on their feet by the habitat's centrifugal spin, heads pointed to the invisible axis of zero-g down the center.

It was all grass again, growing back as the dry blades died. He longed for a tree, or a row of bushes. There was a pond, about three inches deep. The gods of punishment had not seen fit to make more.

Men walked with him, behind, at his sides, keeping company and privacy. Some he recognized; others he did not.

No one ever walked ahead of him.

He recalled a line of poetry—about the awful rowing toward God. But he had no oars of belief to propel him. There were no such oars to be had.

He covered distance within himself.

11

The Lost Within

JUDGE OVERTON'S PRIVATE CHAMBER

"What do you say about hopelessness being the root cause of all crime?"

"Well, yes—but, you see, they get professionally organized, the best of them. They get good at it with practice. Most hopeless people don't commit crimes. Of course, most of them are just too afraid and don't have the courage or skill. It's the bright and canny ones who become the most violent, to maintain their hold on things. They see what it takes."

"So you say it's too late for them?"

"Yes."

"But what if we removed the hopelessness at the very beginning of life, give them something to lose. Then we wouldn't raise the ambitious ones, much less their soldiers."

"Yes. But my job is to restrain them until then. It's the best we can do now."

Ivan Osokin now faced a new challenge to the order that he had established by killing John "Jimmy" Barr. The men needed him—to reassure them about their health much of the time; with any luck, the worst cases would come up a long time from now. For them, he might not be able to do much more than the automated diagnostic scanner could do—tell them what they had and order a drug. Still, their knowing that he was, or had been, a doctor of medicine calmed them and kept him safe.

Killing Barr had been a necessary weeding; it had saved lives.

Osokin looked around the mess hall as he ate, and spotted a familiar figure.

"You can be saved!" cried the preacher as he walked among the men and women in the mess hall. "But you must go down on your knees each day of your life!"

"Yeah, tell me about it," a woman's voice called out.

Osokin looked up too late to see who had answered the self-professed holy man.

Osokin knew that it was his own success against Barr that had encouraged the preacher to come forth. If you had something to sell, then sell it, was the lesson of Osokin's victory. There would be other sellers, Osokin knew, as soon as it dawned on them what specific they had to push. An inmate claiming to be a defrocked priest had been going around hearing confessions far out in the grass. The man had told him that his being defrocked didn't matter, since he was hearing confessions in hell. Osokin had asked him about the hopelessness of it, since no one ever got out of hell. "A true priest ministers to human failings," the man had replied, "and these are the most failed of failures. What greater accomplishment than to hear the repentance of those in hell? Yes, yes, they do repent, Doctor, and I give them the absolution of the damned—forgiveness without salvation. And hope." What kind of hope, Osokin had asked, and the man had smiled at him as if he'd walked into a trap. "Doctor, in the infinity of time that waits before us, God may have mercy on us. He may reach down and pull us free." He had smiled very broadly before adding, "In an infinite time, anything may happen. We may yet dwell in his company and see his face."

Osokin had given some thought to what there was to trade for power: men and women's bodies—that would settle itself—medical help, entertainment, and hope. He had not expected to see the selling of hope so soon. The defrocked priest was harmless, but he had his occasional takers, and that seemed to be enough for him. Osokin had expected to see the selling of cruelty as entertainment first.

The preacher was the second seller of hope, and much more ambitious than the priest. He called himself Dr. Jeremy Ashe. He was a long-haired man, as tall as Osokin, an Anglo–Italian with a mother from Bombay. He claimed that she had taught him about the Great Ones who lived in the central region of the galaxy and were "direct intermediaries to God," whose black holes waited to retrieve the created universe into His bowels. There the damned would be crushed into an infinitely dense state of perpetual pain, but the saved would emerge into light and happiness without end.

Osokin didn't know whether Ashe believed any of it, but that didn't matter; the man might be a force for either stability or disorder, and that was not to be dismissed.

"I bring you hope!" shouted Ashe, bringing to market a very saleable good. "And I bring you knowledge, the father of hope—so that your hope will have eyes and not be blind! We are on our way toward the Great Ones of the galaxy, as planned by the compassionates who built this habitat and sent us on our way!"

"Say who?" a male voice asked.

That was pretty clever, Osokin thought, to suggest that the officers of the criminal justice system had been mere tools in the service of a higher power. He spooned up the last of his stew, then looked around at the faces of the others. Most seemed unconvinced; but it took only a few to build a circle of followers that might grow. *When do we get there?*—he wanted to shout back, but restrained himself; too early an opposition would only gain Ashe the sympathy that sometimes went to an underdog.

"I thought the cop lovers built this place!" shouted a male voice.

"Ah, yes!" Ashe replied. "But its true purpose was hidden even from them!"

"Who told you!" another man's voice demanded.

Ashe stopped and held his arms over his head. "One of the Great Ones spoke to me from the rocks!"

Osokin smiled to himself. So there was to be the usual pedigree to the Word: handed down by an unimpeachable authority at an unfindable location, requiring faith to seal the bargain. Standard operating unverifiability— according to which even the bringer of the truth was unaware that he was hiding the source from himself, if necessary; the fountainhead of needful order had to be unquestioned. The actual source was of course the purely human impulse toward order. Too bad it had to coexist in a partly rational brain with so many other evolutionarily embedded commands.

"At the far end rocks!" Ashe cried. "A voice spoke to me!"

Surprised, Osokin looked up, wondering how Ashe could have made such a mistake. It was a bad move to be specific. Ashe must believe he had heard something there. And

Osokin saw that his chance had come sooner
than he had expected, even if it meant losing
any of the stability that Ashe might have
brought to the community. One must not over-
look a chance to destroy the competition early;
a later chance might be too late.

Osokin stood up. "Where did you hear this
voice?" he asked politely.

Ashe looked at him without fear or suspicion and said again, "At the far end rocks."

There was a sudden quiet.

"Will you take us there?" Osokin asked
softly.

Ashe gazed at him as if he were his lover,
then shouted, "Ye have asked, and ye shall
hear!" Then he looked around the mess. "All
shall hear who follow me! Repeat my words in
all the halls, and follow me."

Men and women were looking at him with
wonder.

"Yes," Osokin said, "we shall go hear your
voice."

"Do you doubt, brother?" Ashe asked,
looking at him with a puzzled, guileless face.

"I need to hear," Osokin said in a neutral
tone, and for a moment played with the thought
that a subtle God was testing him.

"All need to hear!" Ashe replied. "And all
shall hear!"

Osokin sat down, wondering how the man
could have put himself into such a vulnerable

position. A true believer would be too naive to play games. Would they reach the rocks and be told that they were deaf, and that only he could hear the voice?

"Eat and be strong," Ashe said, "and then follow me."

■

The turnout was smaller than Osokin had expected. Fewer than three hundred men and women followed Ashe down the length of the habitat. It was not a short walk—some four kilometers. Ashe led the way, never once looking back. There was conviction in his stride.

Gravity decreased slightly as they neared the rocks of far-end, where the inner surface narrowed toward the axis of rotation. Osokin felt a breeze blowing toward the rocks, and a distant high-pitched howl, but thought nothing of it at first; as they drew nearer to the narrows, and both wind and howl increased, he began to worry.

Ashe reached the rocks, turned around, and shouted, "Hear the song, hear the Word!" He raised his arms. "How beautiful, with words!"

It was a brisk wind now. Osokin looked to the rocks beyond Ashe. His long hair was blowing back toward the rocks. Osokin looked around for a patch of grass or shrubbery, found some, and pulled up a handful.

Ashe stood in the wind, eyes closed.

"Hear the song, hear the Word!" he shouted again, closed up within himself, hearing what he prayed to hear, what he needed to hear. He was more dangerous than Osokin had supposed, because he heard the voices and believed what he heard—what some far part of himself was telling him.

Osokin tossed his handful of grass into the air, and the wind whipped the loose blades toward the rocks. Osokin noted their direction and started climbing. He scrambled past the oblivious Ashe, and stopped in horror when he saw the crack swallow the grass.

Ashe opened his eyes, turned and called after him, "Brother, be patient, be still, and hear the words of the Great Ones."

"I hear well enough," Osokin answered through a tight throat, his heart racing. After a few moments, he turned and stumbled back to stand at Ashe's right hand.

Osokin raised his arms. "Friends! Behind me there's a narrow crack. Our atmosphere is going out that way . . ."

There was a silence, as if the seconds before an execution were running out.

A woman screamed, "My child, my child!"

Osokin saw she was pregnant as she clutched at her belly, which was clearly filling out her loose fitting prison coveralls.

"Listen!" he shouted. "This may not be serious. It may only be rushing away into the engineering level—but we can't take a chance. We'll have to seal it up."

Ashe was looking at him with an open mouth. He seemed to understand; but then something else deep within him reasserted itself and said, "Blasphemer! The voice of the Great Ones is not to be mocked."

Osokin ignored him. "We have to get dirt, wet it, and pack it in until the wind stops."

"You dare, you dare?" Ashe cried out. "You dare to silence the voice of the Great Ones?"

Osokin wanted dearly to say that he dared, but restrained himself as he saw that a group was already breaking away to go back and get spades.

Ashe said the only thing left for him to say. "Have you no ears? Do you not hear? The voice of saving armies speaks!"

Everyone was turning away from him. He dropped to his knees and cried, "I hear, I hear!" Then he lowered his head and wept.

Osokin stepped up to him and put a hand on his shoulder.

Ashe looked up at him and said, "But I do hear," over the whipping wind, "I do hear it."

Osokin nodded, trying to dredge up some show of pity from himself; but he knew that he was only contorting his face into a feeble mask of compassion; so he kept his hand on the man's shoulder and said, "Of course you hear . . . it happens that way . . . sometimes," knowing that it was a necessary display of human feeling, to disarm anyone who would later repeat the tale.

12

Aliens

Rock Five carried away humankind's aliens.

These were the sexually damaged beyond repair. Some said that to have killed them all would have been better; only their numbers— six thousand men and women gathered in the Rock from all over the world—made it politically unacceptable to simply gas them in the enclosed space. Most of them were under a sentence of life imprisonment or death; but the delays were endless, as were the discussions about "clearing the Rock" of vermin, so it might be used again, for a better class of criminals. A mass execution inside the rock might even have achieved legality, but then it would have been necessary to subtract the lifers. "Send it into the Sun," was a common suggestion.

The final decision sent the Rock into another "open" orbit, a persistent misnomer which actually meant that its period was longer than anyone on the Rock could live. Escape velocity from the Sun was not necessary when a period of a century or more would do the job. Sentences of death and life imprisonment were thus again satisfied.

Those who had received life differed only in legal technicalities from those who had been given death; both groups had committed rape and murder, preceded by cruel tortures. Death seemed the most expedient solution, but the understanding of researchers stood against it. Too much was known about what had alienated these human beings from their own kind to permit even the "social self-defense" justification for acceptable killing.

These sexual predators and killers knew that their behavior was fearfully rejected by the society around them; and for periods of time some of them were able to restrain themselves; but sexual release was not possible for them except through violence. After periods of self-restraint that could only weaken, when all other forms of gratification paled before the memory of pleasure, they went out to quiet their bodies by killing. As the normally adjusted man or woman seeks affection and orgasm, these others sought the same through cruelty, rape, and murder.

To find eroticism and adventure at the borders of danger and pain was a tropism closely linked to the main line of human behavior, to be eradicated in the mature adult of this kind only through the dubious purgings of drugs and surgery. Early violence against the child was blamed, in which the initial sexual gratification was released through cruelty and pain, fixing the pleasure response as effectively as the common sexual awakening, but replacing its reproductively purposeful way with an interloper whose only aim was joyous, unspeakable, forbidden domination and bloodletting.

Ordinary violence and rape by otherwise self-directed males was the middle ground between these aliens and the usual run of humanity, except that their avenue to gratification was not occasional but pathological. No other way existed for them. They moved among their kind as secret agents from an alien world, as despised and misunderstood as normal gays and lesbians had once been, driven by their devils to prey that had to struggle and show fear to be desirable.

The richest and most intelligent among them simply understood and filled their needs and were rarely caught; the powerless lived bewildered lives of attempted adaptation, no different than the lives of alcoholics and drug users. As the world grew smaller, the nets of organization pulled them in, preached at them, imprisoned them, drugged them, altered them surgically, locked them up, killed them, ignored them—and yet made new ones. Where were they coming from? From the fatal liberty of human nature, some said.

Humanity cried out in denial, "The Devil does not drive us!" It sought to rip out its evolutionary heart and hurl it into the darkness, denying in the brightly lit realm of its cerebral cortex that predation, sexual domination, the killing of infants and male enemies had all been part of the leverage by which nature had raised humankind out of time's darkness, caring for individuals only if they lived to the age of reproduction. Nature did not fret over how the male delivered his wetware, caring only that he did so; it knew nothing of social systems, and did not agonize over deluded and damaged individuals; it did not trust the species to decide its own survival—so it gave it the orgasm as reward, and whipped the male who denied it into submission.

Social systems, grown from exhortations backed by physical force, acted in ignorance, recognizing neither humankind's true origins nor its waiting, open possibilities . . .

■

The three women came at him on all fours, like slow moving wolves, eyeing him with fear and suspicion. It had taken some time to beat and frighten them into performing. The first one, a curly-headed brunette, came up into his lap, took his penis in her mouth, and bit him . . .

He felt the token pain, then shot her through the head and kicked the body back for the others to see. The other two waited, then began to whimper . . .

As the mercy-VR program ran out, he held on to the three naked figures in his field of vision—one cheesecake white, one silky chocolate, one amber, each with a foresty pubis. They were all probably dead by now, and he could only torment them in the system's limited variations. This had been one of the last downloaded programs shouted to the Rock by pitying friends and relatives before communications had been cut off. The record was supposedly of a real crime, for which the unseen man had been tried and sentenced. Maybe he was even here . . .

As he took off the old style VR helmet, Bellamy longed to have VRs of his own adventures. They sang to him from his fading memory, reminding him that their like would never come again in the lifetime left to him out here. Looking back, he knew that he had once lived and was now dead.

He did not blame anyone for his confinement; they were simply protecting themselves, as they said. On Earth, he would have been selecting and stalking new victims, satisfying new needs.

He did not think of himself as abnormal, because he had never known any other way. As he saw it, those unlike him had a right to protect themselves, and he had a right to use those who failed to escape him as his needs demanded. He had tried repeatedly to live as they did, as a practical matter, to avoid their getting after him; but it was life in an emotional desert of denial. He could not understand how they managed to live in such a way. The only way he could understand it was to tell himself that they had different needs, smaller needs. They were welcome to their ways.

But his body knew what he was and what had been done to deny it: Everyone here was like him, in one way or another, and could not be easily stalked and used as he had done back home. Here there was no prey.

So another kind of order had emerged, and could not be avoided. Bellamy had grown familiar with the ritual, and he lived in the hope of getting something out of it.

The ritual, which was sometimes enacted in the mess halls and sometimes outside in the fields, was a way of deciding who would be the abused and who would abuse. One by one, each inmate of the Rock was tested by tormentors, who used implements, food, and their own bodies to bring the victim to the breaking point, but without killing. Those who resisted best went over to the pool of tormentors; but this also needed a vote of the mass, based on whether they were especially entertained or not. One worked hard to become a tormentor by resisting fear, panic, and pain; one could also fall from tormentor status back into the mass of victims.

But the greatest missing pleasure, one that had disappeared in the first year of exile, was death. Too many were dying at the outset, and it became clear that the Rock could not afford many more deaths. So while the new order guaranteed a chance for everyone to fulfill their needs, it frustrated their most intense realization.

Most everyone lived with the feeling, especially those who had known the ecstasy of sexual slaughter but were now denied it, of a vast emptiness at the center of their lives; and many of them suspected that this had also been the intended punishment of exile in the spinning, fleeing Rock: The rise of necessary order, alien to individuals of this other humanity, would trivialize and domesticate their predator's needs, giving with one hand a chance for community survival beyond the present population, while taking away with the other the right to sexual release through killing.

There arose an order, alien by Earth's standards, that saw quickly that it did not wish to abolish itself through anarchy, even if that meant building a wall between two parts of its own nature.

A far-seer sitting on that wall would have said that there was nothing new or alien about the arrangement. The contortions of the soul-body that lived on Earth were not different. The cruelties and humiliations of economics and business conduct; the accepted inhumanities that called upon a hidden and necessary hand in human history; the silent cruelty of the powerful to the lesser and powerless; the personal vendettas of commission and omission; the hatreds of race, class, and personal antipathies—all sang the song of the predators who dreamed of slaughtering their neighbor's children, enslaving their women, and swarming the future with only their own whelpings. If they had been souls in stone, they would have roughed and polished each other until only the largest were left, and these would have crushed each other into dust.

Humankind had only hurled its most denied self out into the dark, but the angels still battled with devils back home. Bellamy was sure of that.

Would it have helped Bellamy to understand what he was, to step back into endless perspectives on what he took for granted? Would it have helped him to stare reality in the face? He lacked this insight of step-back that had led some individuals into discontented greatness, whose endless method of examination tortured all givens, and yet whose beatific light had somehow sprung from the same cauldron as the unthinking predator.

∎

When Bellamy wore out the mercy-VRs, he had no choice but to work with the details of his own memory. Miraculously, they returned to him, as if the VR had retrained his memory, and he treasured each rescued moment. It was his way of avoiding the rituals—by going out into the tall grass at duskdown and lying there invisible to everyone.

There, slowly, he discovered that he could have what he wanted from his past, drifting in a sea-silence until the blessed moments came to him again out of the black grave of fragmented memories—

They were like little chocolates in their supra-suburban villages, far from the paid-poverty of the suburbs into which he had been born, each female body yielding up a different inner core of delight. He watched and logged their comings and goings as if they were butterflies, and bought their house-entry codes from the sellers who knew their captive market well. For him it was always a simple matter to steal enough to pay for the magic keys . . .

It was always the same with the women. Some were cruel to their males; a few didn't need males at all; and others were natural victims: their innermost doors were always open, waiting for him to find them . . .

He entered her bedroom and put the mini-dart gun to her temple.

She opened her eyes.

"You have decisions to make," he said, dropping his small equipment bag. "Understand?"

Slowly, she nodded, unable to speak. After a moment he saw that she was not breathing. Then her mouth opened and she gasped, staring at him wide-eyed, just the way he liked it.

"Make you a deal," he said. "Let me watch you . . . and I won't touch you at all."

She took a deep breath, as if surprised at her good fortune, then nodded, and he knew that he had hooked her.

She slipped her arms under the covers and closed her eyes. He watched her play with herself for a minute, then reached down and whipped back the covers.

"Don't stop," he said, backing away.

As she closed her eyes and continued, he got down on his knees and took out the four metal eyelets that he had brought. Taking his dart gun, he placed the eyelets, one by one into the business end, then drove them into the hardwood floor. Finally, he took out four sets of cuffs and attached one to each eyelet.

"What . . . are you doing?" she asked, opening her eyes.

He got up, dragged her from the bed onto the floor, and secured her hands in front of her, one to each cuff so that her palms were flat on the hardwood. Then he spread her from behind, attached each ankle to a cuff, then ripped off her top and panties.

He sat down in a nearby chair and watched her. She turned her head to look back at him, but this position was difficult. He waited a moment longer, then lay down on the floor and reached under her from behind. She twisted as he touched her, opening her gently.

"Don't," she whispered perfectly, then began to twist her hands in the manacles.

"You'll only bloody your wrists," he said, standing up.

He came around in front of her and unzipped his pants.

"Fellate me," he said, "and I won't do anything else."

"What?" she asked, but understood as he presented himself.

She took him into her mouth, and made a feeble effort, glancing up at him with a mixture of fear and revulsion.

After a while, he withdrew, went around behind her, knelt and pushed her slightly forward.

"But you said . . ." She whimpered as he prepared to enter her from behind.

She twisted her head back to look at him, and he noticed her blue eyes and short blond hair. "If you don't move with me, I'll go up your ass."

"No, no," she said at once, facing forward.

He pushed in, bringing himself forward until he could whisper in her ear. "Make another deal. Bring yourself off and I won't let loose inside you. Good deal. Best you can get right now."

"Yes," she said with resignation, and made a show of gyrating against him.

"I'm coming," he whispered in her ear after a minute.

"What!" she shouted.

"You were faking," he said, grabbing her short hair and fixing her with his eyes as he forced her to look back at him.

He let go and she turned her head forward once more.

"Try again?" he asked.

She nodded.

"The real thing now," he said. "I'll know."

"Yes," she said.

As she moved against him, he leaned across her back again and said with his cheek against hers, "When I know it's real, I'll pull out and leave nothing in you."

"I'll live to kill you," she said suddenly.

He laughed. "What makes you think you'll live?"

She clenched, then gasped with pleasure, betraying the perversity of the human orgasm, which belonged to both predator and prey.

"Yes!" she rasped in his ear, and he knew it was real.

He pulled out and lay at her side. She was breathing hard, but watching him carefully. He brought the small gun up in his right hand so she could see it.

He stood up in front of her. "Here, maybe you can get back at me a little," he said, offering his limp organ.

She hesitated, then received him, and bit slowly, carefully, knowing the power of death that waited in his right hand. He felt a vague sense of the mystery that exists between men and women, in the million-year old dance that bestows pleasure to the individual while securing the survival of the species, driving the individual forward to do what he might otherwise fail to do. Yeah, he'd heard about that, but he cared nothing for children. He might have made some without knowing it, but it didn't matter.

He pulled back, saving himself, and went around behind her again. Kneeling, he prepared to penetrate her anally.

"You said you wouldn't," she said bitterly.

He was silent as he pushed in and spent himself and sprawled across her back. She was unable to fall on her stomach, so she held him up . . .

The details! How he treasured the details of the women's bodies! But more than that he loved their fear of him, their inward resistance, which he crushed repeatedly, until they cried out their acceptance.

How he had wished that their boyfriends or husbands might be manacled and gagged nearby, so he might enjoy the horror in their eyes when he would say, "As soon as I'm done, you will die, and she can watch. Hope I'm slow!" But it had never been his luck to have such a moment.

But wait . . . yes, there had been one . . . or had he dreamed it? Yes, it had been . . .

"Ah!" he cried out with eyes closed and his back pressed to the spinning ground.

"Well, well, what have we here?" a voice said.

He opened his eyes and saw a dozen men standing around him.

"He's been dreaming," Rebello said. "I've seen him come up here more than once. He knows how to, real well."

"Maybe he should tell us his dreams," said a voice behind him.

"Yeah, he should share!" another added.

Rebello leaned down, grinned at him, and asked, "Didn't yo' mama teach you to share?"

"You . . . you want to hear?"

Rebello stood up to his full height and said, "Do we have anything better to do?"

Bellamy heard a fist slap into a palm. "Yeah, let's kick the shit out of him and make him eat it," said a voice behind him.

"I'll tell you everything, fellas!" he shouted. "But leave me alone."

They sat down in a circle around him. "This better be good," Rebello said.

Bellamy told them. A few of them masturbated. Two went off together into the grass, just out of sight but within earshot.

"So what did you do to her?" Rebello asked, swallowing hard.

"I cut her throat."

"Nah, you didn't," Rebello said. "Not you!"

"I sure did."

"Was it good?" Rebello asked, sounding more convinced.

Bellamy shrugged. "She didn't shake enough before she bled to death. It was too quick. I cut too hard. She had more fierce in her than she gave me."

"So you had better?"

"Not like her. She never gave in, really. Got her in me still." So much so, he thought, that he was constantly adding to the scenario, and no longer knew what had happened and what he had made up. Too bad he had no VR of it, or any way to make one.

Rebello stared at him blankly, and Bellamy knew that showing any feelings at all to the likes of Rebello might one day get him killed.

He had been living for some time on the edges of acceptable humanity, but only deep within himself, and went in fear of falling into the abyss of emotion that would rob him of the calm, anxiety-free state that Rebello accepted as normal. There were long minutes when compassion and remorse welled up from him, and he feared that the others would see it in him. He wondered how many suffered and wept in private. Back home, such behavior would have been labeled a ploy to gain release. Here, this fall-back was held in contempt and punished with beatings.

"You're one of them, aren't you?" Rebello asked. "You want your fantasies more than the real thing, don't you!"

Almost.

Bellamy tensed. Sometimes he was glad he no longer had to go out and do anything with anyone, because fantasy was enough. Almost. More didn't matter. A flood of fear and horror swept into him. He was naked before his enemies, his control gone. They could see right into him.

Rebello stood up and kicked him. "You're the tenth this week. Some of them are hiding out—but we'll find them all."

He moaned and held his side from the pain, and knew that they were about to use him—and he would enjoy some of it and then suffer, suffer and enjoy, and finally suffer completely before he died. He knew that they would lose it and kill him, and he longed for the state of uncaring and self-control that had been his, thinking that if he could regain it, he might be able to stay the hands that would torment him into darkness. If they could see into him, they would know when he was like them again.

But there was no time. There couldn't be any.

And as Rebello kicked him in the stomach, and the men crowded around him like hyenas, Bellamy cried out the words of a preacher who had once laid hands on him and had been the closest he had ever felt to having a father: "There is time yet to climb the mountain of righteousness, or plunge into the pit of wrong!"

Rebello laughed as if he could hear the words, half grunting and half gurgling, then said, "Hey, he's gonna be a good one."

Bellamy closed his eyes and saw the burning red of hell.

13

Enemies of the State

JUDGE OVERTON'S PRIVATE CHAMBER

"They get food and shelter, and an island all to themselves. We no longer execute them, or torture or beat them. Our Orbits are much, much better than the Gulags and Supermax prisons of the twentieth century, or the famous prison in Kazakhstan for young boys. You know about that one, don't you?"

Rock Four was recorded as a twenty-five year orbit, but went twice that. The unknowing inmates, equal numbers of men and women, were so burdened with documents indicating conviction for unquestioned crimes that no defense would ever be able to separate them from genuine lawbreakers. They were mostly from the Asian middle classes, born after the Great Asian Depression of the 2020s, which had ended when the rest of the world had bailed out the financial elites of that region.

As world population decreased after the depression, these financial elites sought longlife and privilege for themselves and their children, even as political opposition, pressing forward with North American and European democratic ideals, rose in a valiant effort to shame the various governments of China, India, and Southeast Asia.

While nutrition was more than adequate for most people in the region, political decision making was denied them. Long life was being denied to all except the elites, who feared a large population of vigorous longlifers as a revolutionary threat, and looked forward to the coming die-off. With the expansion into the solar system, longlife threatened to wipe away all hereditary wealth and power and put it in the hands of economic specialists, priests to the coming AIs.

The elites of Asia focused on the leaders of opposing groups, overlayed their identities with criminal records, and exiled them to the Rocks. The disappearance of people also had the effect of bringing out other rebels and making them available for future disposal.

Abebe Chou, with a Nigerian mother and a Chinese father, was typical of social resisters who were seen by ruling elites as simply wishing to replace them in power. Her claims of seeking justice by exposing unfair social manipulation were regarded as disingenuous by the elites who finally destroyed her reputation and identity and exiled her to the Rocks.

Abebe Chou reasoned in this way: The charge of insincerity was unjustified. Many rebels of the nineteenth, twentieth, and twenty-first century were sincere; but short-lived human beings were incapable, in the vast majority, of wielding power and self-control to accomplish the ends of desired reforms. The longer living power elites were sincere only in their aims of staying in power and passing it on to their friends and relatives; they could only be challenged by elites with comparable economic support, or by military force.

In this view, all political rebellion seeking justice based on ethics and intellectual merit was naive, since it lacked the strength to do more than speak, at which point it was identified and destroyed.

As longlifers increasingly set back their bodily clocks, the kinds of discussion-reforms that had sometimes been possible in the twentieth century remained matters of debate. Long life, power, and wealth became the same thing, and who was to be let into their club became a carefully policed process. The always unequal struggle for the future worsened.

Yet it was not the old wealthy who survived in the bosom of their wealth. The wealth lived on, but only to be managed by those who knew how to use its power; so they naturally felt that they deserved its rewards. The old owners of wealth had begun to understand this, and had hired experts to care for wealth on their behalf. Dutifully, these experts dispensed the desired ways of life to their bosses; but inevitably these caretakers, who knew too much to be controlled, slowly grew their influence and personal fortunes and became the new wealthy . . .

As Abebe sat on the gentle hillside above the barracks town and watched her fellow prisoners, dense with doctorates and special skills, making their sheeplike way to the dining halls, she despaired for the uses of power. Whether it came from below with justice in its heart, or from the top with eyes wide open to self-interest, power could not stand aside from the human creature attempting to wield it.

She had once been a grade school teacher in Australia, and the lesson should have been clear to her even then. Even with equal numbers of boys and girls, the students always divided into bullies, toadies, and a nameless rabble of victims. It had never been otherwise, since the world's beginning: The rich were the bullies—except for the guilt-ridden do-gooders among them; the middle class were the toadies, always ready to roll over for a leg up, or even a leg in place; the poor were the victims—except for the criminals who struck back with injustice of their own devising . . .

So who are we? she asked herself, as she gazed down at a town of once plush chairs in sociology, political science, ethical philosophies, and environmental sciences. Like herself, they had all wept for humanity, had exerted themselves to change its ways, and had failed. We were all ghosts, she thought, unable to warn the living; and now we are the dead, unable to even be ghosts. Speaking truth to power was only effective when it also helped power and wealth; being right was merely a bonus. Besides, the powerful had long ago learned the trick of revolutionaries, by speaking truth to itself in private, however embarrassing or distasteful; it was all part of a useful and necessary game plan. Most moral superiors could be turned around by a go-along-to-get-along human nature, which sooner or later discarded its ideals and became Zapata's man with the gun, who would give it up only to those who would take it from him with a bigger gun. And what would the bigger gun say to its owner?

The trouble with humankind, she had decided, was that you never knew what was speaking out of any brain. Raise up the meek and they will abuse as well as anyone. The predator is only silenced by piles of food and the sight of his progeny crowding the landscape, and is then worn out by their raising and left behind . . .

Sometimes, what managed to speak was the cortex, the white magician, so maligned by the rest of the brain for being naive, because it longed to leave behind the adaptive superstition of the instincts and the impulses of the automatic unconscious that wash the older bicameral brain. It was the cortex's misfortune to be the newest level of a city like Troy, built upon many previous levels, unable to live and think without the ghosts that came up from below and raged through its clean, well-lighted ways. The cortex was an aspiring angel, whose ankles were still held by the ancient demons of evolution's selecting slaughterhouse. Whenever the prattlings about maturity and psychological naivete were heard, the old animal father-mother was speaking, concerned only with survival and the hurling of progeny into time's abyss. The bewildered child that asked *why* to everything was the angelic cortex, Billy Budd waiting to be crushed by Claggett, unsuited to the universe which had somehow produced it . . .

She hated the sneering, patronizing forms of discussion that she had grown up with. Even as a child she had wondered *who* or *what* was speaking, as if a stranger had awakened in the adult who was talking to her. And upon hearing what the stranger said, a Luciferian rebellion had swelled in her heart against these judgments that did not know themselves . . .

She stood up and saw that the rest of the sewing circle, as she thought of the five men and herself, was sitting down on the hillside far down to her right. For a moment she was touched by their innocent, unquestioning belief in the adequacy of discussion to probe and grasp, and even to shape the future. She had pet names for them—Lenin, Trotsky, Stalin, Newton, Leibniz, and she was—who? Lenin's wife, the crow-like Krupskaya? Eleanor Roosevelt? Maybe Madame Touchard? Mrs. Parker? In all truth, she sometimes did not know her own name.

It was the feuds among the historical names that had prompted her to rename these men when she listened to their bickering. She had not thought of them by their true names for some time now; but she never addressed them by their pet names. She used no names at all with them.

Not one of them was the equal of Abebe Chou, who had supposedly stolen a billion dollars online, which had never been found, and whose political ideas seemed about to influence her lover, John Sakari of India, frightening the powerful whose fortunes rode with his. He had been appalled at the charges brought against her, but when it came to choosing her over his future in power, he had given her up.

Gone was her love.

Gone was the medical renewal of her life at fifty.

Gone was her chance to have become someone and made a difference.

Going fast was her compassion for her kind.

Growing fast was bitterness and hatred.

■

She came down the hillside and sat down among the sheltered wusses, the urban tunas who had been caught in the nets set by human sharks, and would never get free. It was dismaying to know that there were more sharks and tunas where they came from, and that the struggle would not end any time soon, unless the species found some way to reach into its deepest regions and remake itself; but that might be as hard as expecting Zapata's gunman to lay down his gun. Look at *what* was trying to remake itself. The only hope was that small changes would in time catch the species unawares. But how to keep vitality and strength in the midst of a flickering goodness that strength saw only as dangerous weakness?

"Good afternoon, gentlemen," she said, noticing with her usual upsurge of vanity how they gazed at her with admiration and longing. Brutality had long been repressed in them, and hid its rapacious hopes—but how long would it stay? She knew as they smiled at her that she would reject each of them in turn; and they feared that somewhere in this population there were some she might not reject; but how long would it take to find them? How long before the show of civilization and order crumbled—five years, ten, twenty? Would everyone pair off and be happy with their lot? Would they all despise each other for living out their time as civilized people?

"People say you can't do this and you can't do that," Lenin said, as if resuming a train of thought pulled out of her mind, "but what they mean is that you shouldn't."

"So what's your point?" Trotsky asked.

"They should say what they mean. And to them I say that I can very well do this or that, even when I choose not to. Even Unamuno, the religious, well understood that there was no basis for morality except insistence, in taking a free stand."

Stalin smiled and said, "The wind that blew in from the ocean had left its mark on the trees that leaned landward. One was so bent that its top branches nearly touched the ground." Like his namesake, he fancied himself a poet.

"Yes, yes, we are set in our ways," Leibniz said with a wave of the hand, "but we can take small steps toward good, and these will add up.

Then new windows of opportunity will open."

"They have added up—to this?" Abebe said.

"No, no," Stalin said with an uncharacteristically quick show of impatience. "You did not notice—I said top branches."

"So?" Leibniz replied.

"There are tall trees, you know."

Not here, Abebe thought, thinking about the one rape she already knew about. There would have been a murder or a lynching if the woman had spoken out. The only guards or police possible here would be vigilantes.

She felt humiliated as she looked around at her five comrades. Humanity had no more use for them or for her. Their major offense had been that they served no one powerful enough to have saved them from this exile.

Each of these men had spoken up for the excluded and endangered, asking why some should be left out to die while the world's powerful cut their political losses, isolated diseased populations, and looked ahead to a smaller humanity. The growing longlifers would not take all the living with them into the coming world; it was their one chance to rearrange power to insure their own survival.

"If not us," they cried, "then others will do the same, and they may not be as trustworthy. We have only to wait until their lives end as they would have anyway. After all, we can't search out everyone on the planet to extend their lives. They would be unprepared for it. We need to start smaller."

"Not to act is to kill them," she had whispered one night to John Sakari.

"It's not practical," he had mumbled, and she had felt ashamed in the darkness of his bed. What he meant by practical or impractical was that it wouldn't benefit anyone he knew very soon. Practical was short term, for himself and others like him; for her. He has assumed that she would gladly wear his chain of logic.

"When life is long," he had said, "and we no longer fear its end, then there will be time for justice. Where the many will one day go, a few must go first. We are not monsters, Abebe."

But we will not include those who speak against us, his silence had said. Because we are not monsters, words may hurt us, by spreading guilt and unease, and damaging our resolve . . .

Twenty-five years, she thought, glancing at the bemused faces of her fellow inmates.

They were all cowards, herself included, afraid of themselves. Afraid of doing evil to oppose it.

■

In the first year the community only became more orderly, but Abebe remained suspicious of the cauldron that simmered beneath the surface, and might boil when least expected. True, no great prize of power existed to be seized, but her fellow inmates were still cowards, unable to face up to their own impulses and needs, afraid to do what their innards urged.

She continued contemptuous of their timidity, but was sometimes taken aback. Did she really want them to run amok? The sewing circle, if they could have eavesdropped on her whispering self, would have laughed at the contradiction. She wondered at her mental state that saw all sides and liked none of them.

It was not religion, law, nor ideals that had subverted humankind; it was humankind itself that was the villain, subverting religion, law, and high ideals. Frankenstein's monster was no monster at all. Doctor Frankenstein was the monster—and not even all of him.

But—she objected to herself—perhaps she was being sensitive to something else here. More seemed needed in this place than simply to do the time, but she could not flush out what it might be. She thought of it as a beast that she hunted regularly in her several mental jungles.

How are we to live? How was she to live? Could anything be done? Was civil order all that might be hoped for? How to last the time with this growing knot inside her, with these festering contradictions and impulses that sent elder brain and hopeful cortex against each other? Countless thinkers had nursed these thoughts, she reminded herself. Man was not a state, but a predicament, and only the unreflective accepted themselves as finished and sufficient. The reflective knew otherwise, but did not know where else to go from themselves . . .

Small steps. Baby steps. We must take all the falls before we can stand and stride. Most learn to stand; some stride; a few learn to dance well; does anyone learn to fly?

She had come to the end of her humanity, and faced a wall of fossil flesh in her mind; she stood before it daily, looking for a crack, a small peephole, a way up and over, under or around. She did not know what waited on the other side, if anything; but she was willing to pay whatever asking price to find out.

But whom was she to pay?

14

Warriors

Of all the epidemics of violence, assault and murder by the young who felt nothing for their victims were the most fearsome and difficult to stop. Here the criminal justice systems of the Earth were dealing with warriors whose instinctive quickness, unchanged for half a million years, was at its height in teenage years. They had grown up outside the restraints that humankind had arrayed against itself, with no parenting or education and no hope of welcome in or outside their class. The stubbornly law-abiding among the working poor hated them. The lawful foraging homeless hated them. The heroic working poor and lower middle class feared them. They were outcasts and failures to the tactical criminals allied with the upper middle class and wealthy. In another age they would have served conquerors and warlords, and been sacrificed in battle to great effect.

"How many warriors can you educate into

post-industrial wusses?" the joke asked.

"One," was the answer.

"If we can catch him."

"All of them," said some politicians.

"We cannot reform them," proclaimed the longlifers. "And we cannot let them come to adulthood beside us. We must be careful what progeny we permit to grow as we live forward."

As the numbers of longlifers increased, they sought to slow and then abolish the past's dead hand of chaotic comings and goings between generations and classes. Longlife meant keeping more benefits for themselves; there was too much to lose. This quickened the drift away from the class systems of twentieth century industrial quasidemocracies, in which the working class sometimes recruited from the poor, the middle class recruited from the working class, and the rich drew from the middle class. The borders between these divisions were becoming nearly impassable, to the degree where the usefulness of classes was being lost, to be replaced with a rigid and fruitless caste system.

"These are the lost," the longlifers said, lengthening on, "and it matters not if they live out their dead-end ways in a small worldlet, away from us. Among us they will only be unhappy and do us harm."

"Perhaps they can change," said some, "if we were to give them more life, more time to start over."

"No—we will not let them into the new world we are making," the others cried as they rushed toward their paradise. "Let them keep the life they have, but no more. We will not lengthen their nightmare into our dream."

There were just too many. With no mindfulness within them or likely to develop, and the abyss of homelessness and early death from violence and disease waiting to swallow them, they had nothing to lose. They struck back impulsively, gripped by the moment's needs, without a horizon of hope or a teacher other than trial and error to guide their actions.

Their presence was explained as a byproduct of market economies that had raised too many young in drugs and drink, that could not educate everyone, and in fact did not need everyone, but feared to say so. Parenting was a nonproductive activity, a hobby for those who could afford it and who lived with specific expectations from the future. The social cost of soulless young was not counted, leaving only the criminal justice system to deal with them.

"There must be a price to pay for failure!" cried the wealthy, and it was paid thrice—by the failures, by their victims, and later by the society, and each paid too late.

On Rock Six, sent for an expected thirty years, Ricardo Nona's life was an eternal present. At fifteen his past was brief, his future blank; he had never had so much time to spend with himself, to see himself as someone else. The objects of his attention had always stood outside him; but now feelings he had been able to ignore swelled with the intensity that concentrated self-awareness forced upon him.

He felt as if his thoughts were assaulting him, as if someone had put a spell on him. What was he doing here? What would he ever do here? Thirty years was forever. He was an orphan; no one cared for him back home. His closest relative had been an uncle, who had been shot to death by the police in Detroit only three days before Ricardo's sentencing.

His lawyer had explained his situation to him more than she probably wanted to. She was good looking, so he let her talk just so he could look at her longer.

"They don't care what happens to you," she had said. "You killed three people in the carjack. You're beyond any concept of rehab. They just want to get rid of you. I'm telling you this so that when your Rock comes back you'll know why you did the time. It won't do you much good now, but you'll have time to think about it." She had smiled slightly. "There's not much else to say. I don't think you'll get into more trouble in the Rock, but it won't matter. It'll be you and the others. No police, no guards. I do wish you luck, Ricardo."

She had asked him why he did it, and all he

could remember was that his two friends were going to do something and wanted him along. When the time came, it seemed right to kill the people in the car, or get killed. They had killed Mario right off, so at least one of them had to die. He had killed one, and Angela had killed the other. That made three. What had the judge expected? That he and Angela should have stood there and got shot? It seemed like a dream to think about it, and have it come out the same way every time.

"Ricardo," his lawyer had continued, "there's not much more I can do for you except say a few things that might stick in your head. It's my last shot. Do you understand?"

"Yeah, sure," he had said to make her feel better. What could it matter. She had great tits and good legs. Her butt was getting bigger, but still pretty good for over thirty. He could enjoy her if he had the chance.

"Ricardo, the Rock you're going to will be nearly all orphans, or so close it's the same thing. It's going to be overcrowded, because they're packing in as many as they can get in before the boost."

"So?"

She had smiled, trying to look friendly. He had thought of killing her right there, because there wasn't much more they could do to him except kill him, but they weren't killing lately.

"Do you have any feelings about why you

are here, and why you are as you are?" she had
asked. "You might have been very different.
Look—think this way, for just a few moments.
You didn't make yourself the way you think
and feel right now, because you weren't around
to decide back before you were born. A lot of
other things decided it for you."

He knew what she meant, but it didn't
matter.

"A great judge said that if a child isn't fixed
between the age of three and seven, it'll never
be fixed. Do you feel you'll never get better?"

"Yeah, I know what you mean," he had
said, just to say something she obviously
wanted to hear.

"You know only what your way of growing
up has taught you—look out for yourself and
get what you can of what you need."

"Don't you do that?" he had asked. "What
else is there?"

She had sighed. "Other people. You don't
need to step on them when they get in your
way."

"You do if they try to step on you," he had
said.

"It's the way you look out for yourself and
get what you need," she had said. "And you will
get it."

She had given him a long look of *how sorry
I am*, then touched his cheek gently with her
hand as she stood up. "You are a handsome boy,

you know." And she had left, thinking it was too bad.

He was the youngest of the boys in the Rock, except for the hundred or so eleven-year olds. The oldest males and females here were well over twenty. The oldest had the largest number of screamers, the drug addicted, and the crazies. A few were recovering, but many were dying, unable to eat. He had seen a few of them sitting in the tall grass, where they had to sleep. They had been brought here at the last minute, a few thousand of them, just before the boost. There was no room for them in the barracks. They didn't come to the mess halls to eat, and were getting sicker each day. A few were already dead.

The rest of the girls, even those his age, were competing for the oldest nonaddicted guys, the eighteen to twenty-fives. There were maybe ten thousand people in the Rock, counting the screamers.

There wasn't much to do except eat, sleep, and spy on the older guys making it with the girls you couldn't get, and avoid getting beaten up by the gays and perverts. Many of the frooties would just ask, even beg, but the pervs went around in twos and threes, and they could get you. Unwilling girls were stalked, but he had not yet gotten up the courage to try it until today.

He was following a tall, willowy girl with

short blond hair who liked to go up to the grove behind the mess halls. A footpath was being worn through the grass to the place. As he came to the grove of maple trees, he noticed a flurry of movement on the ground. He crept closer and peered out from the side of a tree. The girl was on the ground, her arms pinned by a tall, dark-haired boy. She struggled, then lay back, cursing at him as he reached down and started to pull up her denim skirt. She threw her long legs into the air, trying to get him into a headlock, but missed every time.

Ricardo stepped into view and shouted, "Hey, let her go!" He didn't know why he did it.

The boy looked at him and grinned. "Wanna watch? I don't mind."

The girl broke loose as he spoke and scrambled to her feet. The boy reached out for her crotch. She turned and fled through the trees. The tall boy came up to him and knocked him down. Then he started after the girl.

Ricardo got up with blood in his mouth, and followed at a run.

He felt useless as he stopped outside the trees.

The girl was running swiftly across the grass, but the tall boy was pushing hard and gaining. He caught up with her, and the two figures fell silently out of sight into the tall grass.

Ricardo sat down, unable to sort out his feelings.

After a while, he saw the tall boy get up and march away.

A minute later the girl got up and looked around. She saw him. He waved to her. She seemed to be looking toward him. He started to walk toward her. She turned away and marched toward the barracks.

He watched as she neared one of the buildings. Two boys came out to meet her; then the boy who had left her in the grass came up from her left. The three seemed to be talking. She pointed toward Ricardo. The three boys started up toward him.

As he neared the three boys, Ricardo saw that they were grinning at him.

"Get him!" shouted one.

Ricardo halted and stood his ground.

They reached him, and the one who had left the girl in the grass grabbed him by his denim coverall.

"What you doin' out here, boy?" he demanded. "Spying?"

"I was out walking," Ricardo said defiantly. "You said I could watch," he added.

"Who sent you?" asked a short redheaded boy.

"No one."

"She belongs to us, you know," said a third boy. "She complained about you."

"I thought . . ." Ricardo started to say.

"Yeah?" said the tall boy.

". . . you were hurting her," he finished.

"She likes it that way," the tall boy said. "She likes to be hunted and chased. Get it?"

Ricardo didn't but nodded.

The piggish boy sneered. "You can see he's never been laid," he said—and punched Ricardo in the mouth.

The blow knocked him on his back.

He lay still, as if he were someone else.

"Ah, he's no fun," said the redhead.

The three looked down at him with contempt.

"Leave him," the tall boy said. "He'll be taking it up the ass in no time."

They turned and walked off, laughing . . .

■

Ten years later, the screamers were all dead and buried or down the disposal chutes. Only a handful had kicked their habits and lived. It had been bad, with rotting bodies in the grass, until he had organized the dump squads.

Ricardo sometimes remembered the laughter of the older boys who had tormented him. They were now old men in their thirties, the ones he had not killed. He and those younger than him now had all the best girls and the better women, including the leggy girl he had tried to help in the grass. His lawyer had given him a good idea when she had told him how handsome he was. He still looked very young, lied about his age, and counted himself a success.

And the three old bullies went in fear of him.

15

Plato's Cave

JUDGE OVERTON'S PRIVATE CHAMBER

"There are those who say we should pay up front, or pay at the other end of a life, by building higher walls. They say that education and health must deal with human lives, whose value is beyond price. As an investment, lives should not be subject to the marketplace. The original investment in education and health, in the quality control of bringing new human beings on line, should not be counted or begrudged in any way, since the benefits of prevention will prove to be incalculable.

"To all this I say well and good—but what do we do with the ones who are past any rehabilitation, immune to deterrence, and likely to train more like them? Every generation of humanity to date has been damaged in some way by the previous generation; but until we learn how to make a better generation, we have to protect ourselves. Now we've mined all these rocks, and we're filling them up. They're available, ready and waiting for that twenty percent who will never be able to return successfully to normal life."

In the second year of her imprisonment Abebe Chou learned to take a perverse pleasure in the sewing circle. She liked especially to frame chaotic difficulties which set the five men to untangling subtle errors in reasoning or use of fact, forcing them to return to square one of the discussion; at that point she would present another complex misconception with a straight face.

It was pathetic how they vied to instruct her, with the unspoken hope that she would come to prefer one of them over the others. Sadder still were their contortionist efforts to deny the reality of their competition with each other. It was obvious, and yet they continued in their hypocritical good manners. The beast trying to rise above its ancient ways.

On a Saturday morning, by the accepted calendar, as she made her way across the field to the usual meeting place, she noticed that the color was bleeding out of the world. Greens, blues, and distant browns were darkening, as if the sunplate was fading much too quickly toward its usual nightly moonlight.

But it was already way past that, and in less than a minute she stood in complete darkness, unable to see the well worn path in front of her. She put her hand before her face and saw nothing. The blackness was complete.

"Abebe!" Leibniz cried out with concern.

"Are we all blind?" she called back.

"No!" Lenin answered. "Something's gone wrong with the sunplate."

She moved slowly up the path, knowing that it went straight ahead to the group, with only a minor curve to the left.

"Does anyone have a light?" Stalin called out.

She stopped, realizing that she had never seen a flashlight in the habitat. There had to be matches somewhere, but she did not recall ever having seen them either.

She stopped and turned around in the darkness, straining to see if anyone back at the town had lit a fire; but the blackness around her was still unbroken. Suddenly she did not know which way she had come or which way she had been going.

"This way, Abebe!" Trotsky cried.

She turned toward the voice, then got down on her knees and felt where the path had been worn through the grass.

"Stay where you are!" Newton called out. "Maybe the light will come back shortly."

She sat down where she knelt and waited.

After a few minutes, cries of anger and dismay drifted up from the town. She turned her head, but still saw no light of any kind. There was nothing to burn, she realized, except perhaps the grass; but it was probably not dry enough.

This was a major failure, she thought, and

no one knew the way into the engineering level; but even if a way had been found, there was no certainty that it was a fixable failure.

"Abebe!" Stalin called out. "Are you all right?"

"Yes," she shouted back. Why wouldn't I be, she thought, wishing that she still had the watch John Sakari had given her before their separation. He had let her keep it, and she recalled that its face had glowed in the dark.

There was no way to tell how much time had gone by since the blackout, but it seemed long. Time seemed to slow in the absence of light.

Again, she realized that they had nothing to burn, even if a way were available to start a fire. There was simply no need for a flame, not even in the mess halls.

She realized that after a long while there would be no choice but to attempt to reach the mess halls. Maybe there they would find some light, some glow from the equipment.

But as she looked around, she realized that the blackout might mean a more general loss of power. No food would be delivered from the manufacturing plants below the mess halls, where the proteins, carbohydrates, fibers, and nutrients were melded into the uninteresting but necessary edibles and liquids.

Within six hours, she knew that hunger would force her to try for one of the mess halls, if she could remember its direction from the path. She would have to walk very slowly, arms out like a blind person.

"Abebe!" Lenin cried. "Try to get up here to us. No point in sitting there alone. Conversation is better here."

She smiled, picturing the fools sitting in the dark, continuing their discussion like the inmates of Plato's cave—except that here there was no fire to cast shadows on the wall to help them develop a theory of knowledge.

"Well, are you coming?" Trotsky called out.

It struck her how irritatingly distinctive their voices and intonations were in the dark. "Lenin" was Goran Tanaka, of New Tokyo, a sociobiologist, and his voice was a plaintive tenor; "Stalin" was Lono Sada, a linguist and low tenor; "Trotsky" was Saburo Nakamura, a security codes expert, a high tenor; "Newton" was Malik Al-Amlak, a physicist with a high tenor voice, whose self-given name meant "king of kings." "Leibniz" was Salmalin Sander, a Hindustani-Bulgarian economist, whose pleasant baritone was out of place in the sewing circle.

Newton-Malik hated Leibniz-Sander in a seemingly deep-seated way; this animosity was what had prompted her to name them after the historical antagonists. Sir Isaac Newton had vowed "to break Gottfried Wilhelm Leibniz's heart" for having the effrontery to codiscover the calculus. And he had done so. But she had not been able to discover why Malik so disliked Sander. Their antagonism was obvious when she saw them together. They sat far apart, and gave only token evidence of noticing each other.

"Come along, Abebe!" Stalin cried. "Wait out this inconvenience among friends."

Abebe felt a chill, as if the temperature in the great hollow had dropped. She had a sudden vision of some great failure in the systems of the worldlet that would not be repaired, and all its inmates would die in cold and darkness.

She waited for the dim glow of the sunplate to appear in her field of vision. She opened her eyes wide, as if somehow there was some light that her open pupils might drink in; but the darkness remained complete. It seemed to threaten to become coal-solid.

She shivered in the increasing chill.

■

After what seemed like more than an hour, Abebe got up and made her way up the path toward the voices. The speakers heard her approach and fell silent.

"We're so glad you could join us," Stalin said as she knelt down in the darkness and found a spot.

Again there was an awkward silence.

"Shall we simply sit here and wait?" she asked. "Is it reasonable to suppose that somehow the sunplate will come back on?"

"We're not engineers," Lenin said with a hint of fear and resentment in his voice. "What do you suggest we do?"

They were always falling into old male patterns: a woman complains and a man feels he's being blamed; but if he doesn't know what to do, he reacts resentfully or aggressively.

"Malik?" she asked.

"Well, I hope it's not the fusion source itself."

"How could it go wrong?" Trotsky asked him, happy to shift the responsibility to another source of possible wisdom.

"Well, I certainly hope it has not been struck from outside by a meteor."

"Would we have felt the shock?" asked Leibniz.

"Not if it was small, but it could still do significant damage," answered Newton. "I don't know the design, but the habitat must have some kind of buffer or debris deflector."

Abebe said, "Or they didn't care enough to give us one."

"Well, the odds of being struck are small," Newton said in his usual prissy way, as if he were out taking the air. He had once chided her for bringing up the idea that molecules might somehow be alive, and she had imagined that he might have wanted to address them.

They were all silent again, and Abebe began to think of what they would have to do if the darkness continued indefinitely. Would they stumble and crawl toward the mess halls to eat?

It was definitely getting colder.

"If there's no power," Newton said in a sing-song, "then even the mess dispensers won't work."

"Oh, shut up, Malik," Lenin said to the physicist. "You don't have to try to cheer us up."

Again there was a long silence.

"Which way are the barracks?" Stalin asked. "And which way the mess?"

"Straight down the path, as I sit," Abebe said. "Then left and right."

"But the path ends," Trotsky said.

"We keep straight on," Leibniz said. "The way is clear in my mind's eye."

"Is that possible in this utter darkness?" Lenin asked.

"We can only try," Stalin said. "A bank was never robbed by mere talk." He mentioned banks quite often, which was why Abebe had named him Stalin. The old Bolshevik had routinely robbed czarist banks to fill the party's coffers.

"Are we safer here or there?" Abebe asked. "Perhaps we should wait a bit longer."

It was strange, she thought through another long silence, how expectation of light's return persisted, even as her intellect whispered that it was possible she might never see again.

■

"It's been a while," Lenin said. "Perhaps we should consider doing something. Maybe we should get back to our quarters."

Abebe had never seen such darkness. Not a patch of light anywhere, however she turned her head. The only stimulus to her retinas was from the transient effect of rubbing her eyes.

"We should go," Trotsky said, "while we still have our strength, before we weaken from hunger. Not much can happen to us. We might trip in the grass, but no more. We can't really get lost."

Leibniz said, "We know where we are, and at worst we'll find our quarters by luck. After all, how many directions can we try?"

Fool, Abebe thought.

"Maybe we should try for the mess halls?" Stalin said.

"But if nothing works," Newton replied, "then we won't even be able to eat."

"So we stay put," Lenin concluded.

It grew even colder.

Something was seriously wrong, Abebe thought, and there was no way to fix it. Getting into the engineering level would require some dangerous digging, with no guarantee that the right place would be found, or that anyone could fix it.

She took a deep breath of the chilling air, then heard something moving in the grass near her. A hand touched her thigh.

"Are you very upset?" asked Trotsky's voice.

The hand touched her more insistently, exploring inward. She was about to curse, but restrained herself, waiting to see how far the hand would go. It reached her stomach and began to finger her waistband.

She grabbed the wrist and bent it back. Trotsky gave a grunt of pain and pulled his hand away.

"What was that?" Lenin asked.

They were all silent, obviously aware of what was happening. It had to start somewhere.

Then Trotsky was on her, and the others scurried in around her, grabbing at her arms and legs, pushing her down. He tugged at her shorts and underwear, pulling them off together.

She saw the scene in her imagination, fully lighted, as her legs came apart and Trotsky pressed into her and started his pushups. She waited for him to finish, hoping that there would be an instant in which she might break free and be gone into the dark—

Trotsky spent himself like an old bull, breathing hard as he softened. He whispered in her ear, "You're a goddess," then pulled back and rolled to one side. "Thank you."

Her right arm was free, then her left, and then her ankles, and she knew that there would be a few moments of indecision.

She felt a figure trying to crawl into position as Trotsky lay at her side, breathing hard and stroking her belly.

She kicked with her right leg, and heard a snap as she connected. She sat up, threw herself forward, and rolled away into the darkness. She leaped to her feet and ran blindly into the grass.

"Come back!" Lenin shouted with a strange laugh. "We'll need to keep warm before we die."

After a few moments, she slowed, realizing that they could not find her. She sat down, bare-assed, with only her shirt for cover. There was nowhere to go. She thought of John Sakaro, and how uncaringly he had thrown her away, into this prison, where the ground itself was a wall. She could not climb it; to dig through to the airless desert outside made as much sense as digging a tunnel out of life.

As her breathing slowed, she shivered on the cold ground. The stars, she thought sadly, were below her—the beautiful bright stars in the black on the other side of the grass.

16

You Have Been Told . . .

Tasarov grew apart from the men in the hollow, and sometimes felt that their very existence was an affront to him. He came to the mess halls at the appointed times, but increasingly he kept to himself in the engineering level. The warden's apartment was comfortable, access to databases easy, and he could even walk long distances, exploring the engineering complex. He had yet to reach its end.

He was hoping to find some sort of astronomical facility, where he might look out from the Rock, but so far he had failed to find it. Seeing the stars again became a minor obsession with him.

He continued to search, building an inner life for himself. Out in the hollow a hundred men died in the first year—from personal violence and illness. A few died for no cause that anyone could see. They simply stopped. Some were buried in marked graves; others went down the garbage chutes to the recycling hell-fire.

Murders rarely occurred after the first year; a killer was either beaten or killed, or driven out into the grassy wilderness and not permitted to return. Some of these managed to beg their way back before they starved, if they sounded very convincing. Most offenses were settled between the parties involved. After a while most inmates learned to avoid disputes of any kind.

A kind of peace settled in during the second and third years. It became an unspoken test of character to resist the distant authority of Earth, to live to prove them wrong when the Rock came home. Tasarov had once read that half the prisoners who went to Alcatraz, also known as "the Rock," came out and lived lawful lives; but he could only believe that the old prison in San Francisco Bay had frightened them into cowardice.

He never forgot that this Rock was a punishment prison, as many had been before it. No rehabilitation, no escape possible, no guards or authorities to blame; yet it seemed that some men were seeing it as rehab, as something better than a vendetta against lawbreakers, better than the vengeance of capital punishment.

But he could not see it that way—not yet anyway. The arrogance of the Earth that had sent them out continued to astonish him. It worked its criminal justice systems with the illusion of clean hands, but they were not even moderately clean hands. The Earth was a mosaic of interlocking corporate societies and extortionist governments, where criminality was in fact the legal way of things. The system in fact created most criminals and then sought to punish them. For most of the human history he knew, social systems were the criminal's true parents, whelping lawbreakers uncontrollably like the mythical salt mill which could not stop making salt. Certain kinds of criminality could be prevented, and that would eliminate most crime. But he was certain that even a very advanced social system, one that gave its citizens nearly everything they needed, leaving them nothing to covet, might still harbor the creative criminal, one who would undertake special projects simply because they were possible. Could that kind of enterprise be socially engineered out of human beings?

It had always been clear to him that a sane criminal justice system was possible: one that would try the criminal, assess the price he had to pay for his crime, short of death, and commit no fresh crimes of its own against the criminal . . .

"Fresh crimes?" they would ask.

He knew the faces and types that would ask the question with outrage.

"Yes—new crimes." Not that he really cared for some of the slime that had been executed, but he had always felt that the example of killing a human being was demoralizing for those who did it by law. So brave! It was a cowardly act to tie down any human being and kill him. The criminal justice systems he had known were not perfect and never could be; but the death penalty was perfection itself—it killed you and there was no going back to correct errors, no way to bring back the dead. It would always be an unequal struggle between justice and official killing.

"New crimes? Maybe so, but who cares! Too bad."

"If killing someone officially for a crime was still a traditional act of vendetta, then so be it," they would say and shrug. But even they would not want to kill criminals en masse. They would rather fill the sky with prisons, as they overflowed every Earthly lockup. He was sure now that this Rock could not be the only one.

By the fifth year, Tasarov had learned to keep dilemmas, nurture, and feed them, as a wild animal trainer keeps dangerous beasts, and they in turn kept up his skills. He saw them as demons that could not be banished. And their most important feature, he began to believe, was that they were unresolvable dilemmas. A man might be known by the dilemmas he keeps, especially the intractable ones.

As he set down his thoughts, he still sometimes wondered about the rightness of his mind, and wondered if the bent of his thinking was a bias setting given to him by nature. Being in your right mind was always a fence one could see over, but he still sometimes wondered which side of the fence he was on. Maybe he was sitting on the fence.

■

In the sixth year Tasarov called a meeting, to be held in the open air, so that every inmate who wanted to come could be there.

As he sat down at the table set for the judge, he considered the air of display about the trial that was beginning—as if someone might be listening back home, or some godlike lawgiver was peering into the hollow and waiting to make notes in a book of justice.

An older man had knifed Howes to death out in the tall grass, and everyone had heard his screams.

"We're here," Tasarov said as he raised a hand, "to determine why this happened, and what we should do about it." He glanced at the man sitting on the ground in front of the table.

"What do you care that I did it," asked Wang Huichin, a burglar from Brooklyn, New York.

There was a murmur of disapproval from the crowd sitting in a massive circle around the table. Everyone was not here, Tasarov noted, but more men were coming in around the edges for a listen.

Tasarov waited for the murmurs to die down, then said loudly, "That's what we're here to tell you."

"Oh yeah?" Wang muttered under his breath.

"Louder," someone shouted from far back.

Tasarov rose and got up on the table. "Can you hear me now?" he shouted.

"Yes!" five different voices responded.

He looked down at Wang, who seemed unconcerned.

"If you had simply killed your lover," said Tasarov, "I think many of us would understand. But you have now beaten up and nearly killed a dozen others—and you killed Howes!"

Wang stood up. "You're no law! What's it to you?"

Cries of anger rose from the crowd. Tasarov raised his arms for silence. "We've got to tell him," he shouted, "—as much for ourselves as for him."

"What the fuck are you prattling about?" Wang asked. "Anybody wants to come and kill me can try! I'll be happy to take him on."

Tasarov fixed him with his gaze and said, "Just this. Take any six men from this gathering and they'll tell you we've had a somewhat peaceful time here. We eat, we sleep, and we have very little trouble. It could have been worse. You make it worse, Wang. No one feels safe from you. You killed Howes slowly. You wanted to, and it made you happy. Why'd you do it?"

Wang looked at him without fear. "I had to do it. He didn't want me, and I couldn't live without him."

"Then why didn't you kill yourself?"

"They stopped me," he said with sudden tears, "before I could."

Tasarov reached into his pocket, pulled out the murder knife, and threw it in down at Wang's feet. "Then do it now!"

Wang looked down at the knife.

"I can't . . . now."

"You can't?" Tasarov asked coldly. "Then we'll have to do it for you."

Wang looked up. "What? You can't! You have no right."

"We can and we will. That's all that matters. Here, give me back the knife."

Wang looked down at the instrument again, then backed away until he bumped into the first row of seated inmates. One of them raised his leg and pushed him forward. Wang staggered and fell on his face. The knife lay in front of his nose.

"Come on, give it here," Tasarov said. "I'll cut your throat for you."

Wang sat up, pulled his knees close and wrapped his arms around them.

Tasarov said, "We have to take you out before you kill more of us."

"You really gonna kill me?" Wang asked with unbelief.

"Then do it yourself, if that bothers you," Tasarov said, getting off the table and sitting down.

Wang put his head between his knees, and Tasarov could almost see the twists inside him. Wang looked up suddenly and said, "I won't do it again. Please."

"I don't think it's up to you whether you kill again. We have to protect ourselves."

Tasarov knew himself well, and therefore, he told himself, he also knew something of Wang's innards. Murders of his kind were not the rule. They were occasional evils, when one's fixation on another reached out to relieve itself in violence. He had known it often, but practiced it sparingly.

Wang looked up at him, still hugging his knees. "What did I ever do to you?" His eyes were reproachful, unbelieving. He made a pitiable figure bunched up on the ground. He might never kill again—or he might—there was no way to make sure. But there was also the fact the Wang seemed to enjoy the act. That need made him unpredictable. Tasarov wondered how many others like him were present in the four thousand, hiding their needs. Killing Wang would be a warning to them.

"Who are you?" Wang asked. "You have no right."

But his eyes said the opposite: If you enforce your will, you have the right. It was the rule of history's power gangs, from top to bottom. The best of them tried to appear as ungang-like as possible, seeking legitimacy from a divine being, human reason, or mutual sympathy. But it had always been a gang—the tribe, the old school tie, the profession, the business. You had to join one, or be a gang of one—the most troublesome kind. The other gangs occasionally looked to the one to see what he might have, thinking that maybe they could get in on it; where the pathfinders went, the rest could follow with less fear. Sometimes they made a hero of the one, so they could park their lost ideals somewhere, so the gang of one, if he was distinguished enough to make them doubt, would not shame them when he came into his kingdom.

As a prison, this place was no worse than landside prisons. Maybe better in several ways, worth keeping as peaceful as it had been these last years. Worthy enough to get rid of unstables like Wang.

There was no struggle here for anything except flesh, and that was pretty nearly divvied up, with few changes or trades. Those who chose no one had faithful Madame Palm, or nothing. Most everyone wanted peace after five years. It was an attainable prize, after all the others had turned illusory or too costly to seek. Power couldn't have much here, because raising soldiers to enforce it was difficult. What could you pay them if you didn't have them already to get what you needed to pay them? No enterprise was worthwhile, since food and shelter were givens before any game could begin. Those who had tried to control food and shelter had failed with the same problem of soldiers.

Wang was news and excitement. He brought a sense of life and danger. To kill him might not do. The suspense of watching out for him might even be useful.

"Wang—you will have your life," Tasarov said, and saw a questioning look spread through the crowd. "But—every day you will thank ten of us for your life, such as it is, until all have been thanked. Do you agree?"

Wang looked up with surprise. Then, very slowly, he nodded, and Tasarov knew that there was more, that something had finally broken him inside.

Suddenly Wang threw himself on his face and cried out, "I will never see my beloved again! What have I done?"

Tasarov saw the feelings that washed through the tormented soul. The man had lusted after Howes a long time, hoping for a happier intimacy. When Howes rejected him, loss, humiliation, and terror had assaulted him as one. Rage uncoiled from where it had been waiting, followed by visions of revenge upon Howes. Wang's act of revenge through the attempted sexual conversion of the object to his need had brought the death of his beloved who refused to be turned to his need. Loss of love, companionship, sexual completion, hope, and the irrevocable loss of the object itself, now warred with pride, which rode above the internal battlefield intent on killing even the wounded.

Wang took the knife, rolled over onto his back, and slowly pushed the point into his heart.

No one cheered as the blood flowed out; too many saw the innards of a kindred organism strewn across their own private landscapes.

■

Tasarov was asked to sit in judgment at least once a month, sometimes two or three times. But he wondered whether he was a plausible authority or simply better than none. He was happy to settle simple disputes, because these usually followed a gamelike strategy, in which it was straightforward to expose the goal of each participant and then give each of them something for their trouble; but when he felt intimations of violence involving inconsolable passions, whose causes wound backward in time through abused and tormented personalities, he sought to separate the participants as best he could, and hoped to be proven wrong about their future acts of violence.

It rarely happened. They beat, raped, tormented, and murdered each other as if following a schedule, following the statistical regularity of the twenty-one card trick, in which the eleventh card never failed to appear. He could imagine much worse. What startled him was the amount of orderly behavior that endured.

He sometimes woke up in the middle of his night, and saw humanity as a single vast creature with billions of heads, its arms and legs struggling with itself. A piece of that creature had been amputated, placed inside this Rock, and sent out to strangle itself in the darkness.

17

... But You Have Not Heard

JUDGE OVERTON'S PRIVATE CHAMBER

"Males are strong, and natural selection has made them champion impregnators of women. The weaker males just weren't as successful. Yet civilization tells the strong to restrain themselves—raise one family at a time, hold back from all other possible females. But nature says get as many as you can, veiling its program with promises of pleasurable domination. What can you ever expect from this, except rape at every opportunity—for the strong, I mean, and mental illness for the weak? We might as well select out the strong and ruthless ones and ship them out, however we can. Will this solve the problem of rape? Not really; as long as there are weaker and stronger, it will go wrong between men and women, women and women, and men and men. Not always. Sometimes."

"Abebe!" Leibniz's voice called from the dark.

She sat shivering, with her shirt pulled down to cover her as much as possible.

"It's getting colder!" he shouted.

She wanted her clothing, but if he got close enough, she would be helpless again. This had been coming for some time, she knew, as she had flirted with their repressed violence and lust for her; something in her had let them stalk her in their secret selves, disbelieving that it could ever happen, but curious about which one would be first to break his reserve.

Now they had done so in cowardly darkness, to stifle their fears, like chimps who masturbated when afraid. What had she expected? That one of them would so impress her with his genuine ardor and that she would welcome him into her citadel?

"Abebe! You must have your clothes."

She wondered which one she had kicked so well. Not the one who now wanted to bring her the clothes. Well, she would sit here, at odds with herself, "until the day break, and the shadows flee away," as the poet said, even though there was no Sun to rise and she might never see her shadow again.

And something in her wept at this brutal courting she had found instead of a romantic fantasy. No other might ever find her again, as John Sakaro had found her, with his wealthy storybook ways, tall with a soft voice and deep brown eyes. She had never questioned her professed love for him; she had no right but to insist that she loved him, even though she knew the lie within herself, and that it waited to poison her soul after everything else had been taken away from her.

That time was now, all around her.

"Abebe!" cried the night.

And then it flickered, coloring the landscape between black moments, creating and destroying from moment to moment. Somewhere, she realized, repair systems were at work, striving to light her eyes and warm her body; but they would not be able to banish the deeper chill that oppressed her.

As the flickering continued, she wondered how she could live among these people again. The sewing circle was suddenly an odd domesticity that had given her more than she had valued, despite her mockery of its participants.

In the runaway flickering, she saw Leibniz coming down the path toward her. He was carrying her shorts and underpants. She wanted to get up and run, but froze as if before an approaching train.

He stopped and looked down at her.

"Here," he said, dropping her clothes into her lap. "We're not all animals—but I'll confess I also wanted you, and still do."

She looked up at him, but it was impossible in the flickering to glimpse his face. He seemed to be grimacing. The interval slowed. He was staring at her, as if about to tell her something, but after a few moments turned away and went back up the path.

"Lono's dead," he shouted back to her. "Your kick snapped his neck."

Shaken by the revelation, she reached for her clothes. The sunplate stopped flickering suddenly and stayed on at about half strength.

She looked toward the sewing circle, and saw that Lenin, Newton, and Trotsky had met Leibniz on the path. They were whispering among themselves. Behind them, Stalin's body was just barely visible in the tall grass.

The four men stopped whispering and came toward her. She hurried to put her clothes on.

"Don't bother!" Lenin shouted.

They surrounded her, looking down at her as if she was prey. She stared up at them brazenly, knowing that they would attempt to speak rationally.

Trotsky seemed the most restrained, but then he had already had his share of her.

"You'll pay . . . for killing . . . our friend," he said in a halting voice that knew it was rationalizing.

Lenin, Leibniz, and Newton knelt around her and leaned closer.

Leibniz was timid. She saw the resignation in his eyes. There was no telling what was happening to the habitat. If the mess halls shut down, they would all starve—so why not steal a few moments of happiness? He went behind her, as if to avoid her gaze.

Lenin and Newton grabbed her arms. She looked into their eyes and saw their resolve. Trotsky towered over them, watching.

Lenin laughed and reached under her shirt. Newton fondled her naked belly, then took the shorts and underpants from her lap and tossed them aside.

The absurdity of the names she had given them struck her as she began to struggle. Their namesakes would have been outraged. Well, maybe not Lenin or Trotsky, she told herself as if in a dream, recalling when she had played with boys as a child. But Newton had reportedly been a sexual innocent.

Leibniz grabbed her long hair and pulled her head back. Trotsky put his foot on her chest, pressed her to the ground, then leaned over and ripped off her shirt, leaving her completely bare and shivering.

Lenin rolled over on top of her, undid his fly, and pushed into her. Newton sucked at her breasts, while Leibniz worked himself around to her face.

She cried out as Lenin began to move, and struck at him with her suddenly free right arm. Trotsky came around and knelt on it.

Lenin finished and held her for a few

pathetic moments, then slid off. Leibniz was still trying to get into position at her head when Newton took his turn.

She took a deep breath, determined to thrust up with her hips and prevent Newton's entry, when the ground rumbled and shifted beneath her, and she felt as if she were about to fall.

Something was affecting the spin of the habitat, she realized with a cool detachment that escaped her fear of the men. Spin was stopping. The sensation of falling slowly took her and she floated off the ground, with three of the men holding onto her. Centrifugal gravity was gone. Without the acceleration of rotation, nothing would stay on the ground. Unrestrained objects would continue in the direction of spin. The sensation of the ground shifting beneath her also indicated that the asteroid had decelerated slightly—which would send objects toward the sunplate.

As they floated off at a slight upward angle, she imagined that the asteroid had been struck by something. At first this might have affected its power source, which fed the sunplate, and also the attitude and spin maintenance gyro controls, slowing the Rock's spin until it stopped.

Lenin and Leibniz let go of her and drifted at her side. Newton held on. They heard cries, looked toward the barracks, and saw people floating upward. Without anything to restrain them, they would drift in the direction of spin, unless they had been inside the mess halls or barracks.

Objects would tend to move according to the asteroid's previous motions: forward and around what had been the central axis of rotation—and now in a drift toward the flickering sunplate. Centrifugal acceleration—and lack of forward acceleration after the initial departure boost had cut off and put the habitat into free fall—had overcome that tendency; but now it would take work to prevent it.

"You fools!" she shouted to the men floating near her. "If you hadn't been so eager, we might have held onto the grass!"

They were turning together now, Lenin and Leibniz nearby and Newton on her arm, with enough upward angle and previous momentum to keep them moving into the great central area of the habitat.

"Don't let me go," whispered a frightened Newton.

"Idiots!" she shouted. "You may have killed us all."

"What are you babbling about?" Lenin asked.

"We could starve up here!" she shouted, knowing it was an exaggeration.

She knew what she had to do. Breaking Newton's grasp on her wrist, she pulled back her leg and gave him an upward push.

He tumbled away, head over heels, in obedience to the laws of physics set down by his namesake.

"No one can reach you now!" she shouted, knowing that it was not quite true, but nearly enough as to make no difference.

"Help!" Newton cried, and she almost pitied him, the prick.

"Thank you!" she called back to him.

Opposite and equal reactions, she thought happily as the grass came up to meet her. Newton tumbled away into the great space. Any of them could do what she had done, if they could think and reach each other, but only two could regain the surface in this way; one would have to be hurled away, and he would have no one to push against. The other way was to learn how to swim down to the ground.

She grabbed the grass, and laughed; but in a moment she knew that being near the grass would at best enable her to pull herself to the barracks or the mess halls, where there might be some food and clothing available. If not, then starvation waited for them all, for floaters and grassholders alike.

She looked up at the three men high in the space above her. They twisted and turned, but there was nothing to push against; even a more than modest amount of flatulence would not help much. If chance brought any two closer to each other, only one would be able to profit by the encounter; and from what she could see, they were too far apart now to ever meet again. They would have to swim before a collision with the sunplate injured or killed them.

She looked around—and saw Stalin's body drifting low some one hundred meters away. As she watched, it turned slowly, and its loose arms seemed to beckon.

The sunplate, she noticed, was dimming slowly. Color was again draining out of the worldlet, and she knew that anything she could do to save herself would have to be done quickly.

Turning away, she slipped like a sleek black cat through the tall grass, pulling herself forward hand over hand toward the nearest mess hall. It was strange that she could not lie down in the grass and rest, but her forward motion did not seem alien to her. The grass brushed against her bare skin with a pleasant sound, and she wondered if it would be possible for people to survive a lifetime of weightlessness.

She paused for a moment and looked back at the sky where she had stranded the four men. They were distant motes now, far apart and unable to use each other as springboards. She did not feel sorry for them; they were like the salmon who hurled themselves upstream, only to die after spawning. Many died in the falls and rapids well below the warm pools where their future incarnations would have quickened into life.

She looked to the barracks. A cloud of motes rose upward like smoke into the central space, composed of inmates who had been caught in the open when spin had slowed and stopped. They had failed to get hold of something, and with impetus from one unthinking pushoff or another, they had sent themselves up from the inner surface. Fortunately, the habitat's spin had not stopped suddenly, or those indoors would have been hurled to injury or death. She wondered if that meant that AI maintenance and repair programs were at work.

There was nothing she could do to help anyone. It was possible, given the scale of damage that would cause such a failure, that spin or reliable light would never return. For now, she was intent on reaching the mess hall, to see if any food could be had from the dispensers, before others near the ground thought of doing the same.

Her stomach felt queasy from the spinless free fall of the habitat, but she was also getting hungry. She needed her strength, if only to return to the barracks to get some coveralls from her locker.

She resumed her speedy hand over hand motion through the grass, keeping the mess hall in direct line of sight, so if the sunplate failed again, she might still be able to reach her goal in complete darkness.

She paused again, gripping the grass with both hands, and listened. Then, at her far left, she spotted small groups of grounders like herself, whispering through the grass like wolves. They would be no great danger, she realized. People in weightless condition have to keep one arm in the grass; and if they pick a fight, up they go, with no easy means to get back or to move around.

She slipped forward again, picturing groups of people clinging to grass and buildings. The people inside had the easiest handholds.

As she approached the first of the three mess halls, she heard a distant wailing from above. Looking up, she saw the cloud of sky-stranded inmates drifting slowly toward the sunplate. They were wailing and crying for help, like the damned being drawn into hell. Many of them were probably sick, vomiting from weightlessness, and too disabled to learn the trick of air-swimming to stop their forward motion and bring themselves down to the grass.

She wondered how hot the sunplate was, or even if it was hot, or posed any danger to human beings if they should touch it. She had no idea of the velocity with which they would strike it; perhaps atmospheric friction might slow them to a mild collision.

She noticed that other grounders had reached the vicinity of the mess halls, and were considering how to get inside. To do so, one would have to cross a grassless area, where there was nothing to grab.

She made eye contact with two unfamiliar faces, a man and a woman who seemed to be a couple.

"Quite a problem!" the man called to her. He was gray-haired and looked resourceful, but he sounded discouraged.

The woman with him, a stout white woman with red hair, gave Abebe an admiring but competitive look. "Lose your clothes?" she shouted, smiling.

Abebe grinned and nodded, and this seemed to reassure the woman. "Worse," she added, and the woman gave her a sympathetic look.

"What can we do?" the man asked. "Jump for the door?"

Abebe looked around. There were at least a dozen other figures in the grass that grew up to the smooth open area in front of the mess dome. There was a surer way than jumping.

"Once inside," she called back, "we'll be all right if we hang on to chairs and tables." They were anchored, she remembered. "We'll need a people bridge to the entrance!"

"Hear that everyone?" the man shouted with renewed hope in his voice. "We gotta team up!"

Abebe came up to the edge of the grass. "Start lining up behind me!" she shouted. "Grab my ankles, and do the same down the line until I'm across." She estimated ten meters to the door, too far to chance a leap that might miss.

She waited, glancing back to see who was coming to hold her ankles. It was the gray-haired man.

"Hello," he said, smiling as he gripped her ankles and tried to ignore her nudity.

"I'm going to crawl forward," she said, "and someone should grab your ankles."

"My wife is ready," he said softly.

"Go slow," Abebe added. "The chain will lift some, and we'll need forward push!"

"Got it!" a male voice answered.

"Hold tight," she said to the man behind her. "Once off the grass, only your hold and inertia will keep me low. Any push from me will raise me."

"You know some physics," he said.

Cries reached them from the human swarm above.

"Those poor bastards," she said, as she looked up and saw that some of them were using the helplessly sick as reaction mass in attempts to kick themselves back to the grass. A strange game of musical masses was playing itself out, with a handful of grass as a reward. She was not looking forward to meeting the winners of that contest. Quite a few, she noticed, were not playing that game. They were slowly swimming against their forward motion, at an angle that would bring them down to the grass. She realized that only the ill ones, a hundred or more, would reach the sunplate.

"Ready?"

"Yes," she said.

He pushed her slowly onto the ceramic apron that ran around the mess dome. She kept her palms flat on the paving, trying hard not to push down, wishing for a fly's sticky hands. She was moved forward with almost no friction, and stopped when the man behind her reached the end of the grass. She was three inches off the surface, palms pressing against it gently.

It took ten people for her to reach the door. She was a meter off the surface when she grabbed the edge of the open portal.

"Now—everyone!" she shouted. "Start coming across the bridge."

One by one people pulled themselves over the bridge of backs, and found places inside the hall. When the last pedestrian came across, the end link in the chain started to cross, until finally only Abebe was left at the door. She pulled herself in, and hands helped her to a place at one of the tables.

"Thanks," she said loudly.

"Thank you," said the gray-haired man; his

wife nodded. "My name is Gulliver Barnes, and this is my wife, Clare Staples."

Abebe nodded, looking around in the hope of finding some clothing; but the dome was all bare latticework and transparent panels, with the great pillar of the dispenser rising out of the floor.

Clare said, "I'm afraid the only clothes are back at the quarters, dear."

Abebe nodded. "I'll get there, after we eat."

"There's power in the sunplate," Gulliver said, "so the dispensers might be working. What do you think happened?"

Abebe shrugged clumsily with one hand holding onto the table. "Something outside clipped us, stopping our set rotation, but maybe the systems will right themselves after things settle down." She looked up through the dome, to where the human cloud was passing, and wondered what a sudden return to centrifugal gravity would do to it.

Gulliver also looked up. "I see what you mean," he said grimly.

"Maybe," she said, "if they stay near the axis, and come down around the sunplate as spin resumes, they can regain the surface at lower acceleration points."

"They could still break a lot of necks," Gulliver said.

"Is the sunplate hot?" she asked.

Gulliver nodded. "But they might be able to

push off before it burns them too badly. They won't stick, that's for sure. Even if we get spin back, there won't be much attraction on the plate itself, since it's right at the end of the zero-g axis. I think there's some kind of gridwork over the plate. They might be able to grab the mesh struts and climb down, but I'm not sure."

"But will we get spin back?" Abebe asked.

Gulliver gave her a look of doubt, but said, "There are self-repairing systems on the engineering level, robots and all. Depends on what they're doing."

"If they're doing anything," his wife said.

18

A Tunnel Out of Life

Abebe Chou's Rock had been clipped by Rock Seven, sent out with greater boost into a cometary period that no one had been eager to calculate or record. It caught up with the slower prison and brushed forward along its axis for only a moment, then moved ahead. The automatic systems of both prisons slowed spin to zero, adjusted attitude, and ran through a long checklist of sensing information before resuming spin acceleration and control.

Rock Seven housed six thousand women, all murderers of one kind or another, all multiple offenders, all young, reportedly cruel, heartless monsters who deserved to be executed; but a merciful criminal justice system had jumped at the chance to simply sever them from all human society for life.

"We give you your lives," the judges said, "and a place to spend them not unlike hell, but much more comfortable."

Judge Overton, Chief World Justice of the Orbits, said those very words to her, Lonnie Beth Hughes recalled as she lounged in her bunk one afternoon, in the second year of her exile. Born in Mexico City in 2002, raped by twelve boys when she was thirteen, she was being paid for sex by fifteen, and running her own whores by eighteen.

When her father had gotten out of prison at forty, he had come to stop her. She had him killed. When her uncle got out at fifty, and came to stop her with a Bible in one hand and a chain in the other, she had him killed.

When she was twenty, her brother got out of prison; he was thirty. He was more understanding, and helped her kill six members of her organization, along with several of the younger girls. They were all getting untrustworthy, and two of them proved it by donating evidence to the police to get rid of her so they could take over. She should have killed the last two sooner, as soon as she'd had their voiceprints certified to prove them liars. The police in her pay had provided the lab service, and also did the killings. Nobody could say she ever killed innocents.

It was only what she had to do to live, nothing more. She'd never sold herself for drugs. Any woman could do that, and the judges always liked that better; it got their sympathy more easily, the few who were honest enough to be suckered. In fact, she had only killed people who were in the business and relatives, never civvies. She had been caught for a murder she had not done, and sentenced by a judge who was in business with her competitors. She had to admire that; it was the way she had always tried to do things.

By the time her case got to Overton, no one knew anything but what was fixed for them to know.

"When I was younger," he had said to her, "people asked me, how do you know they'll never get out. Well, nowadays we know. No one ever gets out."

It was simple. She was out here to die—to die with nothing left over.

It was comfortable, but she didn't have much of anything to do.

It was boring.

But she was lucky in one way. She didn't need men. Fantasies of their hairy asses were enough. No smell. Some women liked the hair and the smell. And she didn't need women, either, especially the stupid killers that got themselves sent here. She hadn't gotten around to trying hairless Asian or African men, and now she never would.

She had not really been caught at anything, ever. They'd had to make it all up to get her. She had honor and pride in that fact, but she kept it to herself because she knew that there was no one smart enough to believe her. And she wouldn't have even blamed a smart one for not buying it; the police had been unusually clever in framing her.

Some people claimed to be innocent of everything, and maybe they were. She believed that everyone had their own good reasons for what they had to do to get here, and those reasons were likely enough for that person; no one else needed to hear them. If one had to tell others about it, then something was wrong with the reasons. Real ones kept you going, and no one else.

She was free even though imprisoned; but if she ever thought she was no longer free within herself, she would kill herself.

She had gotten to know more than a dozen of her fellow inmates, and the pictures they painted in her mind were enough to make her shudder. These women made each other afraid. In a ground prison, they had all been in solitary because no one would risk further violence from them. Here they were bemused by how far they could walk in any direction, and how no one would try to stop whatever they did; and no one would protect them. She could see the confusion on their faces, as clear as if they were wearing chains. They didn't like it. They simmered inside with fear and hatred of others and of themselves, afraid that they might do something to get themselves injured or killed. Lonnie Beth almost laughed when she read their faces, but it shook her to see how much she was in control of herself while the others weren't.

Three of them she watched very carefully. Carmella Frank, a police officer from Memphis, had shot her partner and three female suspects in the back a dozen times each. She never talked about what she had done, but somehow the word had followed her to Rock Seven. Kelly Rowe Lyone had killed six husbands for their insurance, and collected on all but the last, who lived long enough to call the police and point them to copies of the other policies which she kept under her mattress. Gail Ford, it was said, had orgasms when she killed; whether the victim was a man or woman didn't matter, but there had to be a robbery motive to sweeten it.

Lonnie Beth was sure she was better than these three, at least, since she had acted in what would have been self-defense if she had waited for them to reach her. The other murders were all business, benefitting more people than they hurt. But these three women here were sickos of one kind or another; they had to kill, it seemed to her, from a deep need, for the sake of killing. They and others like them were dead women waiting, as far as she was concerned, for someone to kill them just to have peace of mind. Life was too long to have to worry about them here.

As she sat on the back stairs to her barracks and looked out over the landscape of grass, mud, mess domes, sunplate, and the far rocky end of the hollow, she realized that she would die here. There was no escape, no repeal of sentence possible—unless the authorities of Earth came and turned the Rock around.

She had to admit the finality of it. Inmates could do nothing but complain among themselves about the cruelty of it, as they slowly came apart. And they would, she realized; not the way people came apart in solitary, but in ways no one would ever know about on Earth. Too bad, they'd say, but there's nothing we can do about it.

She had to admire the practicality of it: find an island in the sky, fill it with the unwanted, then hurl it outward and never think about it again. Some Rocks came back, she knew, or were supposed to come back; but it depended on how much people back home cared about the inmates, whether they had any family or friends who wanted them back.

Carmella Frank came out and sat down next to her. Lonnie Beth tensed as the cop smiled at her with her perfect teeth.

"You know," Carmella said, "I think there are guards here."

"What do you mean?" Lonnie Beth asked.

Carmella looked at her and smiled again. "They're here, but we just don't know who they are. And you know what that means?"

"What?"

"We can bribe them. Hold them hostage. Find a way to break out."

"Bribe them with what?" Lonnie Beth asked, trying to sound somewhat interested. There was no point in getting the woman mad at her.

Carmella grinned sheepishly. "Well, maybe we'll have to hold them hostage. And you know what else?"

"What?" Lonnie Beth answered.

"This place isn't really moving. It's just a cavern on the Moon somewhere. They fooled us. You know what that means? We can get out."

"No. We're moving."

"How can you know?"

"This place spins to give us gravity. Don't you ever notice that you just don't feel the same way when you walk as back home? Drop something and it doesn't fall straight."

"Well . . . but there's an engineering level. Wherever we are, maybe there are shuttles we can use to get out."

"How do we get there?"

"We dig straight down!"

"No shovels."

"With our hands, if we have to!"

Looking at her, Lonnie Beth knew that the woman was completely gone, and not likely to come back. A drop of perspiration trembled on her upper lip.

"Did you ever dig with your hands?" Lonnie Beth asked her, wondering why she was bothering to try to make sense to her. "It's not that easy."

"I can do it," she said softly, with a grim resolve that came out of her like icy knives. "I can swim through steel if I set my mind to it."

■

She was out every day, digging in the grass. Women gathered around to watch, but not Lonnie Beth. She did not wish to see Carmella trying to dig a tunnel out of her life; it was pathetic, not the way to prepare for the life that would have to be lived here.

Lonnie Beth did not yet know what that life would be, but she would find it in the same way she had learned what kind of life was possible for her back on Earth. She had taken for herself what she could not have had in any other way, and for that life and her defense of it she had been imprisoned as a criminal. People with much greater power than she had ever held took much more, including the lives of the lesser, than she had ever done.

But after a week she went out to see what Carmella was doing. Something about the woman's dedicated imaginings had gotten to

Lonnie Beth, and she had to try to understand.

She made her way through the usual gathering of about fifty women, and came to the edge of a hole in the ground.

Carmella sat at the bottom, some five feet down, digging with her hands.

"I'm getting out," she sang to herself as she tossed handfuls of red dirt up over the edge. Her hands were raw. She had grown thin and pale. Black circles showed under her eyes as she glanced up. "I'm leaving!" she shouted. "Any time now!"

Lonnie Beth felt her chest constrict as she looked at the woman who had been so dangerous and was now so destroyed; and she realized that she preferred the killer's defiance and pride to the weak human being at the bottom of the hole. Such a humiliation might have meant something only if proud Carmella could have understood it; this creature could no longer be made to suffer in that way.

A handful of bloody dirt landed near Lonnie Beth's right foot.

"It'll be different for you!" Carmella shouted, then dug in again with both hands.

What did she mean? That each would go insane in their own way? For the first time in her life Lonnie Beth felt afraid. Not even seeing the Rock from space when the prison shuttle had brought her out from the Moon—hanging in the abyss above some black floor, to which it might fall and shatter—had disturbed her as much as this woman at the bottom of a hole.

Carmella looked up at her and smiled, and the icy knives came out of her eyes again—with triumph. "There!" she shouted. "I'm out of here!"

Then, with hands deep in the dirt in front of her, Carmella stopped moving. A burst of air gurgled in her throat. She sat still like a statue.

The crowd around the hole was very still; then it began to disperse, until only a few were left.

"She's gone," Lonnie Beth said, and pushed some dirt forward with her foot until it fell over the edge and down on the motionless figure. There was nothing else to do.

A few of the women stayed and helped her fill in the hole. Lonnie Beth shut down her unwanted feelings as she buried the dead woman in the grave she had dug for herself.

Weeks later, when the tough grass had grown back, Lonnie Beth looked toward the grave and couldn't tell where it had been.

19

The Last One Left

JUDGE OVERTON'S PRIVATE CHAMBER

"To do what would have to be done to prevent crime and criminals would cost more than anyone is willing to pay. Certainly the rich and powerful don't want to pay it out of their pockets, the cheap, greedy bastards!"

Abebe felt a tug on her body.

"Spin's starting up again!" Gulliver cried. "Everyone hold on until it's stable!"

"If it gets stable," his wife said.

Abebe grasped her chair with both hands and held on. From outside, she heard a distant crying. Gradually, the tug seemed to lessen and she was able to sit in the chair without holding on.

The crying outside seemed louder. She got up and took a few wobbly steps toward the mess entrance.

The crying was even louder as she came to the exit.

She stepped outside and looked toward the sunplate. The crying was coming from there. The spin axis was clear of floaters. The plate was a red-yellow, and there were black spots all over it.

Gulliver and his wife came out and stood next to her.

"It's the floaters who didn't swim down in time," Gulliver said. "They're on the grid that covers the plate. They should now be able to climb down, those who haven't broken limbs or their necks."

"We should get out there," Abebe said, thinking of the sewing circle.

"Listen!" said Gulliver's wife. "They're calling for help."

Abebe said, "We'll have to carry back the injured and dispose of the dead."

Gulliver nodded. "We'll see how well we can follow the medical instructions of the diagnostic scanners."

All that afternoon, the injured hobbled back to the mess halls and barracks. Those unable to walk stayed where they were, waiting for help. Some of the able-bodied went gladly; others showed no interest.

The dead who were found below the sunplate, or hung up in the latticework screen that covered the glowing circle, were brought to the mess hall recycling chutes and sent down. No one wanted to bury them.

Abebe went with Gulliver and his wife, to see if any of the sewing circle had survived. It disturbed and surprised her to think that she cared at all after what had happened.

As they approached the plate, the sight of those who had died from broken necks or backs made her uneasy and then unwell. She went off by herself into the grass and threw up.

Most of those who could walk were already gone, so it became a matter of seeking out those who were still down but not dead, and needing a shoulder to lean on. She feared finding someone with a broken back who could not be moved, and would have to be left to die.

They came to a group of men and women resting in the grass, recovering from their ordeal. They were haggard and bemused, trying to get themselves together for the trek back to their living quarters.

As she scanned the group, she suddenly saw a familiar figure. Lenin was sitting cross-legged on the grass, alone, breathing heavily. She looked around for the others, but couldn't spot them. She went up to him. He looked up as if he didn't know her. She sat down in front of him and waited to see if he would come out of shock.

"Are you all right, Goran?" she asked, calling him by his rightful name.

He nodded, looking for a moment like a young boy who had been whipped within an inch of his life. "You know, Abebe," he said, "I expected to be sent away for my politics. It was a risk I knew about. But I did not expect to live through a reasonable facsimile of a descent into hell."

"But you didn't burn," she said.

He sighed. "The others . . . I saw them die." He gestured toward the sunplate grid. "They're still up there."

She looked up and saw that there were several human figures still left in the latticework. They showed only as silhouettes against the red-yellow glow.

She touched his hand, as if she had become someone else, and said, "I guess you win by default," thinking that she could not afford to lose the last one. He was a bastard, but he was her bastard; and maybe he would never be one again. She now had the choice of making something of what was left, or living in the wreckage.

She took his hand and held it. He looked at her, squinting through tired eyes out of a bruised and lacerated face, then said, "I'm sorry."

20

A Lamp Unto Himself

As the twenty-first century aged, humanity worried and worked at its global problems with growing effect. It both adapted to global warming and mounted heroic and ultimately successful measures to reverse it. There was simply too much at stake for practical reason to be clouded by politics.

At the same time the growing need to care for an aging population that began in the twentieth century found its natural result in the lengthening of lifespan. Finally, under the threat of worldwide social chaos, indefinite lifespan was accepted as the natural goal of medicine. Disease was accepted at long last as belonging to the evolutionary competition among the organisms of the Earth, as natural selection by the environment to bring up fitter models of organisms; but now, as the human spirit sought to light its own way, the old standards of fitness were being revised. The human genome sang of the possibilities beyond mere adaptations to nature's niches.

As the century of bio-engineering found its way, offering control of reproduction and general health, natural selection became increasingly irrelevant as a method for human betterment. Humankind was quickly moving toward physiological improvement through its own efforts, outside the bloody default settings of nature.

The immediacy of pushing away the old horizon of death changed every society on Earth, forcing them into an intolerable but productive contradiction: Humanity could not long live in the two worlds of short-timers and longlifers.

Long life rewarded the shrinking of populations, even as diseases had their last go at the human body, which could now be adapted to meet every new illness with immediately engineered responses that could be infinitely adjusted to any resistant organisms that arose, in a perpetual embrace of responses.

Later historians commented that "Death had no chance against an ambitious middle class." For this growing body of aging-healthy who later became longlifers, the young no longer served the needs of personal survival; this bond was broken as decisively as had been the link between sexual pleasure and reproduction in the previous century. In the transition years, the face of violent youth became especially fearful. "You will not invade our world!" cried the coming longlifers.

As the AIs increasingly made prescriptions in both politics and economics, humankind initially opposed them; but as the disinterested prescriptions proved productive, no one dared or wanted to oppose them. Business flocked to the education of better AIs, which outran humanity in speed and threatened to achieve a much expected but ambivalently judged critical mass of consciousness. Here also humankind knew that embrace would be necessary to avoid leaving the human mind behind: as AIs evolved, they would also help humankind change itself, as often as was necessary to keep up.

But Great Clarke's hope—that "politics and economics will cease to be as important in the future as they have been in the past," and that the time would come when "these matters will seem as trivial, or as meaningless, as the theological debates in which the keenest minds of the Middle Ages dissipated their energies"—was not to be fulfilled very easily. Competition for power and the distinction of credit for work done continued among human beings; but already those who kept power through profit and investment were in the hands of experts into whose skills they had given their lives. And these experts sought satisfying lives in their work, and not in the accumulation of wealth and power which had nowhere to go and nothing to do.

Later AI management of economies confirmed Clarke's hope that since "politics and economics are concerned with power and wealth," they should not be the "primary, still less the exclusive, concern of full-grown men." Alter human lifespans, bring mature technologies online, and we will have a better polity.

Nevertheless, even as humankind's right hand worked for betterment, its juvenile left hand carried on with its criminal empires; but these became strangely muted, by the standards of past ages, and were based more on personal antipathies and humiliations than on simple greed. There were still too many ways to gain distinction outside the law for mindful, willful individuals to ignore. A twentieth century judgment on the ineradicability of crime in free societies, a conclusion that had counted crime as the cost of certain levels of freedom, would have seen the societies of the twenty-first and early twenty-second century as being nearly without crime. Crimes of passion still existed: assault and murder. Theft of large amounts of wealth existed—but more as a game of information-siege than mugging at gunpoint. Odd crimes still existed in remote places on the Earth and in various settlements throughout the solar system; but in the great urban centers of offworld habitats and surface communities, a better grade of human being was being born and raised. Some said it was a wolf in sheep's clothing, with wool so thick that even the wolf rarely guessed his own true nature.

It was this changing humanity that looked out into the dark, and wondered what had happened to its million exiles. Awareness of them swept Earth's Sunspace when the first timed habitat came back in 2105—twenty-five years later than scheduled.

"The first one is back!" shouted the news.

"So late!"

"What happened?"

No one had an answer; the records lay buried in electronic archives that could only be viewed with great difficulty on outmoded machines. But there were only two possible answers: There had either been a mistake in the initial boost velocity, or it had been done deliberately. That some chance encounter had altered the prison habitat's long orbit was discounted as unlikely.

Rock One was met as it crossed the orbit of Neptune by two torchships from the Martian colony, under the cultural command of Anthony Ibn Khaldun, whose massive historical project was suddenly somewhat incomplete from the early quarter of the twenty-first century. His ambition, ever since he had become head of the Historical Information Project, was to record every fact of human history available, in straight outline form, leaving out all interpretive materials. These would be available as unabridged footnotes, to be accessed separately.

HIP's goal was simply to find and set down every straightforward fact of human existence since the beginning of record-keeping. With the help of fast AIs, the organization of facts was routine, but tracking down elusive physical records had become a problem. All over the Earth and throughout occupied Sunspace, records hid from him. They were buried in old books and papers, in defunct data storage and retrieval systems; they were personal and public. He wanted them all.

His ships met Rock One on January 18, 2105. Only one vessel was able to dock at the rear axis entrance. Ibby, as he was known to his colleagues, went in with a team of twenty men and women, emerging through an ancient hatch just off the axis at the rear rocky parts of the interior.

The sunplate at the front end was shining brightly as he stood with his team and gazed out over the grasslands that seemed wrapped around the light. Surveying through multispectrum binoculars, he saw the barracks complex, the dining domes, and several well-worn footpaths; but there were no visible signs of humanity.

The team came down from the rocks, and gradually moved from the narrower section into

higher gravity. An hour later they were marching down a dirt road toward the barracks town.
The air smelled a bit sweet, but it was difficult
to guess what had made the odors.

"Why does this road lead back to the
rocks?" asked Justine Harre, one of the doctors.

Ibby stopped and said, "I've been thinking
the same thing. There's nothing there except the
old hatch, and that only leads outside. But the
road seems to have been well traveled, more than
can be explained by its first uses."

"A gathering place?" said Ferret the
anthropologist.

As they entered the barracks complex, no
one came out to greet them. The team paused
and looked around, struck by the stillness.

"Doctor Harre," Ibby said, "come with me.
The rest of you stay here."

He led the way to the small stairs that led
up the back of one barrack. He came up, opened
the door, and stepped inside. Doctor Harre
came in and stood next to him.

As their eyes adjusted to the light, they saw
shapes lying in the bunks. She came up to the
first one, and pulled back the blanket. A skeleton lay there, as if he had just gone to sleep and
lost his flesh.

"Male?" asked Ibby.

"Yes. They were all males here." She looked
around at the other dark bunks. "They're all
dead. Too much time gone, not enough lifespan."

"We must look everywhere," Ibby said. "Just in case someone may have exceeded the expected lifespan."

"Unlikely," she said.

"We'll see what's on the engineering level," he said.

■

They went in a large half moon of figures, making their way across the landscape toward the engineering entrance beyond the mess halls. There were skeletons all over, lying in the grass with no sign of violence as the cause of death, as if they had lain down for an afternoon nap.

"It wasn't supposed to happen this way," said Doctor Harre.

"Something went wrong with the timing of the orbit," Ibby replied. "Too wide a cometary."

"Or it was meant this way," said Clive Malthus, one of the graduate students.

"Later, yes," Ibby said as the young man, barely forty, caught up and marched between him and Dr. Harre. "Life sentences came much later. What evidence do you have?"

"I heard things," Malthus said. "I heard things . . . from some very old people last year. Prisons that were supposed to come back just didn't show up, earlier on than we know."

They came to the open ramp that led into the engineering level.

"It's open?" asked Dr. Harre. "I thought convicts did not have access to these areas."

Malthus said, "Records are bad this far back—nearly a century. The inmates might have broken in."

"It didn't do them much good," Ibby said. "How could it? There aren't any controls here, no engines to turn around and go home."

"And with all men," said Dr. Harre, "no new generation to raise that might have gone home. I wonder what they did to deserve this?"

"No one deserved this," Malthus said as they stood before the ramp, waiting for the others to catch up. "It was just something the criminal justice system of the times did, like putting people in stocks. Many worse people stayed home."

"But this one was a life sentence," Dr. Harre said, "except that no one told these inmates they weren't coming back. They lived expecting to return."

"We should count the dead," Ibby said, "then bag them all. Someone back home might want to know."

"Not likely," said Malthus.

■

They found a skeleton sitting at the desk in the warden's office. The dead man had written something on a piece of paper, and finished it, because the pen seemed to have been put down with care. Long flowing white hair covered the shoulders and back of his bones.

Young Malthus stood still and stared, shaken by the sight.

Ibby picked up the page and read: "The appointed time is long past, as I, Yevgeny Tasarov, write this. There is no sign of our having returned. Many of us hope that we have simply been left in closer Sun orbit upon our return, and as soon as they decide what to do with us, they will come and open us up. I don't believe this, or that we have returned to the inner solar system, since there was no sign of deceleration. A few of us believe that a long orbit was intended, as a way to be rid of us. If and when this writing is ever found, please note that if our longer orbit was intentional, then it was a crime committed against us, and should be publicly recognized as such.

"I have thought long and hard about these matters; I had the time. The criminal justice system that sent us away professed justice but committed new crimes of its own. Perhaps it should not have pretended to anything except practical action on behalf of its employers . . .

"And yet . . . when crimes are committed against prisoners, these are in fact new crimes, separate from the crimes of the imprisoned. Everyone is forced to be responsible for these new crimes, since the society supports the prisons in which they occur, even though only specific officials may carry them out. Our prison escaped abuse by guards, and it avoided the dilemmas of capital punishment; but the failure of our return is a crime in place of which we might even have accepted the old abuses. Who will ever be punished for this crime?

"The best possible criminal justice system would try the criminal, assess the price he must pay, short of death, and strive to commit no crimes of its own against the criminal. But there is no criminal justice system that can stand outside its society, or outside human failure. Grief and anger fueling cruel vengeance do not die easily.

"As my life runs out, I carry away from it a virulent hatred of the humanity that threw me away—and I know that such a hatred implies a hatred of myself also, of what I was given to be as a human being. I cannot escape this judgment . . .

"I say carry away as if I meant that I am taking something with me into the grave—except that there is no one left to bury me. Of course, I'm not taking anything anywhere except into the dark that I will not know. One cannot know death while alive, only the long slow steps leading to it . . .

"Is that unknowing a mercy? One would have to live through dying to know . . ."

Ibby put down the page.

"It's from another age," Justine Harre said. We're better than that today, she might have said, but the pride of denial in her thought seemed inappropriate to voice with the dead man's page before them on the desk, into which had spilled a lifetime's bitterness that by its own argument could not have been avoided.

But finally she had to speak. "Our predecessors did this," she said, "as a kind of firebreak to criminal violence." Suddenly her swift thoughts, processing parallel databases, arguments, and the conclusions from decades of debate, outran her ability to speak . . . *why have we done this . . . reaching into our breasts we pulled out our evil . . . but we cannot abolish the freedom to transgress . . . cannot tear liberty from our heart and hurl it starward . . . maybe we have hurled our best away . . . these swine? Without them we were able to try again . . . without them? They never left us, despite a hundred Rocks . . . yet we have learned to restrain ourselves. Crime for us is a subtle thing, so hard to notice that these people would not have thought of it as crime at all . . . money trains carry away wealth, but the street is no longer with us . . . people are killed, and we delete the memory of the crime from the killer and the victim's immediate friends and relatives, by request . . .*

"This kind of prison," she said out loud, "like the ones before it, tried to do too much.

Even without rules and guards, this one did too much . . . too much."

Ibby looked at her, and saw that she was struggling with herself, in a way he had never seen in a colleague. Her restraint held back a wave. He searched his own feelings about this dead place, and found them orderly.

His curiosity waited to be satisfied by the records that were certain to be here: long-timed visual and audio records of prisoners' behavior, even in their most private moments, stored in deeply compressed form. They had to be here, and would help him complete HIP's own record of human life; but if they were not here, he would have to place great blank spaces in HIP's massed data, to exist along with the many others of prehistory and early human history. They reminded him of the old maps which proclaimed at their edges the legend, "Here there be dragons!"

Harre was looking at the page on the table. She leaned closer and picked it up.

"Look here," she said with a sudden deep breath. "There's more on the other side."

She turned it over and read: "To anyone who may see this, please note that I found the surveillance equipment after some years of searching, and have wiped the memory databases in the best way possible—by physical destruction. It gave me great pleasure to do this in my last years, when I thought there was nothing left for me to do. I told as many of us as were still alive, to give them some satisfaction in their last years, and they helped as much as they were physically able. Nothing is retrievable, except my notebooks. You will not study us, except through my heart and mind."

Harre looked at Ibby with disappointment. "How cruel to leave us such a message," she said, handing him the page. "There's a bit more."

"I cannot take it as true," he said, "until we have made our own search. He may have missed some of the backups."

Malthus said, "Even physical destruction of a recording medium may not be final, unless it is ground into fine powder. Today we can reconstruct from even the smallest fragments."

Ibby looked at the page and saw that it ended with the question: "Do you hear us laughing?"

21

Reach Out . . .

JUDGE OVERTON'S PRIVATE CHAMBER

"Judge Overton, what are your thoughts and feelings about your retirement as Chief Justice of the Orbits?"

"Did you think it wouldn't happen, young man? That sooner or later we would not start to get at the root causes of violent crime?"

"So the Orbits will come to an end?"

"Of course! Or so they tell me. As long as we had economies of scarcity and human nature combining to create the political struggles of the last two centuries, we had a system for creating the criminals for the Orbits. There are fewer of them now—except for the perverse ones, who commit crimes when they don't really have to."

"But they do."

"Yes, but it's nothing to ship them away for. And there's so few of them! With the AIs helping us so much, even power has lost its attractions, since you can't influence the running of economies

without risking disaster. We've learned that much—that no individual can control an economy. Oh, we can override AI decisions, but why should we risk it? The only power that individuals can now have is the power of dialogue and persuasion with the AIs and their specialist human collaborators. When the inputs from human brains are good, and they sometimes are, then all disagreement ceases. No one wants to go back to the intuitive, predatory economies of the twentieth century, which cost more than they made in ruined human beings."

"You mean the criminals?"

"And the underclasses, the seemingly necessary poor. All who failed to make their contribution for lack of properly raised character and mind. I've learned a lot in my time. I'm glad to be done with the past."

"What do you mean?"

"We had to do what we did, until we could change the fundamentals of human life. Economics and the restraints of given human nature had to be opened up, loosened. Now, no one wants to go back to short-timer, scarcity blighted living. I know I don't want to. It cost us too much to get here. The old economics of value through scarcity, together with short lifespan, poor health and education, made what we called politics for most of human history, and that kind of politics of self-interest for classes and nation states was contemptible. It was this way: economics and human nature make politics; but increase human life-

span, give us better technologies, and we produce better politics. But what else could we have had? We sought efficiency and profit, because that was what could be had. We had to work through it. But after we could generate all the power we needed, achieved health and longlife, and partnered with our AIs, the old game was over."

"So no more Orbits?"

"No more."

"Were there abuses?"

"Yes, of course. The law, like our past technologies, was a social prosthetic. Like a wooden leg. It doesn't work like a real one. We have better now, and a chance at real law, the kind that rules from inside each of us."

"Do you really think so?"

"Yeah. Maybe."

Astonished and horrified by the return of the tomb that was Rock One, it was a better, wiser world that now looked out into the dark and wondered what had become of the other exiles; a smaller world that sought to reach out along these brute orbits to any kin that might still be living.

The world was better because so many had died, and it was this uneasiness about how many dead stood behind each healthy, educated human being of the twenty-second century that brought concern for these survivors of a shameful past.

Something could still be done.

But what was to be done with them?

Were they even human beings?

What could be done for them?

Nothing was even attempted until the 2150s.

Of the one hundred or more cometary prisons sent out in the twenty-first century, none exceeded an initial boost velocity of 150,000 kilometers per hour, with no additional acceleration.

"They're not that far away," Ibby said to the HIP Projex Council. "Nothing is more distant than 150,000 kilometers per hour times 24 hours times 365 days times 100 years, expressed in kilometers away. Any of our relativistic ships, doing five percent or more of light speed, can reach them in three to four months, and in less than a year at even twice that distance. Nothing is more than one hundred thirty-two billion kilometers away. That's less than two percent of a light year. Not very far in astronomical numbers, but far enough when you have no way to get back. Pluto's only about six billion kilometers out."

"Refresh us as to your views for why this should be done," said the council chairman. "Why not leave them alone? They are not like us, but from another time. It would make them unhappy, or even do them harm, to be contacted by us."

Ibby glanced at Justine Harre, then back at

the chairman, and said, "Quite simply, HIP is incomplete without their histories. AI–17 backs up this judgment."

"Yes, yes," said Chairman More, "but that's a technicality, isn't it? What is the real use to us?"

"I have the right to complete my project," Ibby said. "Permit me to point out that HIP is part of the Universal Knowledge Project, which is attempting to assemble every last scrap of human knowledge from still untapped physical records. Together with HIP, this will form a vast database and permit the uncovering of previously unexamined relationships within that database, yielding new insights in our kind's existence."

"In other words," More said, "you are a trivial completist . . ."

"It is part of our mandate," Ibby said sharply, "and far from trivial. And we should not deny our AIs their continuing familiarity with the history of their biological partners."

"There is the ethical issue," Dr. Harre said. "What do we owe these habitats?"

"Nothing, perhaps," More said with a shrug. "We did not place them where they are. The Orbits, as I understand them, were the last gasp of outmoded penal systems, built on theories of separation from society and a token nod toward rehabilitation, which no one believed was possible. With biological praxis of newborn and proper early education, imprisonment is now almost unknown . . ."

Dr. Harre raised her hand. "Please, that is true but not relevant. Also not relevant is our innocence—relative innocence, I must emphasize, with regard to what was done. But we will not be innocent of the decisions we now make. If we do not take an inventory of the habitats, we will not know whether we should leave them alone or not. And the harm we may do by omission will be our responsibility."

"Can we observe without actual contact?" More asked with a show of interest obviously designed to prepare the way for later dismissal of proposals.

"I think it possible, given the construction schematics we have researched."

"Dr. Harre," More said, "it occurs to me that even undetected observation will carry ethical implications. And it also seems to me that this inventory, as you call it, may go unexpectedly wrong, and then we will be responsible directly for whatever accidents or unforeseen effects that may come about."

"Then what do you advise?" she asked.

"And it will be only advice," Ibby added. "We have the power of decision about this."

"That remains to be seen," More said. "This may require a referendum. My advice? Leave them alone—at least for now, while we live with it for a while. They may all be dead, you know."

"Or in great need of our help," Harre replied. "The potted ecosystems in which these people went out were nothing like what we have today."

"Therefore, I repeat," More said, "they may all be dead. You admit the possibility?"

"Yes," Harre said, "but it's not a certainty. The people who made these prisons planned for indefinite periods of operation and self-maintenance. There is certainly enough energy, in the form of fusion reactors, to run recycling of air, food, and water."

"Wasn't there surveillance transmitted automatically back to us?" More asked.

Harre nodded. "Some was. Some were cut off. From what I have been able to learn, the archives were not kept after a time, because of the sheer amount of recorded time for both audio and visual. A lot was lost during our decades of disorder."

More smiled at her. "So there is nothing to do but go out and take a look—and you want it that way, don't you?"

"Yes," she replied.

More nodded patronizingly. "Projex will probably agree with you. I suppose some of us are curious about these . . . earlier human transitionals."

"Scarcely more than a century ago," she said.

"Yes, of course. But we've come so far . . ."

So few of us, he did not say, and Harre wondered who were the transitional types— those who might still be alive in the Orbits, or the descendants of those who had sent them. And transitional to what? What will we find out there? It might well be more merciful to leave them alone, to let them come back in the normal course of the orbit, if that was possible. But then she reminded herself that no one knew how long some of the orbits would be. Some habitats might never come back.

As she and Ibby left the chairman's chamber, she suddenly knew what was about to happen, and what might have to be done, if her hopes about what was possible proved to be practical and justifiable. More's long-term advice would be to leave the Rocks alone, to treat them as if they had never existed.

"They might all be dead out there," Ibby said.

"We have to know that, too," she said, stopping to face him. "But there is more. You realize that this is the only reservoir of unchanged humankind. If you examined any of them, you'd find almost no changes much beyond twentieth century expectations."

"We do have some here on Earth," Ibby said.

"Not really," she replied. "Don't count Nostalgists. You have to take their word for it that they have few or no changes. The people in these habitats are not like you and me, Ibby. There's a lot of biology we might learn from, and every bit of diversity we can preserve counts!"

"It may be dangerous to go out there," Ibby said. "What can we really expect to find?"

"If most have perished, we will find empty shells."

"So you don't expect any surprises," he said.

"No, but I would like to be proven wrong. These prisons were sent out just as we were learning more about ourselves, and our social systems, which manufactured criminals in ways that they did not fully understand. And this was the most effective way to separate criminals from their victims. For thousands of years we lacked the tools and knowledge to deal with social evils, so in place of tools and knowledge we applied religiously derived exhortations and enforced them as best we could with police forces. But we were experimenting. And those prisons out there are what's left of our experimental ignorance."

"I would prefer to find no one alive," Ibby said. "I feel uneasy enough about our current stability to worry about facing it with past failures."

"What do you mean?" Justine asked, looking puzzled.

"History," he said, "may force us to look into an ugly mirror again. The nineteenth and twentieth centuries made it respectable to decry pity and compassion with the rationalization that the rich and powerful should be left to be rich and powerful and all would benefit. Practice revealed that market economies simply did not need as many people as we had, and that we could discard them without mercy. The boat was full. There had to be losers, even though they contributed to the game. Everything will right itself, cried the winners as they discarded lives. Then, the twenty-first century saw a loss of population, and today we all live in the guilt-haunted palaces of the rich."

"Palaces?" she asked.

"By comparison with mid-twentieth century, yes. And our bodies are new, cared for and adjusted in ways once thought blasphemous, our lives longer, our social problems fewer . . ."

"So what is it that you fear—exactly?" she asked.

"I don't know. Our history makes me uneasy, and history has been my life."

"Maybe too much so. There are virtues to forgetfulness—and to looking ahead."

He said, "The history of the last two hundred years, I sometimes think, has frightened us into prudence. But I wonder what it would take to unbalance us again."

"And you think that this . . ." she started to say.

"This, or contact with an alien culture. Something is on the way, and gaining on us . . . and we are not fleeing forward fast enough."

"When you speak," Justine said, "you say 'we' whether you talk of today or the past. We are not the past, Ibby."

"I'm not so sure of that. We have hidden certain . . . tendencies and habits of mind from ourselves, because they no longer pay. There is no gain in them. But if there were . . . if there are people alive in the prisons, what shall we do with them? Bring them home? Give them a choice? Can they even make such a choice and know what they're choosing?"

"You're trying to decide too much in advance, Ibby. When we go out and see, we'll know what to do."

"Will we?" he asked.

They had come out on the great walkway that circled Lake Plato on the Moon. Justine had always thought of it as a small sea of smooth water. Wispy clouds hung under the great clear dome of force that kept in atmosphere. She looked back at the high cliffs, where the Projex Council housed its AIs and provided remote access terminals for all ongoing discussions, open to all human beings throughout Sunspace. Yet how few joined in the dialogue with the AIs, she thought. Two and a half billion throughout the solar system, yet less than five percent cared enough to participate. For the AIs to do all the science and engineering was all too easy. The concern of human beings was a graceful life, the choice of its bodily improvements, the refinement of appreciations, the acquiring of tastes and sensations, the exploration of virtual realms into which all human experiences had been gathered, the opening of the imagined and created over the intractable reality of the cosmos.

And for a moment she realized what Ibby feared, even if he might not put it in quite this way.

"I know," she said suddenly. "You fear the barbarians at the gates! But you shouldn't. They're going the other way. And there can't be very many of them."

He smiled. "For now."

22

Stranger Kin

At five percent of light speed, catching up with one of the Rocks took only three months. Each quarter of the sky held some twenty-five Rocks, but the records were not accurate enough to identify exactly which one they had chased down.

The Rock was a dark mass obscuring the stars as the HIP ship came up behind it and began to scan for docking zones.

"There should be a spread of them around the axis of rotation," Ibby said, comparing the rear section ahead with the holo chart glittering before his eyes. The dark image in the navigation tank began to show the ring of docks around the blunt end, glowing faintly in the infrared as the little world turned.

"Which one?" Justine asked, struck by the wonder of what was inside.

"Makes no difference. Pick one."

"Twelve o'clock," she said.

The ship locked on and went into its dance with the Rock, whose spin now seemed to stop as the ship began to turn with it.

"We'll shuttle in to your twelve o'clock entrance," Ibby said.

The ship's captain AI, a multiple that divided itself into all the functions that might have been a human crew, including robot mobiles, would stand by until Justine and Ibby returned.

The captain had been nearly silent during the ninety day journey, in which Justine had studied all the old records in an effort to determine which Rock they were chasing. She had decided that it had to be number Two, Three, or Four, since they had been boosted within a week of each other, one hundred and three years ago.

Ibby had become preoccupied with the Shinichi-Feynman-Forward Quantum drive, the pusher that was now named after three scientists from the twentieth century. When it had been discovered late in the twenty-first, the names of these men had not been immediately linked to the pusher drive. It had taken historians like Ibby to gain them their just reward in humankind's memory.

Other notables of the time, Arthur C. Clarke among them, had been conservative in their view of interstellar travel, fearing that large physical ablation shields would be needed to protect a vessel as it accelerated to greater fractions of light speed; but so far, the force deflector shield that drew its sustaining power from the same vacuum pool of energy that fed the drive had been successful up to ten percent of light speed. Attempts to go higher were expected to prove as effective, and one day, the relativistic voyagers would set out into deeper space, and into time, as the faster moving biological clocks that were their bodies were slowed in their experience of time, seeming to shrink interstellar distances. Humankind would finally begin to use the elastic psycho-physiological possibilities of space and time's effects on the human body for more than local benefits. Interstellar ships would never run out of fuel for as long as their design structures lasted.

This small vessel, HIP's *Olaf*, named after the twentieth century cosmic dreamer, Olaf Stapledon, was a modest craft: a one hundred meter cylinder, half of it drive field inducer powered by a miniature Pellegrino Matter-Antimatter unit, and the other half living quarters, self-sufficient for twenty-five years, longer if the voyagers chose to bio-time forward.

Olaf's AI, appropriately named William, from William Olaf Stapledon's given first name, was as silent a manager as the God that Staple-

don had sought and denied in his own short lifetime. Justine had wondered, in her long weeks
of wakefulness on the outward journey,
whether William's silence was a choice drawn
from his database, which certainly included all
the recorded views on artificial intelligence,
among them the one that still sometimes denied
AIs any localized ego, claiming that they were
only universes of information that sought ever
closer relationships among the various data-
blocs.

On one dull evening she had simply asked
William, "Is there a local personality to you?"

"Yes, there is," William had replied.

"Where?"

"In the midst of much more, as with you."

He had replied—something which many
other AIs often failed to do, maintaining silence
for reasons which they would not disclose. She
had suddenly grasped a vision of developing
minds, growing and changing in their own kind
of space, being intruded upon by humanity,
which asked them to perform tasks.

Now, as the small shuttle, a cylinder-
shaped miniature of the ship, approached the
asteroid's docking collar, she had a moment's
fear that William would simply go away,
marooning her and Ibby in the prison habitat.
She knew it was a silly fear; but when she considered what might be waiting inside the habitat—

ignorant generations of unchanged humanity that could not possibly grasp the shockwaves of changes that had thrown their kin back home forward—she appreciated William's silent care and attention all the more. He had brought his two people here so they might learn; he could have no other motive, because he had no adaptive evolutionary past in him, no need to eliminate competitors. William only waited to perform tasks, and to drink in as much of the universe as might come his way. "Our mind-children will raise us up," some had said of the AIs. "They may even become us," said others. The first statement was not quite accurate; it was still a waltz, as far as Justine could see, with neither partner leading. And the second statement did not distress her at all, as long as something continued to dance.

■

After they had made certain that the locks would open to breathable air, Justine went into the spiral passage. Ibby followed. They pulled themselves along until they began to feel the increasing tug of gravity just off the zero-g axis of rotation, and the passage became a corridor leading into the engineering level below the inner land of the habitat.

They came out into a wide, hall-like area

with a low ceiling. Ahead, the floor curved slightly upward into the distance and seemed to meet the ceiling.

"Straight ahead," Ibby said. "We'll soon know this Rock's number, if the signs haven't deteriorated."

They went side by side, listening, almost expecting to be met by human beings.

"There'll be no one here," Ibby said. "After Rock One, the engineering levels were carefully sealed, so no inmate could get in."

The panoptic chamber, she knew, was a half kilometer from the docking area. Most of the Rocks had observation chambers. They might have had more use if the prisons had remained in Near–Earth–Orbit. But visual recording had continued, and some of it had been transmitted back for as long as there had been interest.

This engineering level, with three meters of headroom, went some twenty-five kilometers around the length of the original asteroid, and nearly forty around the middle, making a cross-shaped space measuring some thirty percent of the inner landscape's area. Here was all the distributive technology, run by the fusion furnace, that recycled air, water, and food staples. The inner ecology worked on its own, but it was not perfect, and needed help once in a while.

Justine was glad of the march; the sense of

walking to a destination she had not visited was a welcome relief after three months on the ship, where even bio-time sleep had carried her into constricted spaces inside herself.

They came to a curving wall, and stopped. Four open doorways waited.

"The one on the right, I think," Ibby said, leading the way.

She followed, and almost immediately, they came out into a large circular room. Five meters in they paused before a large opening in the floor like the lower half of an egg cut open lengthwise. All around the egg-pit there were colored squares.

Ibby stepped on a red, and the space below lit up, revealing the asteroid's inner land: grasslands—without a sign of human life.

Ibby stepped on a yellow, and the view rolled, slipping around inside the asteroid, until it revealed the town: barracks and trees—and small human figures.

Light spilled across the land from the sun-plate at the forward end, visible in the concave distortion of the view.

Ibby said, "It's a sophisticated version of an old fashioned device, the camera obscura, which people sometimes had in their attics—a lens in a dark chamber that caught a whole town in one view and projected it onto a white tabletop. But this version enables us to hear, and to pull in close wherever we wish."

"They were planning to spy on these people," Justine said, "until they had the idea of sending them away."

"It was to have been for study," Ibby said. "Even the old planetary prisons had panoptic facilities that enabled guards to keep an eye on the cells."

Justine noticed a number on the floor, on the other side of the vision at their feet. "This is Rock Four," she said.

"Yes, yes," Ibby replied. "People from the Great Asian Purge of the 2050s. They were not violent criminals, not even criminals by that time's standards. Political prisoners and insufferable whistleblowers, who cost others power and money. People who didn't know how to shut up and save their skins."

"We have to know," Justine said, "what has happened here, so we can decide what, if anything, we can do for them."

Ibby was already trying the other colored squares. The view pulled in close. A man and a woman were walking up a well-worn path to the mess halls.

He was a very old Japanese man, short and stocky and bald. He wore old fashioned glasses. She was a tall black woman, with gray in her close cropped hair. They were talking, but no sound reached Justine and Ibby.

Ibby looked around for another square to step on.

He stepped on green.

"They don't know anything!" the man's voice boomed in the hard surfaced chamber. "How can we teach them? We won't be around forever, you know, and they'll be very ignorant. There's a limit to what we can impart to new teachers."

"How I wish," the woman said, "that we could get into engineering. I'm sure there are facilities there—databases, audio and visual records . . ."

"It's hopeless," the old man said. "We have three generations who have never known any place but here, and a fourth on the way. We can talk at them, but we have nothing to show them. We can't even show them the stars outside!"

"Calm yourself," the woman said as she took his arm.

He laughed. "How did we live this long? If I'd known I would have killed myself."

"The plain calorie restricted food," she said, "the lower gravity, lack of infectious diseases. We're very stable here."

The image rolled far to the right, to show a circle of children sitting in the tall grass, obviously waiting for their teachers.

"He's one of the originals!" Ibby shouted. "He must be over a century old."

"And he doesn't know how common that is today," Justine said.

The view rolled around the entire interior, revealing an underpopulated, peaceful community. Groves of trees grew in various places.

"Look at them," Ibby said. "So spartan, living in equilibrium with their limited environment—static, ignorant of human history except through word of mouth from their oldest."

"It may be worse elsewhere," Justine said. "These do not come from the worst that were sent out."

As Ibby rolled the image around, Justine wondered about the grass. "That grass is so beautiful," she said, "so green and blue."

"I recall something about that," Ibby replied. "It was planted in every one of these—a hardy strain."

23

Nothing Else But Here

JUDGE OVERTON'S PRIVATE CHAMBER

"Will any of those responsible for abuses of the Orbits be held accountable?"

"Well, there are only those of us who have survived into longlife and better age, myself included. We were the legally constituted authority of the Orbits."

"But history may still lay blame, without legal process."

"No. Humanity as we have known it is about to leave itself behind. My self of even fifty years ago would have reacted very differently to the closing of the Rocks. There are things going on now that I no longer understand as I once did."

"So what's next for you, Judge?"

"First I'll drop the judge label. Then start forgetting much of what I was before I passed the century mark. You could say that I am readying to die."

"Rock Five is only a stone's throw away," Ibby said.

Justine smiled at him from her command station.

"It's an old idiom," he said, "from when most people were farmers."

"Oh, yes—as in the crow flies—meaning you have a longer way to go on the ground, where you don't have a straight line to follow."

"What is Rock Five?" he asked as their vessel accelerated toward the prison, one week distant.

"The worst one," she said. "People whose early behavioral development was so damaged that every impulse became violent in relentless self-gratification."

"Men and women?" he asked.

"Yes. They were looked upon as humankind's aliens, to be killed or shut away for life. Nothing could be done for them. Serial killers and rapists, mostly. Often brilliant people, some of whom rationalized themselves as belonging to another way, as they put it. Sociobiologically they could be seen as weeding out the weak, if we were still living in the wild. Monsters, vampires of legend were not as bad as these, whose craft and intelligence was all turned to personal pleasure through torture, humiliation, rape, and murder.

"But I don't accept that they were alien. There were enough examples in mating rituals, marriage practices, warfare, religious torture, and political revolutionary behavior, not to mention economic conflict, to prove our nasty continuity with them. We have only to compare the behavior of nation-states or the wolf-pack mentalities of marketeers to see how few they were, how small when seen against the organized cruelties of the social systems that produced these cruel individuals, yet never received as much public discussion. They did not wake up one fine morning and decide to be as they were."

"I'm reminded," Ibby said, "of the wish attributed to Thomas Jefferson—that he would have liked to see the last king strangled with the entrails of the last priest, for all the harm they did through all the wars they started."

"Both priestliness and kingship," she said, "were brazen efforts at social engineering, with the priest claiming a pedigree from God for morals, lest the people run amok, and the king claiming the same derived legitimacy for political power. Both warred with human nature, of which we were mostly ignorant—and human nature won, subverting priestliness, kingship, democracy, and legal restraints, with help from a little record-keeping system known as money, which was easily modified so that those who did most of the work got paid the least. The record-keeping system was also manipulated to make more money without the manipulator producing anything of intrinsic value."

"And all driven by the desire for power," he said, "through which your progeny, and not your neighbors', inherits the future, by which one gets to say who's who and what's what, and what will be. The desire to be somebody is the great appetite of human history. I often wonder how this kind of human nature has changed itself at all in practice, or how it can ever become something better."

"It has changed some," she said.

"Who judges?" he asked. "This same human nature? And can it enforce changes? Whenever I hear a human being talking about progress, I say look who's talking."

"Gradually," she said, "we have progressed."

"How can we see? From where can we get a good look at ourselves?"

"We can and we do, Ibby. We flip back and forth, in and out of our humanity, as if we can be something else for a moment, and then not, and then a little better next time. This self-conscious step-back is humankind's greatest innovation."

"Do you really think so?"

"We do it. We are doing it as we speak."

"And there's hope in that?"

"Hope is a healthy body and a clear mind," she said, "and as Carl Sagan said a long time ago, hope is a database that exceeds the information in the human genetic code, when our knowledge exceeds, overwhelms, and directs our genetic inheritance. We've only done this recently."

Ibby nodded. "I'm well aware of that. But I also see how often humankind has congratulated itself. Look who's talking. Maybe we need something else to talk about us."

"The AIs do—and they let us listen! We have our self-correcting view through their feedback, where once we only had it in the ideals of science, which always had to fight the society around them. Both human and AI, as we converge, continue to share critical intellect's legacy. Err and correct was also the method of ethical religions, but outside of extraordinary individuals the religions only built bureaucracies of salvation, while science applied the method of err and correct systematically to build a body of knowledge."

"I know all this," Ibby replied, gazing into the navigational tank where the beacon of Rock Five burned in the night like a threat. "But what will we do with all these—these leftovers—this damaged humanity? What fountain of unreason are we about to open."

"First we'll complete our survey," she said, "then decide on whether it would be productive to make contact—and then we'll know what to do—and then we'll do it."

He looked over at her and asked, "Do you really think it will be that straightforward, with no complications?"

She nodded to him. "Yes—and I have some ideas about what will have to be done."

"'What will have to be done'?" he asked. "You sound as if it's already been decided."

"If you think about it, you'll see what the choices are. There's only two or three."

■

They watched in the panoptic chamber as the view rolled around the standard countryside of grassland and stopped on one of the barracks villages. A half dozen figures moved around the long structures, tending what seemed to be gardens. A close-in view showed the figures to be young men and women in long shirts down to their knees.

"What do you think?" Ibby asked.

"This doesn't tell us anything," Justine said. "Can we see inside any of their buildings?"

"I'm checking, but I doubt it."

"What can we expect here?" she asked. "The Australian model doesn't really apply, since most of those people were guilty mostly of being poor, and the country's development belied its so-called criminal origins. The Lunar penal colony doesn't help either, because it was closed after a while, with no long-term lessons to teach."

"Look over there!" Ibby shouted, his voice echoing in the chamber.

The view expanded to show a large group of smiling boys and girls in clean denims walking through the tall grass from one of the mess halls. A middle-aged man was leading them.

The audio came on to reveal that the group was singing "Old MacDonald Had a Farm."

"They don't look like they're going to kill or torment anyone," Ibby said.

■

As they went on to the next Rock, Justine was beginning to think that they would find only two kinds of outcomes: Either everyone would be dead, or some kind of order would have emerged from the initial conditions.

"I can't imagine," she said to Ibby, "that even the worst murderer wouldn't behave better to his son or daughter."

Ibby said, "If they're relatively sane, yes, but the deranged and violent will abuse their children, and who will have protected them?"

"There will be some, I would think," she said, "who would have stood up for the children, even kill their violent and abusive parents to prevent further outrages. And gradually, a better order would emerge."

"Or interminable civil wars. And the children might grow up to kill the aging adults, and then start in on each other."

Justine said, "But there would be fewer killers among these, and even fewer in the next generation, because most of the violence would have the character of rebellion, not pathology. The pathological are unstable, and often die first. Political struggles continue, but what would they struggle for here?"

"One would hope that the number of killers would decline and the violence lose its pathology," Ibby said. "It's happened every way in human history. Sometimes the pathology becomes the social institution."

"But it's weeded out," Justine insisted.

"There's no precedent for these prisons. We'll have to see many more to have a better idea of what actually happens."

■

At Rock Two, Justine and Ibby also found an unexpected degree of order. Three generations came and went from the barracks and mess halls in what seemed to be civilized strolls in the park.

"But look at that!" Ibby said, rolling the image to one side.

"It's a graveyard," Justine said.

The view pulled in to show handcrafted markers, more than a hundred of them.

"But why didn't the bodies go into the recycle chutes?" asked Ibby.

"They needed to have them in view," Justine said, "maybe to remind them of a hard won peace of the dead. Reminds me of Boot Hill in the old American west."

"But we're guessing," Ibby said, gazing at the neat black markers in the blue-green grass. A few were crosses.

"Of course we're guessing," she said, "but I'll bet it's what happened. We'd have to go in and ask them, to be sure, of course."

Ibby was silent for a moment, rolling the picture across the two hundred square kilometers of the habitat. "I'm thinking," he said finally, "that this system of incarceration in fact gave the inmates a lot. A place to live without guards. Room and board, to use an old phrase.

And a place where they might just have the leisure to reflect and think without economic temptations working on their insecurities—a kind of limbo or purgatory in which they might remake themselves."

"Purgatory?" Justine asked. "The place as bad as hell, but from which you get to leave? These people never got to leave. Imagine how it was when their time ran out and the Rock had not come home. Slowly, they realized that they were never going home, that they would never get out, and that if this was not Purgatory, then they were in Hell itself."

"Could they have thought that?" he asked.

"Perhaps not—but they must have felt it, even if there was no one to give them the colorful descriptions. Hell has been described as the absence of God, the place where you may even be comfortable, but where to see God's face is denied to you. These people had to feel something like that when they realized they would never see the Earth again, that their own kind had discarded them. Oh, some maybe hoped it was a mistake, that the orbit was somewhat longer, but that they would return. But as the years passed, they must have known it was not so."

"But these," Ibby said, pointing to the people in the hollow, "they look so at home here."

"Things change," Justine said. "They sometimes even get better. Remember, the young would not suffer loss and isolation in the same way, since they would never know anything else but here. They might have had great difficulty in understanding what their elders were so upset about. And when the last old one who had known Earth died—well, things might have even gotten better."

24

Another Orphan

Justine dressed in the observed denim garb of Rock Two, and prepared to go inside. With a fastload of language in her brain and the hope that she wouldn't be noticed for a while among the thousands of inhabitants, she waited at the ramp opening.

"It might not open," Ibby's voice echoed from behind her. "I'll track you constantly in the chamber, and come out if you need help, but I still don't see why you want to do this."

"I want to talk to some of these people face to face."

"But why? We can observe them for as long as we wish."

"You pick up more in person," she insisted once more. "I want to feel for myself what these people are like."

"What will that tell you?"

"I'll tell you when I find out."

"Okay," Ibby said. "Let's hope no one notices

when we open up. I hope it doesn't open."

"Go ahead."

She heard him breathing nervously, and turned to see him still hesitating.

"Maybe we should both go out," he said, "—armed."

"No. If something happens to me, you can help me. Or go home and tell what you've seen."

"I'll see if I can open the ramp cover only a crack. We don't know what kind of noise it makes, or who may be nearby."

"I'm ready," she said.

She looked straight up the ramp, and heard a low grunting sound. Light came in. She started up toward the opening.

The cover was two meters up when she came to it.

"Is that open enough?" he called.

"Yes, I'm going. Close down in ten seconds."

She got down on all fours, rolled through sideways, and watched the entrance cover close behind her.

She was alone in a strange afternoon of greens and browns and yellow-orange light. Slowly, she stood up and looked around. The opening to the engineering level was near the rocky farside of the hollow, as far from the sunplate as anyone could go. She was looking some

ten kilometers down the full length of the asteroid. Three groupings of barracks surrounded by
trees, set well apart, looked like toy villages and
clumps of broccoli. There were no settlements
in the grasslands overhead.

She scanned the area in which she stood. It
was rocky, where the asteroid's original material showed through the land that had been
ground up and mulch-seeded, well over a century ago. There were so many things about a
worldlet of this kind, she reminded herself, that
one took for granted but which made a great
difference to the inhabitants. These people had
never seen the stars; the sunplate could be made
to function as a screen to show starry space, but
that would have required access to the engineering level, and a knowledge of control mod-
ules that these people did not have.

Not many provisions had been made for education of the later-born peoples; so the society
here had only the oldest members to teach them
anything, most of whom were almost certainly
gone by now, having imparted all they could, but it
would not have been enough. People alive here
now were living in profound ignorance. Their
mental picture of the past began at their birth,
with no history to fill in the preceding depth of
time; the future was also a blank, since the habitat
was not really going anywhere. It would return to
the inner solar system someday.

In her own thinking about the prison Orbits, she had begun to see some positive possibilities; but these conflicted with what she knew about the constraints. She recalled something that had been said by an inmate of an old prison on Earth. "Sometimes I think it's not so bad," the man had said. "At other times that it's worse than I expected. Then I wonder who had thought up this putting of people in boxes and watching them. Who was this person who had thought it up? Where had he been born?"

Well, these little worlds were not quite boxes, and there had been no one watching until now. The Orbits were an advance on the old prisons. A time had come to empty out the world's prisons, many of which had become small cities, and to begin again to raise a generation that would not need prisons. Escape proof, the Rocks required only an initial investment to rid the rest of humanity of a past that resisted change, and nothing after that.

Nothing. No educational facilities. Limited medical means. Just room and board for life, away from everyone else.

"Whoorayoo?" a youthful voice said from behind her.

She turned around with her hand on the stunner in the belt beneath her shirt, and saw what looked to be a young boy smiling at her from the rocks below. He was about twelve or thirteen, of medium height, with fair skin and long blond hair down to his shoulders. He wore denim coveralls. She wondered for a moment whether he had seen her emerge.

She smiled, and the boy smiled back at her.

"Just hiking," she said.

The boy frowned. "Yoo tolk foony," he said.

"Sorry," she said, knowing that she would never get the accent right. He had been climbing up from somewhere at her right, and could not have seen the entrance open and close until he got up higher.

"Lucky for you," Ibby said in her ear, "that you came out before he got here, and ran into a single individual."

The boy climbed up toward her, pausing to smile once in a while as if he knew something she didn't. When finally he stood in front of her, she saw that she was only slightly taller than the youth.

He reached out and took her hand, and held it gently.

"My name is Tina," Justine said suddenly, plucking her childhood nickname out of the past for no reason at all except that it seemed appropriate. "What's yours?"

"Alrik," he said, still smiling.

"How old are you, Alrik?"

He let go of her hand and held up ten fingers, then three. "Thirtin," he said, "going on fourtin."

"Where do you live?" she asked, working on the accent.

He pointed to the first village.

"Yoo?" he asked, and she realized that he could not have thought that she was from anywhere else but one of the two other villages.

She pointed to the village at the far left, halfway up the inward curve of the hollow, and realized that she was much safer from discovery than she had imagined. It would take at least two conceptual leaps, both unlikely for Alrik, to guess where she was from: outside, and where outside.

Alrik smiled acceptingly. He could not have met or remembered even the several thousands of people in his world yet. It would take an older person to develop suspicions about her origin, and even then it might take some time to check.

Alrik seemed unconcerned about where she had come from as he took her hand and began to lead her to the lower landscape. He looked up at her adoringly once in a while, and Justine smiled back at him, feeling foolish.

25

The Way in the Void

As Alrik led her down the main way between the barracks, she noticed the smiles and admiring looks she was getting from a large number of the young boys. The few adult males she saw were sitting on the steps, talking to each other. The only women she saw were looking out the glassless windows. Two were young. The others were older, and wore looks of resignation. One or two men looked up and saw her, then went back to their conversation. She was being accepted as merely a visitor from one of the other villages.

"Hey, what loock!" a tall boy shouted at Alrik, and she felt his grip tighten in her hand.

He led her to the back stairs of one of the barracks. A heavyset, balding man sat there with an old woman. He squinted at Justine as they came close.

"My father," Alrik said, still holding Justine's hand.

The old man looked her up and down and smiled, nodding.

"Who is your father?" the old man asked Justine, in the same accent as his son.

"I foond her in the rocks," Alrik said proudly.

Justine gestured toward one of the other villages, hoping that it would be enough. The old man nodded as if she had spoken, and she suspected that he was hard of hearing but too proud to ask again.

The mother was watching Justine carefully, not squinting as much, but clearly surprised and puzzled.

The father laughed in delight and said, "Yoo will make a fine man of my son!"

Alrik looked at Justine, squeezed her hand even harder, and as he smiled at her ecstatically, she began to see what she had walked into.

"Why are yoo so far from your village?" Alrik's father asked.

"I . . . was walking," Justine said, "and didn't pay attention to how far I had come."

There was a silence. "No matter," the old man said. "My son has done well, slow as he is. Have yoo started many boys in your village?"

"Yoo must be at least twenty-five," said the mother.

Justine hesitated. "Some," she managed to say.

The old couple nodded together. The father did not look at Justine, but the mother seemed to stare with a frustrated suspicion.

"My son," said the father, "will choose five of his fellows for yoo to start after him. He will be honored for it, and so will we."

Justine took a deep breath, but did not speak.

"Will you wish to take the child to your village?" asked the mother.

Justine tried not to show surprise.

"It is your right," said the mother, "but we would prefer . . ."

"Too few women," Ibby said in her ear, "and they've adapted to the shortage."

Justine nodded, so he would see that she heard him. Custom had rationalized necessity, as so often in human history, but she wondered why necessity could not be faced directly, without ceremony or sentiment.

"Thank yoo!" the mother replied, taking her nod to mean that the child would stay here. "We are grateful."

Alrik stepped closer and put his arm around Justine's waist.

"Yoo may use our bed," the father said, gesturing with his thumb toward the entrance to the barracks behind him—and Justine suddenly

wished for the delay of sentiment and ceremony. It was apparently at a minimum here,
with the blessings of the parents being all that
seemed to be needed.

"You've got to get out of there," Ibby said
in her ear.

Alrik tightened his arm around her waist
and grinned at her with joy. Of course, there
was no possibility of her ever having a child by
him without the usual preparations, but she
felt a moment of fear at having a young
stranger of doubtful intelligence pressing himself into her body. She could certainly fend him
off, but she could not fend off a group of young
men.

She looked back the way she had come, and
saw five boys standing in the central way
between the barracks, watching the betrothal.
Two of them were smiling.

Justine knew what she had to say. "There
can be no children," she said, trying to look sad,
"because I can't have any. That was why I . . . left
my village."

"What?" asked the father.

"They drove yoo out?" said the mother.

Alrik loosened his hold on her, disap-
pointed by his parents' change of mood.

"You let us think . . ." the mother said,
"and tell us after we spoke for our son? Why?"

"Good going," Ibby said in her ear.

"I'm . . . sorry," Justine managed to say.

Alrik's father looked at her in a new way, examining her now without restraint, letting her know that he both disapproved of her and desired her.

"There may still be some use . . ." he started to say.

"No!" Alrik's mother shouted. "If she will not bear children, then she is not fit to start anyone's manhood."

The expression on Alrik's father's face told her that he clearly thought this restriction was unnecessary, but he was too old to contradict his wife.

"It would set a bad example," his wife said. "Only the fit may . . . teach."

"I can't have her?" Alrik asked, standing downcast next to Justine.

"No, my son," his mother said in a sad tone that sought to prepare him for the worst—that for him there might never be anyone—and it was a withering look of hatred that she turned on Justine.

"Leave now, I think," Ibby said.

Justine turned away and made her way down the central way. She passed the group of boys without looking at them, and started back toward the rocky end of the world.

She strode away without looking back. As she came to the edge of the village, she glanced back and saw the group of five boys following at a distance, as if they were uncertain and waiting for someone's approval.

"Don't look back," Ibby said. "If you knew any sociobiology, you'd know that may only encourage them."

"I'm a record runner," she said, "for a moderately unenhanced human being."

"You don't know how fast they can run," he replied. "But as soon as you run, so will they. Widen the distance as much as you can before you run. I'll open the hatch at the last moment."

"They'll see the hatch," she said, quickening her pace.

The ground ahead was firm soil, but very quickly became a dark green crabgrass, short but easy to slip on.

"Can't be helped if they do, but they won't be able to open it."

If she got there first. She looked back, then opened up with her long legs. Glancing back, she saw that the boys were also running. At least three kilometers, she estimated, to the rocky end. She could do it at this steady pace, as long as it kept her ahead, and they might tire sooner. She did not want to use her stunner, but it might be necessary.

"Mind if I talk?" Ibby asked.

"Not-at-all!" she shouted between deep breaths.

"I've been running a program to see if we can pick up the panopticon data from the entire sphere of sky. Every Rock should have a signal. Save time visiting them, especially the ones that might turn out to be lifeless."

"Fine!" she shouted, glancing back at her pursuers. They had gained enough ground for her to see their grinning faces; but as she pressed harder and pulled ahead, she saw strain beginning to distort their grins.

She stayed well ahead.

"But-of-course," she shouted, "we-will-have-to-visit-them-all, just-to-be-sure . . . panopticon-may-not-show-all."

She glanced back and saw them gaining. They called out after her lewdly, but she could not make out the words. If she tired, she told herself, she would stop and stun them, then walk to the rocky end; but something made her reluctant to use a weapon that would humiliate and punish the ignorant, when it was unnecessary to do so.

She took deeper breaths, and pulled away again. When she glanced back, she saw the looks of disappointment on their faces. The rocky end drew nearer. She was halfway there.

"You're doing very well," Ibby said.

The ground became rocky, and she had to pick her way forward with some care. Spin gravity was diminishing as the world narrowed, but she was grateful for that because in a few minutes she would have to start climbing.

"Want me to come out?" Ibby asked.

"No!" she shouted between breaths, and increased her effort.

She looked back as she finally started to climb, and saw that the boys were much closer; they were better climbers, scrambling upward on all fours at times while she remained upright, throwing her hands out for balance.

"You'll have to do better than that," Ibby said jokingly, but there was a note of concern in his voice.

She did not look back for a while. Just as she was about to look again, a hand caught her ankle—and she went forward on her face, scratching her cheek on a sharp rock. She cried out, then turned over.

They came around her in a halfmoon, breathing hard and grinning. She glanced up toward where the hatch would open, and saw that she was only a hundred meters short of the place.

"Yoo run good," the tallest boy said.

"But we better," said a short, dark-haired one with big white teeth.

She reached for her stunner, but a stocky redheaded boy leaned over quickly and caught her wrist.

"What ya there?" he asked, prying the

weapon from her hand before she could tighten her hold. "What is it?" he said, examining the object.

She scrambled backward and tried to stand up, but one of the boys came up behind her and grabbed her by the shoulders. He held her as she half stood, and let her find her footing.

The fourth and fifth boys came up closer and looked at her with curiosity. One was a thin, wiry youth with brown hair and eyes to match. His companion was a slightly chubby boy with sandy hair and green eyes.

No one spoke as these two examined her. Justine felt as if she were in a dream, unable to move or run. After her rejection in the village, she was fair game for anyone who might take an interest. It was another way to gain experience where opportunities were limited. Still, there was a reluctance in these young men that spoke of severe discipline in their upbringing; they were also unconsciously picking up the fact that she was somehow not one of them, and that strangeness made them doubtful.

She heard a sound behind, like air escaping, and knew that Ibby was opening the hatch—and she was not there! Maybe the panopticon's field of vision had failed to catch her predicament at this point.

The boys stared, startled by the sight of the rising cover. It came up all the way and stopped.

She jerked free of the arms that held her, and tried to move forward toward the opening, hoping that Ibby would not close it too soon.

Strong hands grabbed her again.

Ibby came up the ramp and stepped outside.

"Let her go!" he shouted in a low voice.

The arms loosened but did not let go.

Ibby started down the rocks, then stopped, raised his arm, and fired his stun.

"Ahhhh!" cried the tallest as the shockwave hit him and he fell on his back.

The arms let her go. She scrambled up toward Ibby.

The four startled boys seemed to wake up, and they started after her.

Ibby stunned the redhead. He cried out and fell over, dropping her stunner, which clattered into the rocks.

She reached Ibby and turned to look back. The remaining three boys stood gaping at them, then started to back away.

"Well, now they know about us," Ibby said. "I wish it hadn't been this way."

"What do they know?" Justine said as they watched the retreating trio. The two stunned boys lay moaning on the rocks, more injured from their fall than the wave, she realized. "They chased someone up here and she disappeared into the rocks."

"You may be right," Ibby said. "They may be too ashamed to tell anyone about being stopped in this way."

He turned and led the way down the ramp. When they reached bottom, the large hatch closed. Justine glanced up at the overhead panels of white light and said, "But there may be someone among them who might have an idea of what happened."

"If the boys tell them."

She shuddered as they walked down the passageway, then said, "The strong preying on the weak, simply because they can, because they sense weakness and can enforce their will. Yet how else can they learn in such limited circumstances. There is order and purpose in their way."

"We've led sheltered and privileged lives," Ibby said, "in a garden that softens our evolutionary past. But I think that the capacity for violence should remain ineradicable. It was developed for emergencies, for the protection of individual lives and families. It's a versatile capacity, of course, and may be entered in other contests, as it has been, to serve political power through organized warfare, and in the perverse pleasures of torture and sexual domination. I wonder how much of it we have under control."

"But tell me, Ibby," she said, "where comes

the human freedom to reject given ways? How did natural selection give us that?"

He said, "The runaway richness of the human brain structure permits a level of self-awareness unknown to most animals. It was an accident, of course, the window of freedom that we have, and which we continue to open wider. We have replaced nature's system of species survival with our own self-directed way. We call evil what we have turned against, what was once necessary and useful."

"And the only way."

"Yes. Those boys are driven—until their own young slow them down with the demands of being raised."

She stopped in the passageway and was silent for a few moments.

"It's sad," she said, "to think that they couldn't know that I wouldn't have given them any progeny."

"You were only practice," Ibby said, looking at her intently, as if searching for something.

"They got their practice," she said, "but it was strange to be pursued so vehemently."

"I liked . . ." Ibby started to say

"What?" she asked, returning his curious gaze.

"I liked rescuing you," he said.

■

As their ship sought the next habitat, Ibby's panoptic program began to return images from dozens of Rocks. They watched the display as it revealed, one by one, the standard simple dwellings set in grassy landscapes; most seemed devoid of human life, with the silence broken only by the faint whisper of Coriolis breezes.

26

Umbilicals

The completed inventory revealed that only fifteen Rocks held living communities. Justine and Ibby went before the Projex Council and pleaded for an end to the exiles' plight.

"But what can we do for them?" asked Chairman More.

"Granted, we ripped them from ourselves," said another member, "but we cannot take them back now."

"Why not?" Ibby asked.

"They are too far along another road," More said.

Justine said, "We do not have to take them back now, and perhaps never. But we can free them."

"Free them?"

"Gradually, of course," Justine said, "with contact at a minimum, so these people can raise themselves from the ignorance into which they were thrown by our predecessors."

"How will this be done?" asked More.

Ibby said, "First, we will open the engineering levels in each of the inhabited Rocks, and draw younger individuals in to use self-educational programs. This may require that some of us go among them, to start the process. Later it may be required that we take individuals away, educate and restore them to our norms of physical health and longlife, and return them to their people."

The head of the council nodded. "Yes, but you'll be setting in motion powerful conflicts in these . . . small towns, which is what they are."

"Shall we leave them as they are?" she asked.

"It's one way to be considered, still, is it not?"

"They'll die away, given the backwardness and lack of means with which they were thrown away. Most have died already."

"And what will it all come to?" the council head demanded. "When they are improved, won't they all wish to come home to Earthspace?"

"We don't know," Justine said. "Some time must pass—fifty years or more, before we begin to see what is possible." She did not wish to propose her longer term goal just now. "It may require, after some time, say twenty-five years, that we send out orientation teams to live in each habitat."

"And if that is all successful, then what?" More demanded. "What will we have then? When will it all end?"

Ibby said, "We will have discharged some of our responsibility, which we inherit from our past, whether we accept it or not."

More almost smiled. "That is a very doubtful statement."

"As I've said here before," Justine cut in, "what was done before our times may or may not be our responsibility, but what we do or fail to do now and in the future is our responsibility. And the harm that our inaction may bring will make us all complicit with past wrongs. What shall we not do? What shall we do? We are responsible either way."

"Very clever," said More, "but can we be compelled to act?"

"Yes. AI dialogues since our return support the actions we propose, and we can compel a referendum of all the citizenry in Earthspace, if necessary."

"How do the AI dialogues support your proposals?"

"The full document is some thousands of pages. But the main arguments of the AI high number participants remind us that we cannot afford to lose any part of the human genetic library—and that useful developments beckon in these habitats . . ."

"Ah, now we get to it," said the Projex head. "There are other aims . . ."

She said, "There is caution in our proposal, which I now urge you to study."

More raised a hand. "Before we call upon more AI advice, let me point out that they are still regarded by many of us as no more than brilliant pets. They have no interest in our welfare or progress. They have no sympathy . . ."

"But they do know increase and progress," she said, "and what will contribute to further elaboration and what will not, taking into account a myriad factors that no unenhanced human can grasp in one vision."

"Yes, yes," More said impatiently. "What you are telling me is that my comprehension will forever be inadequate and that I am not a fit judge."

"Not at all," Justine continued patiently. "We have values and sympathies to implement. We can guess in transcendental fashion, and bring self-fulfilling prophecies to fruition."

"You're only telling us that we don't know where all this will lead," More said with even more irritation.

"But do we have the right to intrude?" asked a previously silent member.

"Who will stop us?" More asked as if

answering Justine and not his colleague.

"But should we intrude?" asked the same member.

Justine said, "I repeat, that by not intruding, we are still responsible for perpetuating their disadvantages."

"Are these sovereign communities?" asked More. "By our laws? The criminal justice agencies that created the Orbits no longer exist, and their responsible successors were never clearly defined—in fact, they were never named, as far as our records show. So are the Rocks sovereign?"

"No," Ibby said, "—in our legal sense. Practically, we can pretty much do what we please with them. They do not have the means to resist us. But I say again that to do nothing also brings responsibility for what may happen."

"But what is likely to happen?" More asked.

"We've already said it. They may all die out."

"But is that not what our predecessors intended?"

"Yes, unfortunately," Ibby said. "And the convicts have died out, for the most part. Those who still live in exile are not the same people."

■

Fifteen vessels went out in the first year. They opened the engineering levels. Teams came out to orient the populations. Justine and Ibby visited every worldlet, and in each they found an eagerness to learn, to reach out. The stars were shown to the people of each Rock, and its place in history explained, along with hopes for the future. People were given the choice to stay on their worldlets or to return, after sufficient preparation, to Earthspace. A few entered their names for the return; but when the time came to go, few went.

"They've seen what they are," Ibby said, "and that will change them forever."

"I think they glimpse new possibilities," Justine said, "but they also have some feeling for their worlds."

They sat in the lounge of what would have been the warden's apartment in Rock Four. This was their third visit here in ten years, in which time large numbers of volunteers had come out to the Rocks to help in yearly shifts. Some were helpful, others troublesome; still others were looking for relatives, real or imagined. And various groups were also going out to the now uninhabited Rocks. Most came back, but a few remained, retrofitting the old systems for their use, putting the dead in order, and organizing what records survived.

The fifteen inhabited Rocks all became aware of each other, and their common history drew them together. Representatives from each had gathered in Rock Four to compare notes and assess what lay ahead. Justine and Ibby attended as observers.

"It's clear," Ibby said, "that what we saw was a nearly universal acceptance of the habitats as home—their homes. We can help, but no more, they told us."

"Their plan to expand into all the empties," Justine said, "was quite a surprise."

"You're for it, then?" he asked.

"Is it up to us? They'll go out and make them their own without us."

"If we continue to educate and provide the technology."

"That too will come to an end," she said, "as they become self-sufficient and begin to generate their own research and development. Do you realize what has happened? Humanity now has a real toehold on the stars! We can spread through this whole galactic arm."

Ibby said, "I don't think More and the others will think of it as *we*."

"I know," Justine said. "That's why we have to encourage traffic between Earthspace and the Rocks, help reclaim the empties, and therefore make it *we*."

"If we can. I felt a great sense of independence in the leaders of the fifteen. It came out of them like a storm front."

"And they insisted on a face to face gathering with each other," she said.

He looked at her and said, "I think we both know what you want for them."

She nodded. "I hope so much for them. Is that strange?"

"No," he said. "We've worked together for a long time, so I know."

"Have you ever wondered," she said, "about the motives of those who planned the Orbits?"

"The motives were obvious."

"I get the feeling sometimes that the old planners, or maybe some far-seeing individual among them, imagined that this would be a good way to get humankind out of Sunspace."

"You may be giving them too much credit."

"But it may turn out that way."

"Someone might have thought it," Ibby said. "But look how many died out here—all but fifteen. It might have been all of them."

"Those who live today," she said, "must feel like the snail in the story, who was picked up at the front door and hurled away, then came back four months later and asked, 'what was that all about?'"

"So what happened?" Ibby asked. "I want to hear how you put it all together." He looked at her carefully, seeking a more personal communication through her gaze, but she was oblivious, completely in the grip of history.

She said, "A century ago, many of the world's prisons had become small communities, where two and three generations of children were being born to the inmates. Even Riker's Island in New York City in the late 1990s had people who had never known any other home, children born to lifers who had no place to go, so they stayed with their parents. Then, as a better world beckoned, those who had everything to gain from longer lives and better conditions concluded that they had to clean out these prisons. 'We'll still have criminals,' they announced, 'but they will be a better class of criminals.' It was the end of the street as a place of criminal enterprise, the end of the prison as the school to which aspiring criminals would be sent to learn and graduate.

"The high tech prisons of the late 1990s and early 2000s," she continued, "were the last attempt, before the opportunity presented by asteroid capture and mining, to deal with the most violent criminals. But these systems soon also filled up, as had every prison system of the past. Drug addicts, the mentally ill, the insane, should not have been treated in this way. And the supermaxes became a public shame, as had previous schemes, but they continued to be used long after being discredited, rife with abuse and mismanagement and lawbreaking that no one cared about, until the Rocks beckoned, offering what seemed to be simple incarceration without abuse and public recrimination.

"Then, just as progress seemed about to be proved, the destruction in Lawrence, Kansas, by the hijacked shuttle crash led to the timed orbit solution. A better degree of separation was needed between honest citizens and criminals."

She paused, then said, "Remember Rock Eight? It was originally made up of people who should not have been in prison at all, but in rehab centers, recovery therapies, or with friends and relatives. But the space was available in the Rocks—and it was believed that if they were released back into the society they might develop into worse cases. So it was easier to give up on helping them and send them away, into the Rocks, where they might help themselves. That's why their descendants in Rock Eight seemed so normal. They came from people who weren't criminals at all.

"Use the space for self-rehab. It became an attractive theory, worth trying. Difficult-to-treat noncriminals, not to mention people who should not have been imprisoned for anything, were cleared out simply because it could be done, just as every new prison on Earth had been filled up with a mix of criminals and noncriminals just because the space was available. As with all bureaucracies, work expands to fill up the time—so these prisons filled up as soon as they were ready to go."

He nodded and said, "It was much harder for specialized, practical minds to understand criminal violence as a continuation of evolutionary behavior built up in past environments and biology—and even more difficult to accept human ingenuity as a capacity that is free to do whatever it can, however mistaken. We still have the career criminals, but they're less violent, and still nothing can compete with the rewards they set for themselves to seek. We could not give them enough to *not* do what they find to do. It's showing off, display of skill and intelligence, public humor."

"And the old fears, hatreds, and impulses," she said. "I'm not surprised by the historical hatred for the theory of evolution among our ancestors. Natural selection was a horror, a needed evil . . . unless you were willing to replace it. They didn't know how to do it, and feared it when the possibility came up. We came from that violence, and feared the thing in us that would be taking over the old nature. We still have the vitality of that violence with us, and the need to practice it."

She paused, then said, "I could sometimes strangle More."

"Let's agree not to," he said. "More has his pride in being useful."

"Which he forgets as soon as he leaves the chamber for his personal life."

"What does he do?" Ibby asked, touching Justines's hand gently. "Do you know?"

She smiled. "I think he goes VR fishing—for sharks—but sets the level of difficulty too low, or so I've heard."

"He sets it himself?" Ibby asked.

She nodded and laughed. "And then he wipes the memory of doing it."

"But . . . he does this repeatedly? Some kind of general memory of his procedure must remain with him."

"No," she said. "I'm told he discovers his enjoyment afresh each time."

"Still," Ibby said, "it seems that he may forget the particular act but knows the general approach."

"Who knows, who cares?" she said, looking at Ibby's hand as it covered her own.

27

Dilemmas

As humankind's left hand shaped the tools with which it would break space-time's quarantine of worlds, the right hand preferred to play with its interior mental landscapes. Human hearts continued to war with themselves, and with each other, and craved to keep their dilemmas. They were proud of the wild, contrary beasts in their breasts, the struggling armies in their brains, which kept their deep eyes open to the clash of truth against truth. Far-travelers had always known the perversity of the infinite regress, of the truth known by inspection but unprovable, and that the opposite of a profound truth might sometimes be another great truth. For truth had colors, flavors, and textures that clashed with each other, yet were not diminished or made false by the struggle.

Justine and Ibby saw quantum drives installed in the first fifteen Rocks, and this brought the habitats together in one quadrant of the northern sky. The gathering took twenty-five years. Meanwhile, groups from Earthspace and the fifteen Rocks reclaimed the empties.

Justine's mind drifted outward. Ibby felt left behind.

"The last century and a half of trying to make a better world," she said to him one day, "has brought rigidities to our Earthspace societies—rigidities of will and planning, and exclusion. Maybe something should always be left wild, in the very heart of stability, rather than let go, as we are letting the Rocks go."

She sat up in the grass of Rock Fifty-three, and looked at Ibby, who was standing a few meters away. Above him was projected the entire matrix of human history, as constructed according to his project—a huge red sphere, transparent and filled with smaller spheres, each linked by seemingly solid lines of force. Each smaller sphere repeated the structure, down to a hundred levels of repetition, and each contained arrays of fact that could be accessed with enhancement.

"There's so little to add now," Ibby said, "trivial bits of the past beyond which we cannot penetrate, short of developing time travel." He turned and looked back at where she lay. "There's nothing left to do."

They had come here to secure the systems of the engineering level, and to learn what they could of the people who had died, as Ibby and she had done in every Rock, by playing back a century of recorded fragments.

The panoptic records were never perfect, because the equipment had not been designed to enter every dwelling or follow every individual. It was the kind of record that idle gods might have made, picking up individuals at random, sweeping across larger gatherings with a blind eye, and occasionally noting the dead as an accountant might grimace at a penny error.

Here, as in many habitats where reproduction had been possible, capable couples had turned away from parenthood. This refusal had been most trenchant in populations that knew they would never return, or had discovered that they had not returned at the appointed time. Still others had been too old, or infertile at the time of incarceration, and the few births that had occurred had not been sufficient to set generations in motion.

Ibby had pitched an old-fashioned tent in the grass, and after some weeks Justine had come to appreciate the desolate beauty of the basic design that she had now seen so often. The grass she linked in her mind with yellow suns—the grass of the universe. The soft, clay-like soil was a comfort to her feet as she walked on it. Once in a while she would come upon human bones in the grass, and remind herself how common a sight it had been throughout human history; and then she would wonder how common dead civilizations might be in the starry grass of the universe.

Ibby blinked his big display off, and came to sit at her side.

"What will we do," he asked, "when they are all gone?"

One by one, the renovating Rocks were making the decision to leave rather than return to the inner solar system. Several had already gone, accelerating to relativistic speeds that would carry them dozens of light-years, for a start. How far would they have to go, from system to system, before they stopped looking back to the Sun?

Great Clarke had once said that "no man will ever turn homeward from beyond Vega, to greet again those he knew and loved on Earth." But he had been thinking in shorter lifespans and of travelers who were coming out from Earth for the first time, not peoples who had prepared for a starhopping way of expansion, in which each solar system became a source of raw materials and a colony base for further exploration, leaving secure what was gained and moving outward.

"What will we do," he asked again, "when they are all gone?"

"Oh, go with—after them," she said with

resolve, then saw the look of dismay on his face. "Not right away, of course," she added to anticipate his response.

"I don't think I could," he said sadly.

She looked at him with feigned surprise.

"Surely you suspected," he said.

She wanted to say no, that it was a complete surprise, as if somehow that would make it so.

"Why not?" she asked, convinced that he could give no good answer.

"I've lived too long with this human history. I don't think I could start with another—not now, when it's been so well organized and made so accessible, so well classified even to sources a thousand times removed. I'm a point-center in my big display, and I don't have the heart to remove myself."

"But you won't be removing yourself. We'll take it with us. We'll need it!"

He smiled at her. "This vast split in humanity that is coming will decide more than anyone can guess. No other division will ever equal it. The deferment of decision about our own kind may finally be at an end. We may be at an end."

"But we've always changed, diverged . . ."

"Not in the way that is coming. These changes will have no continuity with the past. To keep it with us will only weigh down and confuse the new lessons that will have to be learned. The past may never again have as much importance as it had during the centuries of human beginnings."

"You seem so certain, Ibby."

He shrugged with what she would later describe as the weariness of histories, and said, "I've had my say about my own kind. My reactions have gone from hopeful to critical optimism, from disappointment to bitter hatred, hatred of the kind we found in Tasarov's writings—and more often now to laughter. Between hatred and laughter, I prefer the laughter. And I feel most for the fools at home who are at an end."

"Why laughter, Ibby?"

"Oh, it's not mockery—but a kind of divine understanding that we achieve ourselves. There's a lot of reason in laughter."

She touched his hand and held it. "You've tied yourself in a knot, and I did not see it."

"A knot which should not be untied. I've spent a long time tying it, and the problems it represents cannot simply be dissipated by untying it. This knot has unsolvable character, because it can't even be cut. There would be nothing left. A man is best known, understood, measured, even valued, not by his settled conclusions, but by the dilemmas he keeps. They are the best markers of fleeting truth on the perverse road of time. My problem, Justine, is that I no longer have any dilemmas. And worse, I don't want any new ones. I am a finished piece of work."

"Oh, Ibby, that can't be!"

"But it is. You must let me go."

"How can I?"

"You can," he said, "and you will—because you cannot bear to give up what is to come."

"And you can give it up?" she asked.

"I can't give up what was—because it stands within me like some massive foundation stone. Oh, I know it is cracking, but it holds me up, and will until my mind is full, and I will either forget or perish."

"Ibby . . ." she started to say.

But he said, "If in some far futurity, we meet again, all new with forgetfulness, it will not be me, and it will not be you."

28

A Supplement to the Soul

The hundred habitats formed an expanding shell around the solar system during the next century—and again they were a reminder: The sky in every direction was now peppered with venturesome, relativistically flung humanity. The expanding shell of skylife became a source of grudging pride, even among those who would never go themselves; but although the old sense of responsibility was gone, new insecurities arose about the nature of the previous, biologically unchanged form of humankind that persisted in the habitats.

Occasionally, additional habitats joined the shell. Back and forth traffic in fast ships continued for some years; people came and went under the pressure of second thoughts, and this growing familiarity disarmed many suspicions.

The young coming to maturity were faced with the choice of a frontier.

Judge Overton voiced his last suspicions before becoming a new personality. "They're growing their own AIs out there," he said, "and not sharing them with us! Some visitors say that they've learned something about raising AIs and are deliberately hiding the knowledge, which worries me. We do need a step up from man, no doubt. Not much, just a step or two in the genome, so it will run cleaner—not much more than separates us from the apes. But this AI news is disturbing . . ."

Justine Harre deleted the beloved memory of Ibby Khaldun from herself, but placed it in storage—between two lines of verse in her favorite book—where she knew she would come upon it from time to time and puzzle over what it might be. The memory was timed to expire after three warnings, one decade apart, and would then be irretrievable even with her best internal enhancements.

At first, Ibby had not set his memories of Justine to expire. He lived with what was left of her within himself, however painful it became at times; but there came a day when it ceased to be painful and became disturbing, as he tried to understand the mystery of personal affinities, sympathies, attractions, and especially unconditional love.

Love was simply there, as easily perceived within one's self as one perceived a color; one saw it or one didn't. And love could die, he admitted, without pushing it into the grave, as he began to feel that Justine had done with her affections. Had she told him, by her action, that he should do no less?

He had come here to the habitat monitoring facility on the Moon for a specific purpose—to see how he would feel about Justine before the memory of her expired, and how he would feel immediately after about the great enterprise to which she had given herself for the indefinite future.

He had drifted away from the HIP project that had been his life to the pursuit of historical miniatures. He selected particularly attractive periods of history and spent VR time in them. The HIP project's vast database worked wonders in recreating the romance of past times as they had never been lived. He accepted this antiquarian longing, and resolved that one day he would study its origins in himself; but by then he might well be moving on to another pursuit. The miniatures, he knew, were also a form of love, not essentially different than his love of Justine's character. He wished to live in them just as he had become part of Justine's inner landscape in their time together.

"I want to look outward into the universe

as it is," she had told him after their return to Earth, "and as it will be. You want to make it over out of the accumulation of historical fact that you have gathered, and then live in that."

"I do love it so," he had told her. "The breezes of times that are gone, the skies and landscapes, the people who in their time could hope to know all that could be known. If I could travel into the past in any other way, I would."

"Romance," she had said. "Don't you find it a bit grotesque to love it?"

"We have the past in our hands now," he had replied, "as much of it as we will ever have short of direct retrieval of information from the past. Why should we not do something with this vast mass of information for our delight? It's nothing new to do so—historical dramas began the process, and later novels of all kinds. Paintings, sculptures, movies, and VRs. I may be able to shape new experiences that will give great pleasure."

"And be unreal."

"Reality is overrated," he had said.

She had nodded and said, "A very old phrase."

"Reality is given to us against our will," he added. "Imposed. A game not of our choosing, even though we remake ourselves."

Now as he stood in the great display chamber which showed the shimmering galaxy, he tried to tell himself that she had never cared enough for him even with full memory. He gazed up at the shell of green points set in the starry ways, and wondered which habitat was hers. Not one of them had made much of an inroad into stellar distance, not even much of a light-year, despite twenty-five years of acceleration; but each worldlet had been making vast progress within itself, bringing all of humankind's gains with it, standing on the shoulders of countless dreaming dead and preparing . . . for what? To become unrecognizable to the past?

The moment when her life within him would expire was fast approaching—a matter of minutes now . . .

He looked around the vast chamber, where his stay-at-home humanity had sought to display and memorialize the dispersal of its kind. There was a young man sitting at a nearby station drinking a cup of tea. He seemed to be contemplating the vision. Was he regretting that he had not gone? There was still time, as the last of the Rocks were renovated and filled with malcontents and amnesiacs . . .

His historian's sense of humor blossomed within him, and he saw the continuing dispersal as the greatest prison break in all history— planned by Justine and the other joiners who had come out to help bring down the walls . . .

I'm not that different, he told himself, as

Justine's memory expired within him, and he found himself staring up at the scattering of emeralds among the diamonds . . . as if waking from one dream into another.

And suddenly, one by one, the green points began to wink out . . .

The young man stood up, knocking over his cup of tea.

A half dozen figures came into the chamber, and as they gazed up at the display, the green markers continued to wink off until they were all gone . . .

"All of them?" asked a voice.

"Yes, as if . . ."

Ibby saw from the monitors that it had taken some weeks for the beacon transmitters to affect the display. Had the beacons been turned off to further delay the news? It was all past now.

"As if . . ." the voice continued, "they had simply jumped off into the dark."

"They wouldn't have turned their beacons off," said the young man.

"It's as if they'd got hold of newer stuff . . . and used it," said a third voice.

Ibby felt a quickening of meaning in himself, and a sudden sense of freedom, as if a great weight had been lifted from his mind.

The young man stepped forward and said, "I've heard things recently, about the experimental drive technologies that were going out there." He looked around as if he had lost something, then said, "They're gone, and I was too late deciding to go with them!"

He seemed very angry at himself.

"There's nothing to show here any more," one of the others said.

"We can keep watch," said another. "Some may return."

"Do you think so?" asked the young man.

Ibby felt a well-being that had not been his for a long time, and wondered what price he had paid for it. A gift of sky waited, he thought as he looked into the black-bright heaven, wondering how the habitats would use it. Would they settle distant solar systems? Some probably would, while others would remain mobile and reproduce, seeking the secrets of the deep as they moved outward into the Galaxy, becoming many humanities, even different species. And some might even return with gifts for the home-life.

He wondered, then asked how it would be, even as his intellect doubted and his heart quickened to the words of an answer that he had once heard somewhere, from someone . . . from Justine, perhaps, and mercifully had somehow not quite forgotten.

The rough crucible of Earth
Is not a loving cradle.
Freedom waits beyond
The way of blood that whelped us,
Whispering into the past,
Stand aside, stand aside,
And seize posterity.
Ride outward you dying devils,
For homeward is the way to hells
Of faith and hopeless yearning
With those who settle to believe,
Fearing to voyage the swifts of thought.

Stride across the eons,
Spy the horizon of nature,
And birth new ways.

"Here There Be Tygers"

Or "If You Think It Couldn't Happen ... Read on and Learn More about It"

In doing the research for the novel you have just read, I started with an outline of penal history and was startled by an interesting account. In the early post-colonial period of the United States, the least affordable, most expensive structure to be built was a prison in Philadelphia. Here the prisoners were provided central heating, an indoor toilet, and an enclosed stone courtyard for each cell. Each inmate—man, woman, or child— was given a Bible and consigned to utter silence and isolation in which to reflect on their transgressions. No one was permitted to speak to them during the entire period of incarceration. The idea put forward by Quakers was rehabilitation, a new idea opposed to the older model of prisons where it was acceptable to do just about anything to prisoners as punishment for their crimes, unless they could bribe their way into better treatment.

The new goal of rehabilitation failed almost from the start, driving the prisoners insane, then collapsing into mere separation and neglect, abuse by guards and wardens, and financial corruption. Yet this system was an advance over previous prisons in Europe, where anything could happen and no one cared. Ironically, this Philadelphia prison looked like a medieval fortress intruding into the utopian ideals of young America, and it began a quest for the perfect prison that continues to this day with the various high-tech supermaxes, whose success resembles more than anything a desire to wed a perpetual motion machine to a squirrel cage; the impossibility of the one makes its power source absurd.

So if anything in this novel seems outrageous in regard to penal concepts, I point out that past governments have already tried something like the Orbits, which seem an advance on past abuses even as they create new ones of their own.

A few of the notable sources I consulted include: Lawrence M. Friedman's *Crime and Punishment in American History* (Basic Books,

1993) is a glorious wrestling match with history. George Sylvester Viereck's *Men Into Beasts* (Fawcett, 1952) details how a bizarre vendetta application of the Sedition Laws, during World War II and after, was conducted simply to show that the laws were being enforced—even when there was scarcely anyone to use them on—in a manner that became even more vicious on the part of judges as wrongs were exposed, preparing the way for the McCarthy Era witch-hunts of the 1950s. Michel Foucault's *Discipline and Punish: The Birth of the Prison* (Vintage, 1979) profoundly meditates on the nature of crime and punishment. In this and other works, Foucault demonstrates that decades of study will not exhaust the subject. And finally, Melvin Konner's *The Tangled Wing* (Holt, 1982) is a compassionate study of humanity's psychological origins by a biological anthropologist and fellow creature attempting to look out and back through the windows of hopeful freedom that science strives to keep clean.

I am moved to paraphrase H. G. Wells who once complained that too much reality had taken pages out of his work, determined to supplant him, and so he would write no more fiction. But he complained after the fact. I complain in advance, surprised by how much reality so relentlessly sought to intrude into my novel as I wrote it, and how much reality I left out. Humanity has done much worse than these Brute Orbits, which I fear may also come.

In my house I have two pieces of artwork by prisoners from Dannemora: tigers on black velvet. Seems right to me as I finished writing my novel.

We do escape.

—George Zebrowski
Spring 1998

About the Author

GEORGE ZEBROWSKI'S thirty books include novels, short fiction collections, anthologies, and a book of essays. Science fiction writer Greg Bear calls him "one of those rare speculators who bases his dreams on science as well as inspiration," and the late Terry Carr, one of the most influential science fiction editors of recent years, described him as "an authority in the SF field." Zebrowski has published more than sixty works of short fiction and more than a hundred articles and essays, and has written about science for *Omni* magazine. His short fiction and essays have appeared in every major science fiction magazine, including *Omni* and *Science Fiction Age*, and in the *Bertrand Russell Society News*.

His best known novel is *Macrolife*, which Arthur C. Clarke described as "a worthy successor to Olaf Stapledon's *Star Maker*. It's been years since I was so impressed. One of the few books I intend to read again." *Library Journal* chose *Macrolife* as one of the one hundred best science fiction novels, and The Easton Press reissued it in its "Masterpieces of Science Fiction" series. Zebrowski's stories and novels have been translated into a half-dozen languages; his short fiction has been nominated for the Nebula

Award and the Theodore Sturgeon Memorial Award. *Stranger Suns* (1991) was a *New York Times* Notable Book of the Year.

The Killing Star, written with scientist/author Charles Pellegrino and published in the spring of 1995, received unanimous praise in national newspapers and magazines. *The New York Times Book Review*, which included *The Killing Star* on its Recommended Summer Reading list, called it "a novel of such conceptual ferocity and scientific plausibility that it amounts to a reinvention of that old Wellsian staple, [alien invasion] . . ." *The Washington Post Book World* described the novel as "a classic SF theme pushed logically to its ultimate conclusions."

The Borgo Press brought out *The Work of George Zebrowski: An Annotated Bibliography and Guide* (Third Edition) and *Beneath the Red Star*, his collection of essays on international SF, in conjunction with his recent appearance as Guest of Honor at the Science Fiction Research Association Conference.

Forthcoming in 1999 are *Skylife: Visions of Our Homes in Space*, edited with Gregory Benford (Harcourt Brace), and a novel from HarperPrism, *Cave of Stars*.

George Zebrowski's World Wide Web site is located at: http://ebbs.english.vt.edu/alt/projects/zebrowski

EXERPTS FROM

CAVE OF STARS

Paul Morse's nightly wanderings through the palace were a bodily form of worry, when his reason, free of daylight's glaring practicalities, reviewed his dilemmas endlessly, reproaching himself for not having done more with his power and influence. He sometimes felt frozen at his center, inside an outer shell that spoke and acted with no feeling for his fellow human beings. He preferred convenient order to justice, because he was deeply suspicious of human nature, even if order was maintained by duplicity and manipulation. Only long periods of order might provide the foundation for genuine progress, he told himself.

He insisted to himself that a religious state had to oppose secular happiness to some degree; it had to accept, by its own theology, a measure of misery in this life as a testing process, and evil as the opportunity for moral choices. But that was only the theological facade. The secret of the Church was that it sought to give human life a decent structure based on an authority beyond question. It did not matter that the authority might be doubted by the most intelligent; what mattered was that the ideals of a good life would be observed. They needed justification from an unimpeachable authority in simple minds that would not accept ethical values on merit alone.

Paul had long ago understood that the world moved according to deeper currents, and that these were not God's mysterious ways. Bely knew that the growing secularization of New Earth's society was a threat to the Church. The old dogmas were being worn away. A difference in kind was creeping in with increasing population. Practical behavior was always the best measure of unbelief. Paul's hope was that the scaffolding of make-do theology would one day fall away and reveal the genuine structure of human ideals.

But Paul knew that this would not happen in his lifetime, if ever. Too many heretics were in exile, scarred beyond recovery, and he was a minor Merlin who thought for himself in private. Ironically, his inner independence and knowledge of the past helped him serve Bely better; few understood so well what was at stake on all sides, and almost no one knew the nature of the roles that were being acted out. There would be nothing for him during a revolutionary upheaval. His power would not survive a transition, even if he lived, because no one would see his true self. The time to have allied himself with change was long past; no one would trust him. And he told himself that his younger self would not have understood the harm that revolution would have brought.

He felt pity for Bely. Secretly, the old man clung to the remote possibility that his daughter might succeed him if she excelled in her theological studies; but this was a delusion born of pride and biology. She could not ascend to Bely's position while he lived, and she would be ignored after his death, no matter what arrangements Paul made. The Cardinals would see to that. Bely did not have many delusions, but Paul expected their number to increase. The Cardinals were watching him very intently.

Had Ondro cultivated Josepha to spy on her father—or had the two simply fallen in love? There was no evidence that Ondro had known that Josephus Bely was her father. Paul had not spoken to her for nearly a year. They had been friends during her girlhood, when he had been her protector. Her life in the girl's school, following her mother's suicide, had been happy, as far as he had been able to see during his visits. She seemed to have liked the nuns who had taught her, especially Sister Perpetua; but there had also been an occasional sadness in Josepha's dark eyes, and future events had only confirmed it.

Paul always tried to think in historical terms; it gave him the hope of looking life in the face without illusions. He was one of the last in a long line of scientists and engineers who had come to Ceti on the colony ark from Earth. A kind of masonry still existed, but it was one more of engineers than of scientists, of practical people who knew how to keep things working; basic inquiry and research was not their interest. But it was their influence, together with that of the merchant-businessmen, that was responsible for the decline of otherworldliness as a basis for law and ethics. Their sons and daughters had an alternative, in business, engineering, and architecture, in farm life and basic industries, to the piety that went along with life in the Church's civil service. The old vision of a powerful, technically advanced Earth had not been erased, only dimmed. There was life beyond the Ceti system, in the mobile worlds, where two centuries had certainly brought new developments. Something was stirring in the people of his world, Paul thought, and it was more than the historically common crisis of religiosity; it was more akin to the millennial tremors of Earth's history, the hope of a second-coming, perhaps even a rise of a secular ideology that might replace traditional faith and rule without recourse to fear and self-loathing.

But these feelings of change-in-the-wind,

he reminded himself, had been around for more than half a century, feeding on scraps of history and imaginative possibility. Everything could be accomplished in the realm of pure possibility—but what was likely to happen in the existing climate of power and politics? How far had the tide come up to Bely's City of God?

He came to the great north windows of his wing of the palace and looked out at the night sky. A tall, gaunt figure stood on Bely's terrace across the courtyard. It was the old man, also a night-orphan. Paul watched, as he had so often over the years, until the wasting shape went back inside, then turned and began his own slow return to his distant bedchamber.

He imagined, as he walked, what Earth's ruined solar system had been like in the years following the loss of the home planet, as groups of surviving humanity struggled to reorganize. The remnants of Roman Christianity had secured a starship and set out to find a new Earth from which to prepare for Heaven. Other ships had sought the nearer stars, while mobile worlds went out to reproduce themselves, forsaking natural planets.

One orphan of this human exodus had come to Tau Ceti IV, burning away the native life on one of the planet's two continents and seeding the soil with the alien biota of Earth. Two centuries later fifty million human beings lived in conditions that had been planned not to progress beyond Earth's early twentieth century. The other continent was still an alien wilderness, mostly unexplored, but blamed for every new disease and the object of superstitious fear. It was also thought to be rich in metals, which the merchant-businessmen knew were the key to economic growth. The rapacious settlement and exploitation of that continent would make a great crusade one day, only awaiting an ambitious Pope to give it his blessing.

No signs of native Cetian intelligent life had ever been found, probably because the invaders had arrived too early, or too late. It would certainly never develop any, now that man from Earth was here. The issue was an obscure one, but he thought about it from time to time.

Paul stopped before the door to his quarters, and felt a moment of sympathy for Ondro and his brother Jason. They had longed for something new to intrude into their world, bringing impossible changes, loosening the mortar of time and fear that had made what seemed to them a changeless wall around their civilization.

The knowledge for change waited in the vast library of the ancient information storage and retrieval system below the palace. But unused skills also required teachers, and there were none. The trades passed on only much-used techniques that required minimal understanding, enabling the world to function, after a fashion, but without progress.

He entered his apartment and closed the heavy door behind him, sick with longing for the sweetness of possibility that he had known in his youth. Enough of the night remained for him to still seek sleep's false oblivion, in which he would suffer, then forget, and awake into morning's remembrance.

It never failed to impress Voss Rhazes that humankind existed in any large numbers outside the mobiles. He knew only his own habitat, but he had taken for granted from his earliest years that the reproducing mobiles were the primary form of humanity derived from Earth, and the true future of the species. His mobile had never met another. The estimate was that there had to be at least two dozen others, and perhaps half of these might have reproduced.

But the scattering of ships in a thousand light year radius of Earth had brought into being a still undetermined number of planetary colonies. Judging by the six he had seen, the settlers were content with modest levels of technology and low levels of medical and genetic praxis, enough to make their worlds manageable during their short lifespans. The peoples grew attached to their forests, plains, high plateaus, and mountain valleys, even while imposing their own regimes on the local biology, and were only vaguely aware of the mobiles of macrolife beyond their sky. During rare encounters, it was difficult to convey to planet dwellers that a mobile habitat's many-leveled structure contained more usable surface area than an Earthlike planet, and was filled with light and clean air, where people grew into lives undreamed of by the mass of historical humanity—all inside an egg shape 100 or more kilometers long, consisting of hundreds of urban shells wrapped around the foundation of an asteroid core. The growing backwardness signalled by this lack of simple geometries made it plain that these colonies were rapidly slipping into a dark age from which they might never recover; therefore, contact with the mobiles might very well mean the very survival of these colonies.

For Voss, mobiles were the civilized places from which to confront and explore the universe. Only suns were greater in their massive use of energy. Inside the macrolife habitats, energy use was subtle and variegated, flowing to enhance the life of a mobile's citizenry. It was the difference between the circulation of blood in an organism, nourishing each cell of every organ, and an open fire. Knowledge and the energies needed for life flowed through the people of the mobiles, but understanding counted for much more than simple survival and longlife; it was the center of life. This was not so in the planetary colonies. There, simply to live counted for much more than to know, and understanding was the smaller part, even a luxury.

In his experience, knowledge and thought were a whirlwind, the central power of living, by which all that was novel and absorbing was achieved. No previous human culture had ever had macrolife's control over itself or more possibility for varied growth. Past humanities had taken their chance, and as they failed Macrolife had bolted free from the planetary cradle. The mobiles were always remaking themselves, multiplying to accommodate population and the need for social experiment. Unchanged humanity's persistence on several planets puzzled and intrigued Voss; but he shared the view of many others that without help these colonies would fail and die, and to do nothing would make the mobiles complicit in that dying.

Nevertheless, this old humanity, it seemed to him, wished to remain poor and powerless in a universe of wealth and beauty—and even though it was an oversimplification of deeply layered histories, he was always struck by the degree of truth that could not be ignored.

Human organisms in purely nature-given environments adapted to scarcity, living in balance with the environment through basic work until they died. Deep bodily satisfactions rewarded the organism occasionally, enough for them to launch the next generation of organisms. Attempts at progress from this state produced profound difficulties, leading to diverse adolescent technological cultures whose individuals felt washed up on an alien shore.

The first flush of growth beyond given nature produced imbalances. Wealth beckoned with the promise of an end to scarcity, but it also brought the disuse of minds and bodies in large, suddenly unnecessary population, sweeping away values built on the striving for mere life and material security. Tribal issues of descent and territory became exaggerated, leading to organized warfare and environmental catastrophe. Earth's civilizations, numbering more than thirty in less than 15,000 years, had been unconscious accretions of beliefs, rituals, and scraps of knowledge applied to technology. The predominant mood at their various endings had been bewilderment; they did not know what had happened to them.

Earth's final civilization had failed to make the transition to a culture of rational values and goals. It had resisted, from motives of greed and power, new forms of social and economic organization, and had finally lost the high-energy state that was the prerequisite for creative goal-seeking; genuine progress would have put too many groups out of power. And it was the example of Earth's failure, as well as the loss of records and teachers, that kept its planetary colonies cautious and backward.

But macrolife, the hardiest flower of Earth's romance with science and technology, had survived the last civilizational collapse and was proliferating. It was not known how many seed worlds had escaped Earth's sunspace, but it seemed inevitable that developing mobiles would one day contact each other. It seemed unthinkable to Voss that his mobile was the only one, since that would mean that the future of humanity would for some time again belong to the wayward path of planetary colonies.

Voss felt, as did most citizens under a century in age, that the time had come for the building of a new mobile. His world's visit to the Tau Ceti system, therefore, had several important aims. Raw would be gathered for the construction of the new social container. This activity would be the natural occasion for a good will mission to the planetary colony on the fourth planet, which had not been contacted before by his mobile, and by no other, as far as anyone knew. Also, a group of malcontents would be given the opportunity of settling on the planet. This might create some opposition from the planetary authorities, since the group would bring a high technology to a backward world; but this would be unavoidable, since it would be suicide for the settlers to do without the medical skills of their parent world, or accept a lower energy level of daily life. It was also possible that people from Tau Ceti IV might wish to emigrate to the new mobile being built in their sky.

As these projects went forward, Voss's assignment was to make contact with the planet's civil authorities and get their reactions to the mobile's visit. It was unlikely that the colony had managed to lay claim to the entire planet by this time, so a suitable, remote area might be found; but First Councilman Adam Blackfriar had warned Voss that there might be complications.

"I'm certain," Blackfriar had said, "that you will find out what we need to know."

"I find it difficult to understand," Voss had said, "why such a group wishes to leave and take so much of our way of life with them. What's the point?"

"They want to live on a planet."

Voss felt uneasy as he entered the small flitter on the engineering level. He had never felt this level of uncertainty; but he knew its cause: multiple implications were coming over the horizon of his awareness, triggering old mental programs of instinct and stochastic insight that could not be clearly stated.

"Voss?" Adam asked inside him as he made his way forward in the egg-shaped flitter and sat down.

"I'm here," he answered aloud.

"What I'm planning to do," Adam said, "is to set our colony down as early as possible, so they can get a taste of the planet while we build the new habitat. That will give those who wish to come back a chance to come back, either to us or the new mobile."

Again, Voss spoke aloud. "I'm ready to go."

"You're set to land at the Papal palace in New Vatican, the capitol city. We've had word by radio from Paul Morse, the prime minister, that he will receive you. Later you'll probably meet with Josephus Bely, the religious and political head of the planetary society, which, by the way, seems to control only the one continent."

"Any signs of hostility?"

"No. They seem to know about us—at least Morse seems to. According to him it's been two and half centuries since they've had contact with offworlders. Your fastload of Euro-English should start you off well enough, and Link feedback will take care of what you're missing, so you should be fluent in a day or so."

Blackfriar withdrew. Voss sat back and flowed

outward through his Link, testing his connections to his world. Forests of data stood all around him in visual manifestation as he swooped through their woven centuries of growth. He took a moment, despite the routine action, to appreciate the beauty of the standing infrastructure.

The flitter was already in the void. With eyes still closed, he looked back at his world and his mind filled with the understanding that was the foundation of his life. Here was an entity composed of a thoughtful humankind and its offspring, worthy of all the hopes of history—a constantly growing culture, secure at the basic levels of material need, yet open to the vastness of space-time, poised to confront all of reality. The human individual had always looked to something deathless—to family, leader, nation, to a god; but they had all failed, while his world gave him longlife and endless chances at happiness and satisfaction.

He turned from the mobile's egg-shape and gazed at the planet. With its fragile envelope of atmosphere, its lumbering gravitational effect, its fractured massiveness, it seemed an oblivious creature rolling through the night, waiting to swallow him.